My Book of Pony Stories

My Book of Pony Stories

GILLIAN BAXTER

Illustrated by Elisabeth Grant

containing
Pantomime Ponies
Save the Ponies
Ponies in Harness

DEAN

Pantomime Ponies *first published 1969*
Save the Ponies *first published 1971*
Ponies in Harness *first published 1977*
This edition published 1991 by Dean
A division of Reed International Books Ltd
Michelin House, 81 Fulham Road, London SW3 6RB
Reprinted 1991 and 1992.
Text copyright © Gillian Baxter 1969, 1971 and 1977
Illustrations copyright © 1969 Methuen & Co Ltd
© 1971 and 1977 Methuen Children's Books
Printed in Great Britain by The Bath Press

ISBN 0 603 55000 2

A CIP catalogue record for this book is
available from the British Library

Pantomime Ponies

Contents

1 · Uncle Arthur

Ian and Angela Kendall gazed anxiously out of the taxi window as it turned yet another corner. The street was still drab and grey, as all the streets had been since they left the High Street, but here there was a little more life about it. People were walking to and from a short row of shops at the farther end, and the lights in the shop windows glowed warmly in the damp, grey dusk.

"Do you think one of those is Uncle Arthur's shop?" asked Angela.

"I should think so," replied Ian. "Aunt Mavis said that he'd got a paper shop."

Angela was silent again, as the taxi slowed down to swing across the road. She had long fair hair and her eyes were blue, and at the moment her face was pale and nervous. She was eight years old, and Ian, who looked very much like her, was nine. Their mother and father had died so long ago that Angela could not even remember them. Ian said that he could remember their mother, but Angela did not think that he could, although she enjoyed listening to his stories about her.

It was the thought of another new home, although a temporary one this time, that was making Angela nervous. She and Ian seemed to have had so many. Since their parents died they had lived with Grandmother, with Auntie Lorna and Uncle Sam, with Cousin John and Aunt Carrie, and with Aunt Mavis. And now that Aunt Mavis had gone to Ashby to look after her mother, who had fallen and broken an ankle, they were to stay here in south east London with Uncle Arthur until she returned. It seemed an awful lot of homes in less than eight years.

The taxi stopped outside the first shop in the row, the paper shop. A board above the door read "A. Perry. Newsagent, Tobaccon-

10

ist and Confectioner". In the lighted window were boxes and jars of sweets, packets of cigarettes, tins of tobacco, magazines, cake-decorations, and plastic toys. It was the first week of January, and the Christmas decorations were still up. Blobs of cotton wool were stuck to the glass, and strands of tinsel hung behind the goods on display. It was rather a haphazard sort of window, looking as though someone had arranged it in a frightful hurry. On either side of the door, racks held copies of evening and local papers, and there was a board behind the glass in the door for small postcard advertisements.

"Here you are, then," the taxi driver told them. "Shall I take your stuff inside?"

"We'd better ask, first," replied Ian, and he and Angela climbed out.

The shop bell jangled loudly as Ian pushed open the door, and Angela followed him uncertainly inside. The shop was very small, with two counters: one for sweets, cigarettes, and oddments, the other for news-

11

papers and magazines. Paper chains hung across the ceiling, and there was a cluster of balloons suspended over the door. In spite of the noise from the bell, no one appeared.

"I'll try the bell again," said Ian.

He opened and closed the door again, with the same loud jangle, but still nobody came.

"Had we better try knocking on the other door?" asked Angela. There was an inner door, with a piece of green curtain hung over the glass in the top half.

They were about to try this idea when the shop door opened, and a woman came in. She was short and stout, dressed in a black coat, bedroom slippers, and curlers under a head scarf.

"No one about?" she asked them cheerfully.

"No," replied Angela.

"He'll be out the back," the woman told them.

Without hesitation she went behind the counter, opened the inner door, and yelled "Arthur. Shop." Then she came back and leaned against the counter, beaming at them.

"You'll be Cousin Jack's kids, come to stay," she said. "Angela and Ian. You've had him in a right state, I can tell you."

"We have? Why?" asked Angela.

"Arthur looking after kids?" the woman laughed. "Frightened him to death. He's probably hiding out there now."

There was a sound of hurried footsteps beyond the inner door, then it swung open, and Uncle Arthur came hurriedly into the shop. He was a tall, thin, red-faced man with grey hair going rather thin on top, blue eyes, and bushy grey eyebrows.

"Sorry, May," he began. "I was just. . . ." Then he noticed the two children, and stopped short.

"The kids are here, Arthur," the woman told him. "Angela and Ian. Thought you'd run off or something."

She laughed again, and Uncle Arthur's face became redder.

"Oh my goodness," he exclaimed. "I am sorry. I wasn't expecting you just yet. Your

13

luggage. What about your luggage?"

"It's outside," Ian told him. "The taxi's still here. Shall we let the driver bring it in?"

"Yes, yes, of course. Better use the side door. Awkward through here," said Uncle Arthur. "May, would you mind? Just a few minutes. Shan't be long."

"I don't mind," May assured him.

Uncle Arthur followed Angela and Ian outside, showed the taxi driver the side door, and then hurried back into the shop to unlock it. Angela and Ian looked at each other uncertainly. Uncle Arthur seemed awfully disorganised. And was it true that their coming had really scared him? The other relations that they had stayed with had sometimes been unwelcoming, or irritable, but never scared.

The side door opened with a jerk, and the driver carried their cases into the narrow passage, before returning to his taxi. Uncle Arthur led the way down the passage, past some stairs, and into the back room.

"Must just see to the shop. Make yourselves at, er, home," he told them, and vanished through the green-curtained door. Angela and Ian looked around them.

Uncle Arthur's living-room was different from anywhere that they had stayed before. To start with it was very crowded, while Aunt Mavis's home had been spacious and tidy. Chairs, tables, a sagging settee, a huge sideboard, an ornate upright piano, and towering shelves of books fought each other for space. A blue budgerigar in a big cage chattered above them, his cage suspended from a hook in the ceiling. A hot coke fire burned in the grate, and there was a huge ginger cat spread out on the hearth in front of it.

On the mantelpiece, on top of the sideboard, and all round the room were photographs and old playbills of music hall performances and circuses. Many of the photographs were signed, and looked like old-fashioned film stars.

Out in the shop the bell jangled as May

went out, and Uncle Arthur came back into the room. He beamed at them rather anxiously, and said, "Well. So you're Angela and Ian?"

"Yes," agreed Ian.

"Isn't he a lovely cat," said Angela. Usually she was very shy, but knowing that their uncle was shy of them made it somehow easier to talk to him.

"Oh yes. Partner. He helps me run the shop. The mice are his department," replied Uncle Arthur.

The ginger cat raised his head at the sound of his name, and stared at the children with large golden eyes.

"Well now," Uncle Arthur started towards the passage door, "we'd better take your luggage upstairs. See your rooms."

The stairs were very steep and narrow, and led on to a tiny landing with a door on either side. Ian and Uncle Arthur struggled with the cases, and Angela followed.

"On the left," instructed Uncle Arthur.

The room had been divided at some time

16

by a hardboard partition which did not quite reach to the ceiling. Half of the window was in each half of the room, and each part contained a bed, a chest of drawers, and a curtained corner for hanging suits and dresses. There was a rag rug beside each bed.

"Not what you're used to, I expect?" said Uncle Arthur. He bounced one of the beds up and down anxiously, and Angela said, "It's lovely. Does it matter which half we choose?"

"No, up to you," replied Uncle Arthur. "Er, well, come down when you're ready. Bathroom's downstairs. Had it built on."

He went off with obvious relief, and Ian and Angela looked at one another.

"I like him," said Angela decidedly. "He isn't like the others."

"No, he isn't," agreed Ian. "It might be fun here."

They unpacked a few of their things, and then went downstairs. There was a strong smell of cooking, and a haze of blueish smoke was drifting in through a door on the far side of the living room. Angela and Ian went to investigate, and found Uncle Arthur cooking sausages in a small, surprisingly bare kitchen.

"Hope you like sausages?" asked Uncle Arthur.

"Oh, we do," Angela assured him.

The sausages were well cooked by the time Uncle Arthur put them on the table. They were so well cooked that half of them were black, and Angela wondered if all Uncle Arthur's cooking was like this. If so, she would ask if she could do some herself, for her mistakes would hardly matter. She might even manage to do better.

There was plenty of bread and butter to eat with the sausages, and a luscious cherry cake to follow. Angela and Ian wondered where it had come from. It seemed too good to be from a shop, and it did not seem likely that Uncle Arthur had cooked it himself.

While they ate Uncle Arthur asked rather stiffly polite questions about Aunt Mavis, and how they got on at school. It was still the holidays at present, but if Aunt Mavis had to stay away for very long they would go to school near Uncle Arthur's. There had been some talk about them being sent to boarding schools, but Aunt Mavis had decided that they were not really old enough yet. Also a boarding school would be expensive, and Angela and Ian knew that their aunt was not very well off, in spite of her beautifully kept and furnished home. Aunt Mavis had said that she might try to get Ian into a State boarding school later on.

The shop bell rang several times during tea, and Uncle Arthur went to serve the customers. Partner sat by his master's chair, waiting regally to be handed bits of sausage and cake.

After the meal the children helped their uncle to wash up, and then he went to close the shop. He came back into the living room beaming and rubbing his hands.

"No more demands tonight," he said. "Open at eight tomorrow. Now, time you met the rest of the family."

Angela and Ian looked up in surprise. There was no one else in the house, and Partner and the bird, Bluey, had already been introduced to them. What more family could Uncle Arthur have? But their uncle was putting on an old jacket which hung behind the kitchen door, and taking a large, red, electric lamp down from the top of the dresser.

"Better slip your coats on," he told them. "Bit chilly down the yard."

Angela and Ian did so, and followed Uncle Arthur down two steps into the dark yard. There was a high fence on either side of them, and the backs of other houses faced them, with lights in many of the windows. Further away, a towering, skyscraper block of offices loomed against the sky, many of its windows still lighted. Behind it the night sky was pink and luminous with the lights of London.

Uncle Arthur's lamp showed them a long shed with a slanting roof built against the wall at the end of the yard. There was also a gate in this wall. It was only a few steps from the house to the shed, and when Uncle Arthur's hand touched the door latch there was a rustling noise inside, and something made a soft, deep, blowing sound.

"Hello then. I've brought you some visitors," said Uncle Arthur, opening the door. "Not fans yet, but they soon will be."

Angela and Ian followed him into the shed, and Angela gave a small shriek of delighted surprise. The shed was divided into two halves by poles and wooden partitions, and in each half was a tiny, cream-coloured pony with a flowing mane and tail and big, dark eyes.

"Magic and Moonshine," said Uncle Arthur. "My pantomime stars."

"Pantomime?" asked Ian. "Do you mean they go on the stage? Like at the Palladium?"

"Just like that," agreed Uncle Arthur. "Mind you, we haven't quite made the Palladium yet, but there's time. At the moment we're appearing at the Corry Empire, in

'Cinderella'. Got Donnie Shaw as Buttons."

"Donnie Shaw? The one who makes records?" asked Ian.

"That's right," agreed Uncle Arthur.

Angela was stroking the ponies, who had both thrust their noses over the partitions, and were nuzzling her gently.

"Which is Magic and which is Moonshine?" she asked.

"The one on the left is Magic," replied Uncle Arthur. "He's got a star on his forehead, look, and he's a bit smaller than Moonshine."

There was a white, star-shaped marking on Magic's forehead, and he was more pushful than Moonshine. The shed smelt sweetly of fresh hay and straw, and clean horse, and the light from the lamp showed bales of hay stacked in the space between the two partitions. Partner had followed them from the house, and now he jumped up on to Moonshine's partition. The pony nuzzled him with a gentle nose, and the big cat rubbed his whiskers against the pony.

22

"They're great friends," said Uncle Arthur. "Partner often sleeps on Moonshine's back if he wants a nap in the day."

"When are they in the pantomime?" asked Ian.

"Every night except Sunday and Monday." replied Uncle Arthur. "It's Monday today, of course. There isn't much of a house on Monday, so they don't open tonight."

Two short poles at one end of each partition took down to make a doorway, and Uncle Arthur lowered Magic's top pole.

"Shake hands with the lady, Magic," he instructed.

Solemnly, Magic lifted one forefoot, and offered it to Angela. She took it in her hand, feeling the cool hardness of the pony's narrow leg. His ankles, or fetlocks, as she later learned to call them, were little thicker than her own wrist. Not wanting to be left out, Moonshine too was lifting his forefoot in the air, and Ian shook hands with him between the poles.

"Can they do a lot of tricks?" Angela asked Uncle Arthur.

"Oh, a good few, a good few," replied Uncle Arthur.

"Did you teach them?" Ian wanted to know.

"Oh, er, well, yes, I did," Uncle Arthur looked embarrassed. "Always have liked to have an animal to train, you know. I used to have a dog, big Collie. He was never as good as these, though."

He refilled Moonshine's water-bucket at a tap in the yard outside, and gave both ponies a large armful of hay.

"That's it until tomorrow, then," he told Angela and Ian. "Come along. Now, what about your bedtimes?"

2 · Magic and Moonshine

In spite of being in strange beds, Angela and Ian both slept well that night. They were woken while it was still dark the next morning by the sound of Uncle Arthur moving about downstairs, and by shrill whistles as the paper boys arrived. While they were getting dressed they heard one of the ponies whinny, and Uncle Arthur's voice in the yard as he talked to them.

"Do you think we might be able to go to the theatre with them one day?" Angela asked Ian, as they went down the stairs.

"We can ask Uncle Arthur," replied Ian.

The big wooden clock on the living-room wall pointed to seven o'clock. There was no sign of breakfast, although Bluey was eating seed in his cage, and scattering it over the floor with little shakes of his head.

The children washed in the tiny pink and white bathroom which opened off the kitchen, and then hesitated in the doorway.

"Do you think it would be all right if we went outside?" asked Angela.

"I should think so."

Ian opened the back door. Outside, it was just starting to get light, and they could see a few details of the yard. A dustbin stood in a corner at the bottom of the steps, and on the other side was a concrete coal-bunker. Partner was sitting on this, washing his paws, and light shone from the ponies' shed. Inside they could see Uncle Arthur moving about, and Ian led the way down the steps.

"Hello," exclaimed their uncle, as they paused rather uncertainly in the shed doorway. "Early risers, I see. Say 'Good morning,' Magic, Moonshine," he instructed them.

The ponies lifted their heads from their piles of hay, and Magic whinnied.

"Come on, Moonshine," urged Uncle Arthur.

26

Moonshine made a soft wuffling sound in his nostrils, and then turned back to his hay.

"He's not so talkative as Magic," explained their uncle.

He had already sorted the dirty straw out of the ponies' beds, and it lay on a split sack between the two stalls. Uncle Arthur was spreading the clean straw back over the floor in Magic's stall. Moonshine's was finished, and looked neat and comfortable.

"Can I fill the water-buckets?" asked Ian, seeing them empty.

"Oh yes, yes, of course, if you'd like to," agreed Uncle Arthur.

Ian went out with the buckets and Uncle Arthur folded the sack so that all the dirty straw was inside, swung it up on to his back, and carried it round to the side of the shed. The small manure pile there was neatly and carefully covered with sacking.

Partner strolled in, and jumped up on to Magic's rail to have his head stroked by Angela. Ian came staggering back with the buckets, slopping water over his shoes.

Both he and Angela had decided to wear jeans, so that it would not matter if they got dirty.

"Well, that's all," announced Uncle Arthur, a few minutes later. The stable was clean and tidy, both buckets stood, full, in position, and Magic and Moonshine were eating hay with comfortable munching sounds. "Time for our breakfast now. Do you both eat boiled eggs?"

"Oh yes," Angela assured him, as they walked across the yard.

In the house Uncle Arthur exclaimed with surprise at seeing that it was ten past eight.

"Must open the shop," he told them. "Back in a minute."

He hurried through the green-curtained door, and they heard him unbolting the outside door. Someone came in at once, and they heard voices and the clang of the till. Uncle Arthur just had time to come out and put the saucepan on to boil for the eggs before another customer came into the shop.

"Shall I set the table?" Angela asked, as

he hurried towards the shop door.

"Oh, yes, certainly. Be a great help," agreed Uncle Arthur.

Angela and Ian set the table, hunting in drawers and cupboards for the cloth and the cutlery. They found the plates and cups on the plastic draining rack in the kitchen. The saucepan was boiling by now, but Uncle Arthur was still in the shop. Angela decided to put the eggs in herself. She found the box of eggs and a large spoon and lowered three carefully into the water. Then she looked at the living-room clock and carefully began to time four minutes. Ian cut bread, and put it under the grill to toast, and filled and switched on the electric kettle. Uncle Arthur came back to find everything ready.

The eggs were done perfectly. Angela felt very proud of them as she dipped her spoon into her own, and Uncle Arthur congratulated her on them.

"I'm not very good at eggs," he told them. "Always get them too hard or too runny.

I'll have to leave them to you."

"I like cooking," Angela told him eagerly. "I've done a little bit, when Aunt Mavis had time to let me. I'd like to do some."

"Oh well," Uncle Arthur looked rather worried. "I suppose you could. Mustn't burn yourself, though. Your Aunt Mavis would be after me if I let you hurt yourselves."

"I'll be very careful," Angela promised him.

Partner came in through his own cat-flap in the kitchen door, and was given milk and half a tin of cat food. Everyone helped to clear away, and Ian offered to do the washing up. Uncle Arthur had to dash away to serve in the shop, and when he came back Ian asked if they would be able to go to the theatre with the ponies one day.

"I don't see why not," replied Uncle Arthur. "Have to ask permission though. I'll do that tonight. Grace, or rather, Miss Lawley, is coming in to stay with you while I'm at the theatre."

"Miss Lawley?" asked Ian. "Is that the lady we saw in the shop yesterday?"

30

"In the shop? Oh my goodness, no, that was Mrs Pearson, May Pearson, a neighbour," replied Uncle Arthur. "No, Grace is quite different. You'll like Grace; she's a very nice person. Very nice indeed. Not that Mrs Pearson isn't nice, of course, but still Grace is different."

Ian and Angela thoroughly enjoyed their first day at Uncle Arthur's. After the washing up was done and the beds made Uncle Arthur's assistant, Mrs Randall, arrived to take over the shop for two hours while he took the ponies out for their exercise.

"Can't leave them shut up all day," he explained. "It wouldn't do them any good. It's not natural to keep any animal shut up all the time. They need exercise and fresh air just like we do."

Before going out Magic and Moonshine had to be groomed. First Uncle Arthur brushed them over with a stiff, yellow brush called a dandy brush. This removed all the bits of straw and stains from their coats. Then he picked up a softer, flat brush and

31

a flat metal comb with a lot of teeth and began to rub the brush over Moonshine. After each stroke he cleaned the brush by pulling it over the comb, and every few minutes he tapped the comb on the floor to knock out the grease.

"Could we try, do you think?" Ian asked, when he and Angela had been watching for a bit.

"Yes, of course you can, why not?" asked Uncle Arthur. "Ladies first."

He handed the brush and comb to Angela, and she tried to imitate the way that he had used them. It was much harder work than it looked, however, and she did not seem to be getting very much dirt out of the ponies' thick coats. Ian tried, but he was not much more successful. Uncle Arthur assured them that they would soon learn, and gave Magic a quick brush over.

"They've got their winter coats at present," he told the children. "It's easier in summer, when they've got less hair."

He went to fetch the ponies' bridles from

the back of the shed, and Ian and Angela watched him slip the metal bits into their mouths and the leather straps over their ears. Magic and Moonshine followed him eagerly out of their stalls and into the yard.

Uncle Arthur was much too big to ride the ponies, of course, and even Ian and Angela would have been rather big, and so the ponies were led. There were white webbing leading reins clipped to their bits, and Uncle Arthur led them one on either side of him. Ian opened the yard gate, and they all went out on to the cinder path which ran between the back yards of the two rows of houses.

Ian and Angela soon discovered that Uncle Arthur and his ponies were very well known in the district. A lot of people waved or spoke to them when they came out into the quiet street at the end of the path, and children came running to pat the ponies.

Magic and Moonshine seemed to enjoy all the attention. They pricked their ears and arched their necks to enjoy the patting and "asked" by lifting one forefoot and waving it in the air. Their feet made a soft thudding sound as they walked, and Angela remembered that most horses and ponies clattered on the roads.

"Don't they wear iron shoes?" she asked Uncle Arthur.

"Oh no. Not for the stage," replied Uncle Arthur. "They do in the summer, when they go to fêtes and horse shows and things. For the stage they wear rubber shoes. Rubber doesn't slip."

"Don't they go on the stage at all in summer?" asked Ian.

"Oh, sometimes, sometimes," said Uncle Arthur. "I have them shod specially then."

Their walk took them round a lot of quiet little streets, through a square with a rather overgrown garden in the centre, and over a canal bridge on to a big recreation ground.

"Like to lead one?" Uncle Arthur asked Ian.

"Please," agreed Ian.

Uncle Arthur handed him Moonshine's

34

leading rein, and Angela felt very envious. Perhaps her turn would come in a few minutes.

"I'll just give Magic his run," said Uncle Arthur.

He let Magic's long leading rein out to its full length, and the little pony began to circle round him, breaking into a quick, gay trot. Moonshine shook his head, and put his nose down to smell the damp, trampled winter grass.

The recreation ground was very quiet. It was a dull, slightly misty morning. The only other people there were a man in a blue track-suit, running slowly round the football ground, and a woman with a small dog. The woman waved to Uncle Arthur, who waved back, and Angela and Ian realized that here, too, the ponies were a familiar sight.

After about ten minutes Uncle Arthur stopped Magic, and handed him to Angela to hold while Moonshine had his run. When the bigger pony had had his turn Uncle Arthur brought him back, and stood just in front of Magic with his back to the pony.

"Good boy, Moonshine," he said.

He patted the pony's neck, ignoring Magic, who pricked his ears and then took a step forward. Reaching out his nose, he nudged his master in the back.

"What? Who did that?" exclaimed Uncle Arthur, looking round.

Magic pricked his ears, and gazed innocently into the distance.

"Was that you?" Uncle Arthur demanded, looking severely at a startled Angela.

"No, it was . . ." began Angela, but Uncle Arthur quickly turned away again.

Doubtfully Angela looked at Ian. Was Uncle Arthur cross about something? But Ian was grinning, and looking back at their uncle Angela saw him wink. Suddenly she understood. This was part of Magic and Moonshine's act.

Again Magic nudged Uncle Arthur, and again he turned round to see nothing but an innocent pony looking away across the big, misty field.

"Did you see anyone? Who was it?" he asked the children.

"I didn't see anything," said Ian. "Did you, Angela?"

"No," agreed Angela. "I didn't see anything either."

"Funny," said Uncle Arthur. He turned back to Moonshine. "Did you see anything?" he asked the pony.

Moonshine shook his head vigorously. Magic went up closer to Uncle Arthur, and gave him a harder push. This time he went on pushing when Uncle Arthur turned round, and his master put his hands on his hips and nodded.

"So it was you, was it?" he said. "I suppose you want some attention as well?"

Magic nodded his head, and Uncle Arthur put his hand in his pocket and brought out a slice of carrot. Moonshine immediately nudged him as well, and Uncle Arthur brought out a second slice for him.

"Clever, aren't they?" he asked the children, while Magic and Moonshine munched. "Magic does that routine with Donnie Shaw in the show."

"Does he do it all on his own?" asked Angela.

"I give him signals," replied Uncle Arthur. "Had to teach Donnie the same ones, of course, and get them working together. Now watch."

He turned his back on Magic again, and patted Moonshine. This time, watching closely, the children saw that he also quickly put one hand behind his back as he turned. Magic pricked his ears, and immediately went to nudge Uncle Arthur again. This time he got his slice of carrot at once.

"Always give a reward," explained Uncle Arthur. "Rewards, not punishments. That's how to train animals."

"Is there a signal for everything?" asked Ian.

"Yes. A signal or a word," replied his uncle. "Watch."

Angela and Ian watched carefully as Uncle Arthur turned to Moonshine.

"Do you like sugar?" he asked, holding one hand in front of him. He moved it up and down slightly, and Moonshine nodded his head.

"Do you like vinegar?" asked Uncle Arthur. This time he moved his hand sideways, and Moonshine shook his head.

"Do you see?" he asked the children.

Ian and Angela said that they did.

"Why don't you carry a long stick with them?" asked Ian. "In circuses the people with horses always do. Don't they give them signals with that?"

"Yes, in circus," agreed Uncle Arthur. "But it wouldn't look right in our kind of act, would it? It's a bit harder this way, but it looks a lot better, I think." He looked at his watch, and then began to gather up Magic and Moonshine's reins. "My goodness," he exclaimed. "Ten to twelve. Must

40

get back. Mrs Randall has to cook her husband's dinner by one o'clock. Come along."

Ian was allowed to lead Moonshine for part of the way, and Uncle Arthur let Angela lead Magic up the cinder path to their gate.

"Which is the cleverest?" asked Angela, as they watched Uncle Arthur give the ponies their mid-day feeds. These consisted of half buckets of greenish-brown cubes, which looked rather like thick, chopped up bits of stick.

"Oh dear, not in front of them," exclaimed Uncle Arthur. "One of them might be hurt."

Angela stared at Magic and Moonshine.

"Can they really understand that much?" she asked.

"You never know," replied Uncle Arthur. "Mustn't risk it. Might have one of them going on strike."

As they went across the yard he said, "Cleverest? Well, I don't know. Moonshine's very reliable, never gets excited. I can leave him standing on his own in the middle

41

of the ring at a show. He won't move until he's told. But Magic—he's the quick one. He learns quickly, and he's got a sense of humour. Loves to get the laughs. He's a real showman, in fact."

"Which do you like the best?" asked Ian.

"Now, you mustn't ask that," Uncle Arthur told him. "Never have a favourite. They might know, you see. Now, I must go and let poor Mrs Randall get home."

He hurried through into the shop, and Angela and Ian looked at one another.

"I bet he has got a favourite," said Ian.

"Yes—Magic," said Angela, and they laughed.

3 · Grace

For lunch they had chops, frozen peas, and potatoes, all rather over-cooked, and followed by cold apple pie and some ice cream from the shop fridge. The apple pie was delicious.

"Grace made it," explained Uncle Arthur, when Angela said how nice it was. "Cooking's one of her hobbies. She said you'd probably starve if you had to live entirely on my cooking, and so she made a few things to help out."

It began to rain after lunch, and so the children stayed in the house. There were some games in one of the drawers in Uncle Arthur's big dresser, and they played Snap, draughts, dominoes, and Snakes and Ladders. Uncle Arthur joined in when there was no one in the shop, but the bell was busy

43

for most of the afternoon.

People came in for a packet of cigarettes, a bar of chocolate, a magazine, or to change a book at the little lending library. This filled three shelves in one corner of the shop.

Uncle Arthur let the children go into the shop with him, and they both found it very strange to be on the wrong side of the counter. Angela was allowed to work the till, and Ian scrambled up and down the ladder to fetch things from the higher shelves.

At half-past four Angela made some tea and put out cake and biscuits which they ate in a short lull from the bell. The shop was supposed to close at half-past six, but it was ten to seven before it was empty long enough for Uncle Arthur to lock the door and pull down the blind.

"Have to hurry now," he told them. "Must be at the theatre by a quarter to eight."

There was tinned meat and tomatoes for supper, with bread and butter and the cherry cake to follow. Uncle Arthur ate his very fast, and Ian and Angela were still eating their meat when he said that he must fetch the van round.

"Do the ponies go in a van, then?" asked Ian, who had supposed that Magic and Moonshine walked to the theatre.

"Oh my goodness, yes," replied Uncle Arthur. "Can't have them walking there, especially on a wet night. I'd never get them looking clean again. Have to groom them again at the theatre anyway. Besides, I don't like having them out on the roads after dark. Not safe; there's too much traffic."

"Can we watch them go into the van?" asked Angela, and their uncle said that they could.

Uncle Arthur backed his van up the cinder path to the back gate, and Angela and Ian went out in their mackintoshes to watch. The van was very gay. In the light of a nearby street lamp they could see the red, green, and yellow paintwork. The mudguards were red, the bodywork green, and the doors yellow, and big yellow letters along both sides read "Magic and Moonshine". In smaller letters beneath the names was written "Wonder ponies of stage and screen".

"Have they been in films?" Ian asked Uncle Arthur, when he had read this.

"Well, they once made a commercial for television, advertising shampoo," replied Uncle Arthur. "That's the screen, isn't it?"

Ian agreed that it certainly was.

The shape of the van was rather tall and narrow, and the original back doors had been changed to a ramp for the ponies to walk up. Inside it was divided into two halves by a padded partition, and the sides were also padded. A padded bar went across in front of the ponies, very low down as they were so small. Beyond this there was a space for equipment to be stored.

Magic and Moonshine had heard the van arrive, and they were waiting eagerly in their stalls. Magic especially looked excited: his little creamy ears were pricked, and his dark eyes shone. Moonshine looked interested, but calmer.

46

Uncle Arthur led Magic into the van first, while Ian held Moonshine. Both ponies went in happily, without any hesitation, and certainly the van looked comfortable with its bed of straw on the wooden floor. A net filled with hay hung in front of each pony, for them to eat on the journey. A little light in the roof made it easy for Uncle Arthur to see to tie the ponies up.

Uncle Arthur had got out, and come round to raise the ramp when a voice behind the children said, "Hello. I'm just in time, then."

"Hello, Grace," exclaimed Uncle Arthur, turning to beam at her. "Meet Angela and Ian. This is Miss Lawley," he told them.

Ian and Angela turned to see a nice-looking, dark-haired woman in a green mackintosh smiling at them. She looked younger than Uncle Arthur, and her dark eyes were warm and friendly.

"Just Grace, please," she said. "I see you've become fans already. When is Arthur taking you to watch them on the stage?"

"I'm going to ask Mr Woodward about

it tonight," Uncle Arthur told her. "If he agrees, they can come backstage with us."

"I'm sure he will," said Grace. "Aren't you going to be late, Arthur? It's twenty-five to."

"Is it? I must be off," exclaimed Uncle Arthur. "See you later. Goodbye, all. Look after Grace, won't you, kids?"

"Goodbye," said Angela and Ian, and Grace waved. Uncle Arthur got into the cab, and the van moved slowly away down the path.

"Come on," said Grace. "Let's go into the dry."

The yard seemed suddenly empty without Magic and Moonshine moving and snorting in their shed. Partner was waiting on the top step to precede them into the house.

"You'd better finish your tea," Grace told them, when they had taken off their wet mackintoshes. "Trust Arthur to be in such a hurry you didn't have time before he went."

She laughed, felt the tea pot, and put the kettle on to boil for more. Then she sat down at the table with them, and asked them how they liked it at Uncle Arthur's.

Ian and Angela found Grace very easy to talk to. She was not shy with them, as Uncle Arthur had been at first and still was a bit. Nor was she stiff, like Aunt Mavis, and she seemed really interested in them. Soon Angela especially felt that if Grace was really their aunt she would be happy to stay with her for always. She felt much the same about Uncle Arthur, but living with him might be rather a responsibility.

When they had finished tea Grace sat down at the piano and asked them if they liked music.

"Well ..." said Ian doubtfully, trying to be polite. "We do sometimes."

Grace laughed. "I mean songs, and things like that," she said.

"I like singing at school," said Angela.

"Do you know this?" Grace began to play, and Angela recognised *Bobby Shafto*. Soon they were all singing. Grace knew dozens of songs and tunes. She played old ones like *Mollie Malone* and *The Grey Goose*,

49

songs from musicals such as *Oklahoma* and *Mary Poppins,* slow traditional ones like *Greensleeves* and *Over the Sea to Skye* and jazzy ones like *Yellow Submarine.*

Angela and Ian hummed the ones that they did not know the words to, and the time flashed past. They had never realized how much fun a piano could be. Aunt Mavis had one, a polished beauty that stood in her front room. It was very different from this battered instrument of Uncle Arthur's, and they were strictly forbidden to touch it. It was certainly not considered a thing to have fun with.

"Do you play the piano a lot?" Ian asked Grace, when they finally paused for breath.

"Yes, I'm a piano teacher," explained Grace. "And I play for dancing classes at a school twice a week. Then there are Arthur's film shows. I play for those as well. That's a lot of fun."

"Film shows?" inquired Angela, puzzled.

"Yes. He's got a projector, and he shows old silent films sometimes, in here," replied Grace. "All the neighbours come, and we

50

have quite a party. I play the piano to ac-
company the films. Cinemas always had a
pianist before films had sound."

She played a few deep, sinister notes on
the piano.

"That's the villain's music," she explained.
She played a pretty, tinkling tune. "That's
for the heroine."

Some fast, exciting music like horses galloping was for the chase, and there was a
slow, sad piece of music for when things
went wrong.

"Do you have to watch the film, and make
the music fit in, then?" asked Ian.

"Yes. And you mustn't get left behind,"
replied Grace. "The wrong bit of music at
a dramatic moment could ruin everything."

It was getting late by now, and Grace said
that it was time they went to bed. She got
out milk and biscuits, and said that she would
come up to look at them after they were in
bed.

"Isn't she nice?" whispered Angela, as
they went up the stairs. "It is fun here. I

hope Aunt Mavis won't come home too quickly."

"So do I," agreed Ian. "It'll seem awfully dull back in Surbiton."

Next morning Uncle Arthur asked them if they had enjoyed themselves with Grace. Ian and Angela told him that they had.

"Thought you would," said Uncle Arthur. "Couldn't help liking Grace, could you? I've often thought I ought to marry her. Don't suppose she'd have me, though." He laughed, and got up to answer the shop bell. Angela and Ian looked at each other.

"I wish Uncle Arthur would marry Grace," said Angela. "Perhaps we might be able to stay here, then, if she was here to look after us."

"It would be terrific if we could," agreed Ian. "But he might only have been joking."

Angela was afraid that he might be right. It was a nice thing to dream about, however. Living with Uncle Arthur and Grace would be much nicer than living with Aunt Mavis.

"By the way," said Uncle Arthur, when they were washing up, "I asked about you two coming to the show. It's all right, so you can come along and see the performance tonight. Backstage, of course. I'll fix you up with seats out front another night."

"Oh, thank you," cried Angela, and Ian said, "Gosh, how marvellous. Thank you."

They grinned at each other in excited delight. It had been fun at home with Grace, but how much more exciting it would be to see Magic and Moonshine on the stage, and to be with them backstage as though they too were part of the show.

The second day at Uncle Arthur's passed as quickly and as interestingly as the first. Mrs Randall came to look after the shop again while Uncle Arthur and the children took Magic and Moonshine for their walk.

In the afternoon Angela and Ian went to do some shopping at the other shops in the street. The other shopkeepers knew who they were, and all about them, and were very friendly. It was as though they really belonged, thought Angela, as they walked back to their uncle's.

It was very exciting that evening to watch Magic and Moonshine climb the ramp into their van, and to know that tonight they were going as well. Grace had called round to see what was happening, and she was there to wave them off.

There was plenty of room in the cab beside Uncle Arthur, and the children discovered a little window behind them through which they could see into the back. Uncle Arthur had a switch in the cab which turned on the inside light over the ponies, so that he could see them whenever he wished.

It was not far from Uncle Arthur's to the theatre, and Ian and Angela thoroughly enjoyed the ride. They were soon in a much busier, more brightly lighted district than the one in which Uncle Arthur lived. From the high cab they had a good view of the traffic and the lighted shop windows.

It was a cold evening, and everyone seemed to be hurrying along the pavements with their coat collars turned up, but a lot of people glanced at the van, and paused to stare at its gay paint, and to read the words painted on the side.

The theatre stood half-way along a wide road of shops, its glass doors open to the warmly lighted foyer. A big sign across the front read, "The Corry Empire presents *Cinderella*, a grand pantomime spectacular, starring Donnie Shaw."

"It doesn't say anything about Magic and Moonshine," exclaimed Angela, disappointed.

"Not up there. We're not stars yet," replied Uncle Arthur. "But they've got their names on the other posters, the ones by the doors."

To Angela and Ian's surprise he did not stop outside the theatre, but drove straight past.

"Got to go round to the stage door," he explained, seeing them exchange glances. "First turn on the left."

The van turned, and a few minutes later they entered a dimly lighted yard, behind the massive back of the Corry Empire. Uncle Arthur parked the van beside a row of cars, switched off the engine, and opened the cab door. In the back one of the ponies whinnied, and Uncle Arthur said, "That's Magic. He knows we've arrived."

The ponies came out of the van as eagerly as they had gone in. Ian was trusted to lead Moonshine across the yard, and Uncle Arthur handed Angela one of the hay nets to carry. There was a huge pair of iron doors set in the wall of the theatre, with a dim light beside them. Uncle Arthur explained that the big pieces of scenery were taken in that way. Their way in was through a smaller door set into the large ones. Magic went through first, lifting his feet neatly over the step, and Moonshine followed. Angela closed the little door behind them, and they were backstage at the Corry Empire.

4 · Backstage

The door opened into a long, wide corridor, stone-floored, and with whitewashed brick walls. Uncle Arthur turned right, and a little further on they came to another pair of doors. Beyond these lay what really seemed to be another world.

Backstage, the children soon discovered, was a confusing place. Tall pieces of canvas and wood, the scenery "flats", and the huge canvas "back-cloths" on which were painted the background to each scene, hid the stage from view. Ropes and pulleys dangled from the high, shadowy roof, and the lighting was dim and dusty.

One big, dark opening led to the scenery store room, and through a gap between the "flats" the children caught a glimpse of the stage. The red curtains were down, hiding

57

the audience, and there were gay market stalls in position, ready for the opening scene.

There were a lot of people hurrying about behind the stage: men in jeans and sweaters carrying stage properties and bits of scenery, and other people in strange costumes and thick make-up. Most of them spoke to Uncle Arthur, and patted the ponies, and one thin, pretty girl wearing a red skirt with big patches and a white, loose-sleeved blouse gave Magic an apple core.

"Was that Cinderella?" asked Angela, when the girl had gone.

"No. That was Julie. She's a dancer in the chorus," replied Uncle Arthur.

He was making his way right round the back of the stage, and the ponies seemed to know where they were going.

"They've got their own corner, you know," said Uncle Arthur. "Just round here."

Magic and Moonshine's corner was an empty alcove which Uncle Arthur said was sometimes used for storing extra scenery.

58

There was sand on the board floor to prevent them from slipping, and to soak up any moisture, and two rings were fixed to the wall. Magic and Moonshine were fastened to these, and Uncle Arthur took the hay net from Angela and tied it between them. He filled an empty bucket with water, and the ponies were settled.

"When do they go on?" asked Ian.

"Magic does his bit with Donnie Shaw just before the interval," replied Uncle Arthur. "The transformation scene, where they pull Cinderella's coach to the ball, is near the end."

Angela remembered the story, and how the rats and the pumpkin were supposed to turn into the ponies and the coach. She could not imagine how it would be done.

"Are there really rats?" she asked. "To turn into ponies?"

"Oh yes, there are rats all right," Uncle Arthur told her. "You'll see. It's all done with the lights—lights and a gauze curtain. Very clever."

It sounded impossible to Angela, but she supposed that they would see what happened later on.

"Hello, Arthur," said a tall man with a beard. "Got your helpers with you, I see."

"That's right, Frank," agreed Uncle Arthur. "Angela and Ian. Couldn't manage without them."

"No. Need someone to help you to hold those fire-eaters down," said Frank, smiling. "If you want to watch later on," he told the children, "you can stand over there." He pointed to the right hand side of the stage. "Behind the prompter. But stand well back and keep quiet, won't you?"

Angela and Ian promised him that they would, and Frank went off.

"Stage manager," explained Uncle Arthur. "Nice fellow, Frank."

"What is a prompter?" inquired Ian.

"The person who reads the lines to himself as the performers act on the stage, and tells them what comes next if they forget," replied their uncle.

60

A bell rang somewhere, and he said, "Five minutes to go."

Moonshine was eating hay calmly, his ears relaxed and his eyes half closed. Magic, however, was trying to look round, his ears sharply pricked and his eyes bright. He did not seem interested in his hay, and as the space behind the stage began to fill up with people in gay costumes he began to paw the floor with one small front hoof. Uncle Arthur went to stand beside the pony, putting one arm round his neck, and talking to him softly. Magic grew a little quieter, and Frank said, "Everyone on stage, please. Opening number."

Most of the gaily dressed girls and men went on to the stage, and from beyond the curtain Angela and Ian heard the exciting sound of the orchestra tuning up.

"Quiet, please," warned Frank, and the instruments were suddenly playing a merry, dancing tune. There was a swish and a rattle as the curtain went back, and the children jumped as the chorus began to sing only a

61

few feet away from them, beyond the scenery.

"Why not go and watch?" whispered Uncle Arthur. "I'll warn you when it's time to get Magic ready."

Angela and Ian nodded, and crept round to stand where Frank had suggested. The prompter was a girl with long, dark hair, dressed in slacks and a sweater. She was sitting on a low canvas stool, a typewritten script on her knee, reading the words silently and intently as the people on the stage spoke them. It was easy for the children to see over her head, and they found that they had a good view of most of the stage.

The pantomime at the Corry Empire was not really a very big one, but to Angela and Ian, watching from their dark corner, the warm, bright stage seemed enchanted. People in costume stood in the dusty wings, waiting to go on, just seeming ordinary in spite of their make-up and fancy dress. Then they stepped out into the light and colour, and suddenly they were people from a fairy

62

story. The change was dazzling and confusing, and the nearness of the music and singing made the children feel almost part of it themselves.

There was not a big audience, but there were enough people in the seats to fill the theatre with laughter and clapping, and this helped to give the show life. Angela and Ian had almost forgotten the ponies when Julie, from the chorus, touched Ian on the shoulder and said that Uncle Arthur was getting Magic ready.

It did not take much work to get Magic ready for his first appearance with Donnie Shaw. Uncle Arthur was polishing his creamy coat with a soft body-brush, and Ian and Angela were allowed to brush out his silvery mane and tail. Then Uncle Arthur unfastened his rope, and led him round to the opposite side of the stage from the prompter, ready for his entrance.

Magic knew that it was time for his special bit. His eyes shone, and he arched his neck against the pull of the rope. The scene was in the forest, and the back-cloth was painted with green trees, yellow and blue flowers, and red toadstools. The canvas "flats" were shaped and painted like trees. Donnie Shaw, as Buttons, was helping Cinderella to gather sticks. Cinderella wandered off the stage, still searching, and Donnie stood looking at the big pile that they had collected, wondering how to carry them.

"Oh dear," he said. "I shall never be able to manage all those on my own. I wish I had someone to help me."

This was Magic's cue, the moment when he had to go on to the stage. Donnie clasped both hands behind his back, and Uncle Arthur unbuckled Magic's head collar. Completely loose, Magic trotted on to the stage. He went straight up behind Donnie, or Buttons, and pushed him in the back.

"Here, who did that?" exclaimed Buttons, turning round.

As he had done on the recreation ground with Uncle Arthur, Magic stared innocently into the distance.

"Was it you?" Buttons asked him. He was holding his hand out, and he moved it sideways slightly. Magic shook his head. Buttons turned his back again, and once more Magic gave him a push, and then looked innocent.

The audience was starting to laugh now, and Buttons turned away again. Once more Magic pushed him, and this time he went on pushing with his nose when Buttons turned back. Buttons shook his fist at the pony, and Magic jumped sideways and trotted off. Buttons chased him round the stage, in and out of the "trees", until, at another signal from Buttons, Magic swung round and began to do the chasing himself.

The audience roared, and Angela glanced at Uncle Arthur. He was watching his pony carefully, and proudly. Angela thought that he was right to be proud, after training a pony like Magic.

At last Magic stopped chasing Buttons, and they stood and looked at one another.

"Look," said Buttons. "Why don't we make friends? You carry my sticks, and I'll introduce you to the most beautiful girl in the world."

Magic shook his head, and then lifted his nose and curled back his top lip.

"Oh, so you don't think much of that?" asked Buttons. "Well then, suppose I tell you about the dancing classes everyone is going to, ready for the Prince's ball?"

Again Magic shook his head.

"I bet you can't dance, anyway," retorted Buttons.

The orchestra struck up a rumba, and Buttons dropped his hand to his side, moving so that he could touch Magic's flank. Magic pricked his ears, and as Buttons began to dance a rumba the pony began to swing his hind quarters from side to side as though he, too, was dancing. The tune changed to a waltz, and Magic and Buttons circled the stage, twirling round in circles to the music.

The fairy story enchantment of the stage worked on Magic as well, and Angela found it easy to imagine that he really was a fairy pony, part of the mysterious forest, and not

66

one of Uncle Arthur's pantomime ponies at
all. The soft, warm lighting darkened the
colour of his creamy coat, and his silver tail
swirled behind him, shot with red, blue, and
green from the footlights.

Then the waltz came to an end, and Magic
and Buttons faced the audience in a low bow,
Buttons with right foot extended, Magic

down on his right knee with his other leg stretched in front of him.

"I know," said Buttons, when they were on their feet again. "If you carry my sticks, I'll give you a bag of carrots."

Magic nodded vigorously, and went to stand beside the pile of sticks. Buttons swung the bundle on to the pony's back, and Magic followed him off the stage to where Uncle Arthur was waiting.

The applause for Magic was long and loud, and Uncle Arthur fed him on carrots while Ian and Angela patted him.

"He's wonderful," Angela told her uncle, and Ian agreed. Uncle Arthur's face was red with pleasure as they praised the pony, and Magic looked smug as he buried his nose in his hay. Now that his first, and most exciting, appearance was over he was as ready to eat as Moonshine was.

It took much longer to get the ponies ready for their appearance with the coach in the transformation scene. Both Magic and Moonshine's manes and tails were plaited, and the plaits were threaded with ribbon. They wore tall ostrich feathers, coloured silver and blue, on the headbands of their bridles, and the bridles and their harness were also silver and blue. The leather was studded with shiny things that looked like rubies and diamonds, although Uncle Arthur said that they were made of glass.

When the ponies were plaited and harnessed they had to be fastened to the coach. Cinderella's coach was made of wood, and the framework was set on big wheels. There was a single narrow seat inside, and the roof was arched. As it was supposed to be made of glass there was no covering over the wooden struts, and Uncle Arthur said that Cinderella and her attendants had to remember not to put their hands between them.

"Give the show away if they did," he said. "You can't put your hand through glass."

The coach was painted silver, and the woodwork was set with gold and silver sequins and more bits of coloured glass. It looked so light and fragile that it did not seem possible that anyone could really ride in it.

The coach was already in position at the back of the stage when Uncle Arthur led the ponies out to harness them. The second, or drop curtain, was down, hiding the comedians who were making the audience laugh at the front of the stage.

Between the ponies and coach and the main part of the stage there was a thin curtain made of gauze. Uncle Arthur said that while the lights shone on it from the front the audience could not see through. It was when those lights went out, and the ones at the back came on, that the ponies and coach would be seen.

This seemed incredible to Ian and Angela, for when the drop curtain went up they could see the stage, with its set of kitchen fireplace and cupboards, and the table with the cage of white rats and the pumpkin, quite clearly. They could also see the audience, and it was hard to believe that they themselves could not be seen at all.

Uncle Arthur and the children waited with the ponies while on the stage Cinderella's fairy godmother appeared, and granted her wish to go to the ball. Magic and Moonshine stood very quietly, seeming to understand that they must not make any noise. Then all the lights went down, and part of the chorus danced a fairy ballet. They wore luminous frocks, and shone blue, green, and red in the dark.

Then Cinderella came quietly back on to the stage, and two members of the chorus came to take the ponies from Uncle Arthur. He hurried the children off the stage, and the lights came up behind the gauze curtain. The audience gasped, and then began to clap as the ponies and their lovely little coach became visible, and as they saw Cinderella in her beautiful ball gown. Then the gauze curtain rose, and Cinderella stepped carefully into her coach. Led by two members of the chorus the ponies drew Cinderella's coach away, off the stage, to the ball.

"So that's how it's done," exclaimed Ian.

71

"I've always wondered."

Uncle Arthur laughed as he began to unharness the two ponies. "Not very magical really," he said. "But clever. Very clever."

The pantomime was almost over. Cinderella met the prince, lost her slipper on the stairs at midnight, and was found again in rags by her kitchen fire. The entire cast, including Magic and Moonshine, went on to the stage for the finale, which took place at Cinderella's wedding to the Prince. Then the curtain came down for the last time.

Angela and Ian helped Uncle Arthur to make sure that all the harness and trappings were safely back in their box, then they were ready to go home. Uncle Arthur and Ian led the ponies back along the corridor, and Angela followed them out into the damp and chilly yard.

It felt very cold outside after the warmth inside the theatre. The children were shivering as they watched Uncle Arthur load the ponies, and the thought of the living-room fire and of bed was very inviting. They could not remember ever having been out so late before.

The streets were very dark and quiet as they drove home, and there was hardly anyone about. It was very welcome to enter the yard at Uncle Arthur's and see the kitchen light shining, and the back door open. Grace had waited for them to come home. She had everything ready for hot chocolate drinks, and the cake tin was on the table. Partner lay stretched out luxuriously in front of the glowing fire, and Bluey was dozing with his head under his wing.

Angela was almost too sleepy to eat her cake, although Ian was still wide awake, and asking eager questions about things they had seen at the theatre. Angela hardly remembered Grace taking her upstairs, and tucking her into bed, but there was something very comfortable about it all.

5 · A new trick

For the first time since they had come to Uncle Arthur's Angela did not wake up when the paper boys arrived in the morning. Ian woke her in the end.

"It's half-past nine," he told her, as she sat up, rubbing her eyes. "We had breakfast ages ago. We left you some bacon and toast, but I expect it'll be pretty hard by now. Oh, and there's a letter from Aunt Mavis."

"A letter?" Angela was wide awake at once. "She doesn't want us back yet, does she?"

"Oh no, not yet," Ian assured her. "But she says she hopes she won't have to be away too long. She says her mother's leg isn't very bad, and she'll be able to get about again in two or three weeks. She doesn't want us to put upon Uncle Arthur for any longer than we must."

"But we aren't 'putting upon him', are we?" asked Angela anxiously. "He seems to like having us here, now he's getting used to us."

"I think he does like it," agreed Ian. "But Aunt Mavis doesn't know that."

"Oh, Ian, I don't want to go back," wailed Angela. "We're always moving about. When we do go back to Aunt Mavis's we'll be sent to stay with someone else again when she has to go away the next time."

"Perhaps we'll come back here next time as well, if Uncle Arthur does enjoy having us," said Ian hopefully. He did not like thinking about going back to Aunt Mavis's neat, tidy, silent flat either, but he supposed that it was unavoidable. But it was no use starting to be miserable about going back yet. They had hardly been with Uncle Arthur for any time at all, and there was no sense in spoiling their stay by thinking about Aunt Mavis's all the time.

By the end of their first week Angela and Ian really began to feel as though they had always lived at Uncle Arthur's. The whistle of the early paper boys and the clang of the shop bell were familiar sounds, and so was Bluey's chatter above their heads as they had breakfast.

They went to the theatre again, to sit in front this time, and applaud with the rest of the audience when Magic did his act. On Sunday they went to church with Grace in the morning, while Uncle Arthur looked after the shop.

In the evening Grace came to tea, and afterwards they all sang round the piano. Then Uncle Arthur set up his projector and showed some short, silent, slap-stick comedies. Grace played the piano while Charlie Chaplin, Little Titch, and Buster Keaton went through their antics, and Angela and Ian laughed until they were helpless.

After Grace had gone home the children went out into the frosty night to help Uncle Arthur to settle the ponies. It did not seem possible that only a week ago they had not known the yard, and the ponies' shed, and Magic and Moonshine drowsing or eating inside. It seemed even less possible that they had not known Grace or Uncle Arthur, and even to Ian it was their old life with Aunt Mavis which began to seem less and less real.

Although it was Uncle Arthur who was supposed to be in charge of them it was Grace who did a lot of the jobs that were too hard for Angela. She took all the washing home with her, saying that it was easy, as she had a washing machine. She also did the more difficult mending. Angela could sew on buttons, and she quite enjoyed doing it, but mending a long tear in Ian's jacket was harder, and Grace did that. She did not come every day, as sometimes she had music lessons to give in the evenings as well as during the day, but usually she called in at some time to make sure that all was well, and that they did not need anything. Uncle Arthur said that he did not know how he would manage without her.

Wednesday was early closing day, and that week Uncle Arthur said that he intended to teach Magic a new trick on Wednesday afternoon. It sounded great fun, and Angela was horrified when she woke up with a sore throat. By lunch time her nose was running, and she was sneezing. Uncle Arthur looked at her anxiously, and awkwardly felt her head.

"Do you often have colds?" he asked her.

"Quite often," Angela told him. "They aren't usually bad. I don't always stay in," she added.

She looked imploringly at Ian, who wished that Grace was there. He suspected that Angela ought to stay in, but it did seem hard on her when Uncle Arthur was going to work with Magic.

"She's not usually ill with colds," he said, after thinking for a moment. It seemed the fairest thing to say.

Uncle Arthur looked relieved. He had no wish to make Angela stay in either.

"That's all right then," he said. "Business

78

as usual. Now, let's get washed up, and then we can start on old Magic."

"Where will you teach him? Here, or on the recreation ground?" asked Ian.

"Oh, here," replied Uncle Arthur. "They've had their walk for today. Best to train an animal in an enclosed place that it's used to. Nothing to distract it then."

"What are you going to teach him to do?" asked Angela.

"You'll see," Uncle Arthur told her happily. "It isn't anything too hard; he'll have it in half an hour, but it'll dress up."

"Dress up?" Angela was puzzled. She imagined Magic in a hat and ribbons.

"That means it's the sort of trick that can be made to look difficult and exciting," explained Uncle Arthur. "It's simple enough really, like that business of pushing someone, but more can be made of it for the stage."

Angela and Ian understood vaguely. They would soon find out, anyway, when they saw what the trick was going to be.

Uncle Arthur put a head collar on Magic,

and Angela was allowed to lead him out into the yard. Magic knew that something interesting was going to happen, and he looked round with shining eyes. Partner jumped on top of the shed, and settled down as though he were in a ringside seat.

There was an iron rail on either side of the steps up to the back door, and Uncle Arthur took Magic's rope from Angela and tied him to this. He used a simple quick-release knot, leaving a long, loose end. Then he took a carrot out of his pocket, and tied it to the free end. Magic started nosing for it at once, and Uncle Arthur said, "Go on, then. Pull it off."

Magic did so, pulling the carrot free with a quick jerk. The knot, of course, came undone at the same time, and Uncle Arthur made no move to re-fasten it.

"Let him realise he's free first," he explained to the children.

Magic finished his carrot, looked round, and pricked his ears towards his master.

"Come here, then," said Uncle Arthur.

80

He was standing some distance from the steps, and Magic started towards him at once. Suddenly he seemed to realize that he was free, and he paused, looking back at the steps. Then he walked on to push his nose into Uncle Arthur's hand.

"Let's do that again," said Uncle Arthur, and led Magic back to the steps.

This time Magic seized the carrot at once, and pulled it free. When he had eaten it he paused for a moment and then walked straight across to his master.

"Good boy," Uncle Arthur told him, patting him. "He's getting the idea," he added to Angela and Ian. "It never takes him long to catch on."

By the time they had repeated the same thing six times Magic was grabbing the carrot and walking off loose almost before his master could move away.

"Now," said Uncle Arthur, as he tied Magic up again. "This time we won't use the carrot."

Magic reached out his nose eagerly to the rope, and then stopped in surprise. No carrot.

"Go on," Uncle Arthur encouraged him. "Pull. Here then, Magic. Come on, boy." He held a carrot out towards the pony, and Magic tried to move towards it. Discovering that he was still tied up, he stopped.

"Come on," urged Uncle Arthur. "Pull. Here, Magic."

Magic looked at him, ears pricked, and nostrils wide. Angela and Ian could almost see him thinking. There was no carrot on the rope. There was one in his master's hand, which was held out temptingly, but to get to his master he must get free from the railings. Before, he had found himself free when he had pulled the carrot.

Magic reached out his nose to check again that there was no carrot on the rope. Experimentally he nibbled it with his teeth. Angela almost held her breath. Would Magic realize what he had to do?

Suddenly, Magic decided to try. He seized the rope firmly between his teeth, and gave it a sharp pull. Uncle Arthur had fastened the knot very loosely, and it came free at

82

once. Delighted with himself, Magic kicked up his heels and gave a little squeal before trotting over to get his carrot.

"Good boy. Very good," said Uncle Arthur, patting him hard. He found another carrot in his pocket for the pony. His face glowed with pride in Magic, and Angela and Ian came to praise the pony as well.

They repeated the procedure twice more, and it was obvious that Magic had got the idea.

"Is that the whole trick?" asked Ian. "Or has he got to do anything else?"

"Well, it isn't really the whole trick," replied Uncle Arthur. "But it's enough of it for one day. We'll practise that with him for a bit, and then we'll have Moonshine out as well, and get old Magic untieing him."

"Oh, I see," Ian suddenly understood how the trick would appear. "Magic will sort of rescue Moonshine on the stage."

"That's right, that's it," agreed Uncle Arthur, pleased that they understood. "Good ending to a ring act. I leave Moonshine tied up, pretend to forget him, bow to the audience, and walk off with Magic. Just at the exit we remember. Magic gallops back, unties Moonshine, and they both canter off after me."

"Lovely," exclaimed Angela. "Do you teach him all his tricks like that, with carrots and things?"

"Oh yes. Plenty of encouragement and reward," replied Uncle Arthur. "There are lots of ways of training animals, but that's always been my way. Taught them to bow with carrot. Held it between their front legs, so that they had to bend their necks and knees to get at it. Held it further and further back until I got a bow. After that they soon caught on without the carrot: just a signal with my hand or a stick behind their front legs. Magic, he hardly needs a signal now. Knows when I bow he bows, and that's it. Moonshine still likes to be told."

"What other things can they do?" asked Ian.

"Well, let me see. They can lie down or

84

sit down, count, open a box, and pick up a handkerchief or take off my hat," listed Uncle Arthur. "And the things you've seen, of course."

"They are clever," said Angela. She sneezed, and pulled out a damp handkerchief to blow her nose. Uncle Arthur looked at her doubtfully and said that they'd better put Magic away and go indoors.

While they were helping Uncle Arthur to settle Magic there was a knock on the yard gate. Ian opened it, and three of Magic and Moonshine's young "fans" came into the yard. Angela and Ian knew them quite well, and had played with them once or twice. Although living with Uncle Arthur had helped them to meet some of the other children, they were not yet really accepted by them.

Magic and Moonshine's fans had been visiting them for a long time, but Uncle Arthur had never trusted them to do more than offer the ponies tit-bits, and sometimes to fill up the water-buckets. But Angela and Ian were allowed to lead them at exercise, and Uncle Arthur had taken them backstage at the theatre with him. The other children had not yet decided whether or not this was quite fair.

"Mum sent some scraps round for them," Jane, who was Ian's age, told Uncle Arthur. She handed him a brown paper carrier bag, and Angela saw that it contained stale bread, cabbage leaves, a few withered carrots, some boiled potatoes, and apple peel. She knew from watching Uncle Arthur before that he would break up the scraps and mix them with Magic and Moonshine's other food.

"My goodness, that is kind of her," Uncle Arthur told Jane. "Coming in to say 'hello' to the lads, are you?"

Jane and her two younger brothers, Simon and Daniel, were allowed to pat Magic and Moonshine and shake hands with them. Ian could not help feeling rather superior when he remembered that they had just helped Uncle Arthur to teach Magic a new trick. He knew that their Uncle did not usually let anyone watch him training the ponies. Angela merely felt rather uncomfortable. She did not like knowing that the others were a bit jealous.

Grace came round while they were having tea. She took one look at Angela's red nose and watery eyes, and said that she hoped Uncle Arthur had kept her in that day. Uncle Arthur went red, mumbled, and looked uncomfortable.

"It isn't very bad, really, Aunt Grace," Angela told her.

"Well, perhaps not. But I do think you'd better stay indoors tomorrow, to give it a chance to go," Grace told her. Angela promised that she would. Staying in was not a very welcome thought, but at the same time it was rather nice to have someone to make a decision like that. It felt comfortable and secure. Angela liked staying with Uncle Arthur, and doing some of the household managing, but it was nice to have Grace about as well.

6 · The pantomime is over

Angela stayed in for two days in the end, as the weather turned very cold. Showers of wet sleet blew over the tall buildings and down the street, and Uncle Arthur gave the ponies extra straw in their beds at night. Partner spread himself out in front of the living-room fire, and hardly moved away from it at all.

Surprisingly Angela enjoyed those two days indoors, although at Aunt Mavis's she would have hated it. Aunt Mavis dreaded them making a noise or a mess, and she would not allow them to use paint or Plasticine in the house. Nor did she like Angela to try her cooking in the shining kitchen except on the few occasions when she had agreed to it as a special treat.

88

During the holidays the children usually went for a walk in the park every afternoon. In the house they had their rooms to tidy and books to read, and they watched the children's programmes on television. Aunt Mavis never allowed them to watch anything that was later than six o'clock. School, in Surbiton, was a welcome release, but if they stayed here long enough to go to school in the district it would be far less welcome, Angela knew.

There was plenty to do at Uncle Arthur's. Angela spent most of her first morning indoors making jam tarts in the kitchen, while Ian and Uncle Arthur took the ponies out for a short trot round. She cooked chops for lunch. Afterwards Uncle Arthur fetched out a box of photographs of the dog he had owned before the ponies, and of Magic and Moonshine. In between serving in the shop he told them stories that went with the photographs, and he also found some old programmes with the ponies' names in them. Later they got out the games, and had an

89

exciting session of Snap and Snakes and Ladders until tea time.

The second morning was too cold and the sleet was too wet and icy for anyone to go far. Angela was finding paper and pencils to do some drawing when there was a knock on the back door. Opening it she was astonished to find Magic standing on the steps, his hind feet still on the ground, and Uncle Arthur behind him with his mackintosh over his head.

"Open the door wide, Angie," called her uncle. "Go on then, Magic."

Angela pulled the door wide and stood back, and Magic came neatly up the steps and into the kitchen. Uncle Arthur followed, and Ian came running across the wet yard from the shed to join in the fun.

"As you can't come out to talk to him he's come in to see you," explained Uncle Arthur. "Well, Magic, lad? Want some sugar?"

Magic nodded, and his master fetched a bag of brown sugar from a shelf in the kitchen cabinet.

"He's been in here quite often," he told Angela, as the cream-coloured pony licked the thick, dark sugar off his hand. "Not Moonshine, he doesn't like the steps, but Magic's a bit smaller. It's easier for him."

When Magic had finished the sugar he explored the kitchen, reaching up his nose to examine the table and the draining board, and sniffing at the sink. Ian turned the tap on very slowly, and Magic put his nose under the water, and then shook his head. He scattered drops of water over everyone, and Angela giggled. Magic put his nose back under the tap, and reached out his tongue, catching the water on it, and lapping like a cat.

"He's been watching Partner," said Uncle Arthur, laughing. He gave the pony a friendly slap on his round hind quarter. "Well, Magic? Think you're a pussy cat, do you?"

They were still playing with Magic in the kitchen when Grace came through from the shop carrying a basket. She had been doing

92

their shopping for them along with her own.

"Oh, Arthur," she exclaimed. "You and those ponies. I really think you'd give them beds upstairs if you could get them there."

Magic went to meet her with a pleased snuffling noise, but Uncle Arthur looked slightly hurt.

"I don't really think I'm unreasonable with them," he said, rather stiffly.

"No, of course not. I didn't mean it," replied Grace at once.

Uncle Arthur's expression softened, and he smiled. "Oh, I know," he told her. "Just touchy, that's me. Come along, Magic. Time you went out again. Home, boy."

He opened the door, and Magic went down the steps after him and trotted across the yard to his shed. Grace put her basket down on the table, and closed the door.

"How's your cold, Angela?" she asked. "You look a lot better."

The kitchen needed tidying after Magic's visit, and his muddy hoof prints had to be mopped up, but it did not take long. The afternoon was very dark, and at tea time they built up the fire, and toasted crumpets on a long brass toasting fork. On the whole, thought Angela as she lay in bed later, it was almost worth having a cold at Uncle Arthur's.

Angela's cold was much better the next day and she could obviously start to go outside again. This should have made the day very cheerful, but there was a letter from Aunt Mavis at breakfast time which cast a shadow over the morning. In it she said that her mother was recovering quickly now, and she did not expect to be away for more than another week or ten days. The only good thing about this was that it meant there was little point in them starting school. Not that school was so bad. Ian had even found himself missing maths, for he rather liked working with figures. But Angela thought miserably of going back to the rather cold, tidy flat in Surbiton, and even Uncle Arthur seemed unhappy at the idea of them going.

"We shall miss you," he told them. "My

goodness, it will seem quiet. Still, it hasn't happened yet, has it?"

"I wish this was where we always lived," said Angela boldly. "We really do like being here."

"Do you? Do you really?" Uncle Arthur looked pleased. "Glad to hear it. Do you know, I never thought you would. I told Grace you'd think it a pokey place after your aunt's nice flat. She thought I was wrong. Trust Grace to know."

That Saturday was the last night of the pantomime. Angela and Ian had seats in the audience to watch it from, and Grace came as well. Although they had seen it twice before, the children still enjoyed it. Grace had also seen it before, but she laughed and clapped as much as anyone.

At the end the whole cast came on to the stage, including Uncle Arthur with Magic and Moonshine. Bouquets and boxes of chocolates were handed up for Cinderella and Prince Charming, and Uncle Arthur was called forward and given two big bags of carrots for the ponies. Magic and Moonshine bowed in thanks, and then the red curtains swung down for the last time.

"Are you sorry that was the last night?" Angela asked Uncle Arthur, as they drove home. They were all squashed into the cab of the van, with Angela on Grace's knee, and Ian sitting on the gear box between the seats.

"I'm always sorry to see the last of panto-mime for the year," replied Uncle Arthur.

"But there'll be plenty of jobs for us in the spring. Old Magic'll miss it for a bit; he likes to be working, but he'll soon get over it."

On the following Monday morning Mrs Randall did not turn up to take over the shop for the morning. Instead she sent a message round to say that she had 'flu, and could not come.

"Oh dear, oh dear," exclaimed Uncle Arthur. "What about their exercise? Magic's going to be bored anyway, when he finds out there's no pantomime any more."

"Isn't there anyone else who'd look after the shop?" asked Ian.

"No. Grace would, but she's teaching most of the day. The school she plays for has got dancing exams next week too, and so she's doing extra time there this week."

"Uncle Arthur, couldn't we take them for their walk?" asked Angela. "We often lead them, and we know the way you go."

"Yes, we could do it," agreed Ian eagerly.

Uncle Arthur looked doubtful. "They've never been out without me," he said. "I don't know. No, better not. It won't hurt them for a day. We'll let them wander about the yard this morning. It'll give them something to do, anyway. Might try taking them out after dark, though I don't like doing that. It's too easy to get run into round these dark roads."

Magic and Moonshine spent the afternoon wandering about the yard, and seemed to enjoy it. Uncle Arthur decided to try taking them for a short walk after dark, but it was not very successful. Ian walked at the back, carrying a torch covered in red cellophane to warn passing traffic about them, but some of the cars still came uncomfortably close.

"Let's take them home," said Uncle Arthur, after the particularly close passage of a taxi. "I never did like having them out after dark. These streets are too narrow."

Even Magic and Moonshine seemed quite glad to get back, and Uncle Arthur said that he hoped Mrs Randall would not be away long.

There was no sign of Uncle Arthur's assistant next morning either, and Ian was

sent round to inquire how she was. The news
was not very promising.

"Her daughter came to the door, and she
says Mrs Randall's still in bed," Ian told
Uncle Arthur when he got back. "She doesn't
think her mother will be back this week, anyway."

"Oh, my goodness." Uncle Arthur ran his
fingers through his hair until it stood up in
a grey bush. "What are we going to do?"

"I'm sure we could manage them on our
own," said Ian. "Couldn't we try?"

"Oh dear. I don't like asking you to take
so much responsibility." Their uncle looked
unhappy. "I suppose it is the only way,
though. I can't let my customers down by
closing the shop. All right. But do be very,
very careful, won't you?"

The children promised that they would be,
and Uncle Arthur told them exactly where
to go. This was round all the quietest streets
in the district, and should not take them
more than half an hour.

"And tomorrow we'll give them a really

good run during the afternoon," said Uncle Arthur.

He put on the ponies' bridles, and clipped a leading rein to each pony's bit. Then he fussed around them, brushing pieces of straw out of their tails, and cleaning the dirt out of their hooves. He obviously hated to let them go out without him. He was still tidying them when the shop bell clanged distantly inside the house.

"Now remember, walk one behind the other," he warned the children. "Keep between them and the traffic. Let Magic go first —he likes to see where he's going. Ian, you're taking Magic, aren't you, and Angela's having Moonshine."

"You there, Arthur?" shouted a distant voice. "Shop."

"Shall we go?" asked Ian.

"Yes, yes, go on then. Be back in half an hour, won't you? You've got my watch, Ian," said Uncle Arthur.

"Arthur," shouted the voice again, and Uncle Arthur had to go. Ian opened the gate, and he and Angela led the ponies out into the path.

Magic looked back once as though he was wondering where his master was, but after that he and Moonshine accepted the children as being in charge of them. At the end of the path they turned left down the road, and left again almost at once. This brought them into the very quiet road which was on the other side of the houses behind Uncle Arthur's. Jane and her brothers lived here, and so did some of Magic and Moonshine's other fans. They would be at school today, or so Ian and Angela thought.

But as the ponies went past the door of number eleven, where Jane lived, it opened, and she came out. One of her younger brothers, Dan, was with her, and her older brother, Alan, whom the children did not know very well, was also there.

"Where's your uncle?" inquired Jane at once.

"He's looking after the shop," replied Angela. "Mrs Randall's ill."

"Have you got a holiday?" asked Ian.

"No. Simon's got chickenpox, so Mum thought we'd better all stay at home," replied Jane.

Her older brother, who was a year or so older than Ian, was staring at the ponies with his hands in his pockets.

"Fancy him letting you take them out," he remarked. "I didn't think old Uncle Arthur ever trusted his precious ponies with anyone else."

"He does us," retorted Ian, who did not like the look of Alan.

"They're sweet," Jane was patting Moonshine. "Can we come with you?" she asked.

"I suppose so," said Ian unwillingly. Jane and Daniel were all right, but he did not like the idea of Alan coming along.

The street came to a dead end, but there was a narrow footpath through to the next street. Magic and Moonshine followed Ian and Angela between the posts that were meant to keep out cars, and Jane, Dan, and Alan brought up the rear.

7 · A stupid thing to do

It was a cold, sunny day, and the muddy garden in the middle of the square that they had come into looked quite green. Alan climbed the railings and jumped down inside the garden, but Jane and Daniel stayed beside the ponies.

"Why don't you let them walk side by side?" asked Jane. "That's how Mr Perry always leads them, one on each side."

"Uncle Arthur told us to keep them one behind the other," explained Angela. "It's safer if a car comes."

"I bet he told you everything," said Alan, arriving beside them again. "Where to go, how long to be, how many breaths to take. I thought they were supposed to be clever. If they're that clever they ought to be able to take themselves for a walk. They wouldn't need a couple of kids tagging on."

"That's stupid," retorted Ian. "They are clever, but they're still ponies. They don't do their tricks on their own. They have to be told what to do."

"Can you make them do tricks?" asked Jane.

"Uncle Arthur showed us how," replied Ian, warily.

"He's never shown us," said Jane, rather jealously. "And we were here the first day he brought them home. Mum said she thought they'd smell, but at least they wouldn't bark all night, like the dog he used to have."

"They don't smell," exclaimed Angela.

"No, not really," agreed Jane. "Even Mum says they don't often. Only if it's very hot."

"I bet you can't make them do their tricks, even if you do know how," said Alan, who was bored with the conversation.

"We've never tried," Ian told him.

They had reached the end of the square now, and were going along the other side.

104

"Haven't you even tried to make them shake hands?" asked Jane. "Oh, do. I'm sure they would. Mr Perry always makes them shake hands with us when we go to see them."

"They can't," jeered Alan. "I expect they only do it for old Uncle Arthur Perry because they're scared of him. Mrs Crosbie at number fifteen says all performing animals are trained by cruelty."

"That's not true," cried Angela. "Uncle Arthur would never be cruel to any animal. All you do is this." She stopped Moonshine, stood in front of him, and held out her hand.

"Come on, Moonshine. Shake hands," she said.

Moonshine did as he was told, raising one forefoot, and holding it out to be shaken.

"You see?" said Angela. "And he couldn't be frightened of me, could he?"

"I don't see why not," said Alan darkly, but Jane was praising Angela, and saying how clever Moonshine was.

"You see?" she said. "You can make them

105

do things. Oh, please do. Go on, Ian, make Magic do something. It can't do any harm, surely."

It was very tempting. After all, Uncle Arthur had not said that they mustn't make the ponies do their tricks, and it would show Alan that they were not merely "kids" tagging along with the ponies. Also, Ian liked Jane and her smaller brother, and he knew that she really did want to see the ponies do some tricks.

Angela guessed what Ian was thinking, and felt worried. Although she had started it by making Moonshine shake hands she did not think that Uncle Arthur would like them playing about with the ponies' training.

"I don't think they really do know how," said Alan, who was getting tired of Angela and Ian and the ponies. He would go and find something else to do in a moment, he decided.

"I'm sure they do, really," insisted Jane. She could see that Ian was wavering, and it would be such fun if he stopped being

106

stuffy and let them all play properly with the ponies. "Go on, Ian, please. Just make Magic do something. Make him push you, like he does Donnie Shaw on the stage."

There did not seem to be any possible harm in the idea, and Ian gave in.

"All right," he said. "Just once. Come on, Magic."

He turned his back to Magic as they had seen Uncle Arthur do, and began to pat Moonshine. Then he put one hand behind his back. Magic looked at him for a moment as though he was wondering if Ian really meant it. Then he took a step forward, and gave him a firm push. Daniel squealed with delight, and Jane laughed and clapped. Even Alan looked slightly impressed.

"Again," pleaded Jane. "Go on, Ian,"

Ian did it again, and for the second time Magic pushed him obediently. It was an exciting feeling, knowing that the pony would obey him so easily. Ian began to enjoy himself.

"Make him chase you," urged Jane.

"Do you think we ought?" asked Angela anxiously.

"I suppose it really can't do any harm," said Ian. After all, he thought, Uncle Arthur made the ponies do some of their tricks when they were out for exercise. The square was very quiet, traffic hardly ever seemed to come this way, and there did not seem to be any danger. The few parked cars were almost always there, no one ever seemed to take them for a drive, and some of them were clearly abandoned, with flat tyres and missing wings and windscreens, and there were no delivery vans about.

Ian decided that it was safe, hooked Magic's leading rein through the bridle, and moved away, leaving the pony loose. He kept one hand behind him, and Magic followed immediately, and gave him another push. Ian pretended to be indignant, and walked faster. Magic broke into a trot, and even Angela laughed at his ferocious expression.

Jane and Daniel were urging Magic on,

and Alan began to grin. Magic flattened his
ears more closely to his head, and poked out
his nose. Encouraged by their success, both
he and Ian were beginning to get excited.
Ian dodged on to the pavement, and Magic
hopped up the curb after him. Ian jumped
down again between two of the parked cars,
and Magic dived after him.

"Quick, Ian; he neárly had you," cried
Jane.

"Go on, Magic," shouted Alan.

Ian dodged round the front of one of the
abandoned cars, and Magic, determined to
catch up with him, broke into a canter. He
whipped closely round the bonnet of the de-
crepit old car in pursuit.

There was a sudden hollow bang as the
pony collided with the wing of the car, a
squeal from Magic, and a rending noise.
Then Magic was standing on the pavement,
holding up one hind leg from which blood
was dripping. The rusty front bumper of
the car hung down to the road where Magic
had ripped it off.

"Oh, Ian, look," wailed Angela.

"Oh, Ian, look what he's done," gasped Jane.

"Gosh, look at that," exclaimed Alan, in an awed voice.

110

Daniel burst into noisy tears, and Jane picked him up. Ian and Angela looked at one another, and at Magic, in frozen silence. Ian's face was very white, and Angela thought that she might be going to be sick.

Magic put his hind foot gingerly to the ground, and Ian took hold of his leading rein. The blood was still trickling down the inside of the pony's leg from somewhere above the bent part that was called the hock. His pale, creamy hair was turning dark and sticky, and there seemed to be a lot of blood on the pavement.

Moonshine watched the scene with pricked ears, looking surprised by the sudden air of trouble. Magic half-pricked his own ears, and decided that he was still interested in his reward for doing his trick. He began to sniff at Ian's pockets.

"He wants his carrot," whispered Jane.

She was almost as white as Ian and Angela, and her eyes were enormous. Even Alan looked shaken, and Daniel was still crying, though more quietly now.

111

"Have you got one?" Ian asked Angela. His voice sounded queer, and Angela knew that he felt as awful as she did. She found a piece of carrot in her pocket, and Magic ate it quite happily.

"What shall we do?" asked Angela shakily. "Do you think he can walk home?"

"It doesn't seem to be hurting him very much," said Ian. "We'd better try."

"We'll come too," said Jane. "After all, it was our fault for wanting to see him do tricks."

"Yes. We were a bit stupid," said Alan bluntly. "Come on, let's all go and face old Uncle Arthur."

"I was the most stupid of all," said Ian miserably. "I knew I shouldn't do it, but I went on."

He led Magic off the pavement, and the pony followed stiffly. He was not very lame, however, and the blood did not seem to be running terribly fast. Slowly and sadly they started towards home, Jane, Daniel, and Alan trailing behind, and Ian and Angela not daring to imagine what Uncle Arthur was going to say.

Uncle Arthur had been watching for them, and he came down the kitchen steps as they opened the gate. He saw at once that something was wrong, and it only took him a moment to spot Magic's leg.

"Whatever have you been doing?" he demanded. "What happened? Oh my goodness, what a mess. Give him to me, Ian."

All the children began to explain at once, but Uncle Arthur was hardly listening. He knelt down to examine Magic's injury, and told Angela to put Moonshine in the stable.

"It was our fault really; we wanted to see Magic do some tricks," said Jane.

"Ian, fetch me some hot water from the kettle," instructed Uncle Arthur. "Bring it in a clean basin. And bring the first aid box as well. Then you can telephone the vet—his number's on the card."

"We were a bit stupid," said Alan. "But it seemed all right round there."

"Yes, all right. I don't want to hear it all

113

now," replied Uncle Arthur shortly. "It's done and now it's got to be dealt with. You three had better go home. Off with you, now."

Jane, Alan and Daniel knew better than to argue. They let themselves rather thankfully out of the gate. Inside the stable Angela stayed where she was. She could not bear to face Uncle Arthur at the moment.

Ian brought the water and the white box marked with its red cross, and Uncle Arthur poured disinfectant into the bowl. He got out the cotton wool. Ian hurried back into the house to telephone the vet.

"Angela," called her uncle. "Come and hold Magic, please."

Timidly, Angela did as she was told. Ian came back after a few minutes to say that the vet was on his way. Then he stood miserably watching while Uncle Arthur bathed the cut, and washed away the drying blood from Magic's leg. The pony flinched slightly as the disinfectant stung the cut, but he did not try to kick or move away. His patience made Angela feel even worse. How could they have

114

let him hurt himself?

"Well," said Uncle Arthur eventually, "can't do much more until the vet comes. You two go indoors. It won't help, all of us hanging around watching."

In Uncle Arthur's crowded living-room Angela and Ian looked at each other unhappily.

"Do you think Magic will be all right?" whispered Angela.

"I hope so," replied Ian. "After all, it is only a cut." He did not feel as confident as he sounded, but he wanted to reassure Angela.

"Uncle Arthur won't want us to come to stay again now," said Angela miserably. "Or live here, if there ever is a chance. Though I don't suppose there will be."

She sat down in the armchair by the fire, clasping her arms round her knees, and pressing her chin against them. Her long fair hair fell forward, hiding her face, and Ian knew that she was really wretched. She only sat like that when something went really wrong, such as the time when they heard Uncle Sam say that they would be better put in a Home, and the time when Aunt Mavis took the stray kitten that they had found and gave it to the pet shop. It made Ian feel horribly guilty, for this time he was the main cause of the unhappiness. If only he had been more sensible.

The vet came, and only stayed for a few minutes. After he had gone Uncle Arthur came into the house.

"What did the vet say?" asked Angela anxiously.

"He thinks Magic should be all right in a few days," replied Uncle Arthur. "He gave him an anti-tetanus injection, and said the cut didn't seem very bad. He was in a hurry —he had an emergency to go to somewhere else."

"I really am most frightfully sorry," said Ian. "It was all my fault. I just didn't see how it could hurt to have him do some of his tricks. Jane really did want to see them."

"Oh, it's not your fault," said Uncle Arthur,

rather vaguely. "Too much responsibility for you. I shouldn't have asked you to do it at your ages. It's my own fault for expecting too much. Hope Magic won't move around too much on that leg. I'd better pop out and have another look."

He went, leaving Ian staring miserably at the floor. So Uncle Arthur did not really blame him at all. He just thought him too young to behave sensibly. It hurt even more than Uncle Arthur being really cross would have done. And of course it made no difference to the future. Uncle Arthur would not want them again if he felt that they were merely irresponsible.

When Grace was told about the accident later she took a slightly different view. She said at once that Ian was old enough to have had more sense. She also said that she was sure Magic would be perfectly all right in a day or two.

"It doesn't even matter if it leaves a scar," she pointed out to Uncle Arthur. "It won't show on the inside of his leg. And as there aren't any tendons or anything damaged I can't see that any of you need to worry. He's a healthy young animal, and it'll soon heal."

She went on firmly to talk about something else, and by the time she went home they were all feeling a lot more cheerful. Uncle Arthur even got out the Snakes and Ladders board for a game before bed, and the cloud which had hung over them all afternoon no longer seemed half as heavy.

8 · A real home

Magic seemed as bright as usual next day, although Uncle Arthur said that his leg seemed rather hot. He was not supposed to walk much, although he could wander round the yard to stretch his legs a little.

As it was early closing day Uncle Arthur took Moonshine out for half an hour after lunch, leaving instructions that neither of the children was to touch Magic while he was gone. It was not nice to know that they were not trusted, and Angela and Ian stayed in the house, attempting to play draughts, although they did not feel at all like it.

Magic did not finish his evening feed. There was not a lot left, but enough to worry Uncle Arthur.

"Always loves his food," he told the children anxiously. "Oh dear. That leg is hot.

119

Can't call the vet at this time unless I'm sure."

Magic nuzzled his hand, and accepted a carrot, and Uncle Arthur's anxiety faded a little. He decided to wait and see how Magic was next morning.

Angela did not sleep very well that night, and several times she heard Uncle Arthur get up and creep down the stairs and out into the yard to look at Magic. By the time she and Ian went down next morning it was obvious that something was wrong. The pony did not want any of his breakfast, and his leg was hot and swollen, with the infection running right up his leg. Uncle Arthur went indoors to telephone the vet, and to start making a bran mash to encourage Magic to eat.

When the vet came he agreed that an infection had developed from the cut.

"There may have been a scrap of metal left in it," he said. "Or the piece he cut himself on may have been very dirty. I'll give him a penicillin injection, and open the wound again. That should drain it and get

120

rid of the trouble. He has a temperature, so don't let him get cold and give him plenty of chilled water and warm mashes. If he won't eat he might drink skimmed milk with a little water."

"Do you think he'll come through it all right?" asked Uncle Arthur anxiously.

"Oh, there's no reason why he shouldn't,"

replied the vet. "But he'll need a bit of care. I'll call tomorrow and see how he is."

Magic was certainly not very happy. After the vet had gone Uncle Arthur found an extra blanket for him to wear under his rug, and put extra straw down in his stall. He stirred up the cooled mash, and offered that to the pony, but Magic was not interested. Uncle Arthur tried warmed water, and the pony took a few mouthfuls of that. While Uncle Arthur was busy with Magic the shop bell clanged.

"Oh dear, Ian, you go, will you?" said Uncle Arthur.

Ian did so, and managed to weigh out a quarter of fruit drops, and take the right money. Then he went back to the stable.

Magic looked very miserable. His thick, soft coat looked harsh, and the hairs were standing on end. His usually bright eyes were dull and half-closed, and obviously his leg was hurting him. In the other half of the shed Moonshine watched curiously. Now and then he made soft, snuffling noises, ask-

122

ing for attention himself, and Angela rubbed his ears and patted him.

"I'll stay with Magic," said Uncle Arthur. "He shouldn't be left alone in this state. Besides, if he lies down his bad leg will make it hard for him to get up. You two keep away. Best if he's as quiet as possible. If he doesn't improve we'll have Moonshine out in the yard. Rig up some cover for him. He won't hurt there for a night or two."

Angela and Ian went back into the house. The remains of breakfast were still on the table, and it was almost lunch time. The bell clanged in the shop as they went inside, and Ian said, "I'd better go. I don't expect Uncle Arthur will want to come."

"I wish Mrs Randall was back," said Angela. "And I do hope Grace comes round today."

"She often doesn't come on a Thursday," replied Ian. "And she is extra busy this week because of the dancing school's exams."

There were impatient shuffling and coughing sounds coming from the shop, and Ian went through to serve the customer. Angela began to clear away the breakfast things. She very much hoped that Grace would find time to come round that day.

Magic was certainly no better that evening. Grace had not been round, and Uncle Arthur had only been into the house to fetch milk and warm water for Magic, or to find tit-bits with which to tempt the pony. He had not even stayed inside to eat his lunch, and Angela had taken some out to him on a tray. Even then he had hardly touched it.

Ian had looked after the shop, without making any serious mistakes, and Angela made all the beds, washed up, and cooked. Several customers asked Ian where Uncle Arthur was, but Ian just said that he was busy outside. He was not very eager for the whole district to know about the accident.

Uncle Arthur came into the house while Angela was getting the tea. He looked grimy and tired, and he had not shaved that day.

"I'm going to put Moonshine outside," he said. "I don't want Magic disturbed if he does rest tonight. Ian, come and help, will you?"

There was an old tarpaulin in the loft, and Ian helped his uncle to get it down. They carried it into the yard, and with Ian's help Uncle Arthur fixed one side to the roof of the shed. From there he slung it across to the fence, and he fastened the other corner by a rope to the roof of the bathroom. This made a three-sided shelter for Moonshine, one side being the shed wall, the second the back fence, and the third the loose flap of the tarpaulin. Uncle Arthur anchored this to the ground by putting two bales of hay on the edge where it touched the yard. Then he and Ian spread thick straw under it for Moonshine's bed, and Uncle Arthur fetched the pony out.

Moonshine did not seem to mind his temporary stable. He was tethered to a ring in the fence, with his tail to the open side of the shelter, and given plenty of hay. He began to munch straight away. Magic hardly seemed to have noticed him going.

"What about your tea?" asked Ian, when Uncle Arthur turned to go back into the stable.

"Oh, Angela can bring me something out here," replied Uncle Arthur. "Mind you two eat something, though. And then get to bed. I shall be staying with Magic, so don't wait."

Ian and Angela ate their tea almost without speaking. After they had cleared away Angela went out to get Uncle Arthur's tray. She also took him some more hot water to make Magic a fresh poultice and to add to bran to try him with another mash. The shed door was closed, but Moonshine whinnied softly to her from his place under the tarpaulin.

At Angela's soft tap Uncle Arthur opened the door and gave her the tray. She handed him the kettle of hot water.

Inside the shed the light was on, but shaded by a piece of sacking, and Magic stood miserably in the shadows with his head hanging down.

"Shh," hissed Uncle Arthur, when she started to speak. "You and Ian go to bed."

"You haven't eaten your tea," Angela whispered.

"Never mind," Uncle Arthur whispered back. "It won't hurt me to go without. I'll fetch something later if he seems better."

He closed the door, and Angela took the tray indoors.

"He didn't eat much dinner either," she told Ian. "He must be awfully worried."

Ian nodded. He felt more guilty than ever, but there was nothing at all that he and Angela could do to help get the pony better. If only, thought Ian for the hundredth time, it had never happened.

Ian and Angela were already awake when Uncle Arthur came into the house next morning to get the papers ready for delivery. They went downstairs in their dressing gowns to ask how Magic was, but they knew at once from his face that the pony was no better.

"But he isn't any worse," Uncle Arthur told them. "That's something, my goodness it is."

He yawned, shivered, and pulled his coat

127

more closely round him.

"Very cold this morning," he said.

"I'll make some tea," said Angela.

Uncle Arthur looked cold; his hair was standing on end, and his eyes were red from staying awake all night. Ian went to help with the papers, and Angela put the kettle on. She felt very worried. Uncle Arthur looked as though he, too, might be ill if he had to sit with Magic much longer.

The papers were ready very quickly that morning, and Uncle Arthur swallowed a cup of tea before hurrying back to the stable. The vet called just after breakfast, as he had promised to do, and said that it was a good sign that the pony was no worse.

"Oughtn't we to tell Grace what's happened?" Ian asked Uncle Arthur, when the vet had gone. "She could help you with Magic, couldn't she?"

"Dear me, no," exclaimed Uncle Arthur. "You're not to go bothering Grace. She's been more than good. I can't possibly ask her to do anything more. Besides, she's got enough to do this week, with those exams to play for. And I couldn't ask a lady like Grace to sit out in the stable. As for the shop, if it gets too difficult I'll shut for a day or two. If you have any real problems there, come out and ask me. But don't make a noise."

He hurried out with a fresh kettle of warm water, and Angela and Ian looked at each other helplessly.

"I wish he'd let one of us sit with Magic for a bit," said Angela. "But he won't trust us."

"I don't blame him, after what happened the last time he did," replied Ian gloomily.

Already, the house looked a mess. Uncle Arthur might not seem to do any housework, but he was clever at putting things back where they came from, and clearing up any litter he made before he started to do something else. He would flick over the sideboard with a duster while he was talking, and sweep up the hearth each time he rebuilt the fire.

Now, everything looked dusty, and the hearth was thick with cinders and ash. The fire was not burning very well because it had not been properly riddled, and several drawers were partly open where they had searched hurriedly for something. There were crumbs on the floor around the table, and Partner's milk had been spilt on the kitchen floor, and not wiped up.

Drearily, in between washing up and cooking, and serving in the shop, Ian and Angela tried to clear up a bit. Once or twice, as she struggled with a carpet-sweeper that needed emptying, and as Ian tried unsuccessfully to get the fire burning properly, Angela almost found herself wishing them back with Aunt Mavis. It was all so difficult, and she had a terrible feeling that Magic was not going to get better, and that Uncle Arthur would never forgive them. Their dreams of staying with him again, or perhaps even living at the shop, seemed very far away now, and very impossible. This was not their real life, and never could be now that they had made

130

such a mess of things.

The afternoon dragged past. At about five o'clock, though time was vague because the clock had stopped, Angela took some tea out to the stable. Uncle Arthur opened the door at her knock, but to her alarm he did not seem able to stand up properly.

"All right. Nothing much. Cramp," he explained, seeing her scared expression. "Been sitting too long."

"How's Magic?" asked Angela timidly.

"Oh, about the same," replied her uncle. "About the same. You two managing all right?"

"Yes, we're all right," Angela assured him. "You will eat some tea, won't you, Uncle?"

"Yes, don't worry about me. Go on now, don't want to disturb him," said Uncle Arthur.

Ian came in from the shop as Angela returned. He looked flushed and cross, and explained that he had just given someone the wrong change.

"She was awfully cross," he said. "I think

131

she thought I'd done it on purpose. She wasn't a regular customer."

"Oh dear," Angela sat sadly down at the table. "It's all so awful."

"Jane came in, too," said Ian. "She wanted to know how Magic was."

Angela nodded. It was kind of Jane to worry. It seemed as though Jane was probably rather nice. But she was too miserable to be really interested.

After tea they discovered that the fire had gone out completely. Partner, disgusted, was curled up deep in an armchair with his nose in his tail. There was no hot water to do the washing up. Then Angela picked up the tea pot to clear away, the handle came off, and the half-full pot fell to the floor, flooding the carpet with tea. It was too much. Angela flung herself on to the settee, and burst into tears.

"Angela," exclaimed a voice from the door. "What on earth's the matter? Whatever has been happening?" and to Ian's great relief Grace walked into the room. She sat down beside Angela and put her arms round her, and Ian began to explain.

"But why didn't one of you come and tell me?" asked Grace. "I'm never that busy."

"Uncle Arthur said we weren't to bother you," sobbed Angela. "He said you'd been more than good, and anyway, he couldn't ask a lady like you to sit out in the stable. Oh, Aunt Grace, Magic looks awful, I'm sure he's going to die, and Uncle Arthur looks as if he's getting ill as well."

"Honestly," exclaimed Grace. "Sometimes, I despair of Arthur. Now, stop crying, Angela. I'll go out and talk to him. I'm sure it isn't that bad. I can stay with Magic while Arthur gets some sleep. I expect that's all he needs. As for Magic, he's a tough little animal, and I don't see any reason why he should die."

She left her basket on the kitchen table and went out into the yard. Angela and Ian waited anxiously, Angela still sniffling, and Ian staring out of the window. For about five minutes nothing happened, and then Ian saw the stable door open.

133

"Uncle Arthur's coming out," he exclaimed. "And Grace."

"Do you think he's going to let her help?" asked Angela anxiously.

"I don't know," replied Ian.

"Angela," called Grace, from the kitchen. "Heat your Uncle some milk, and see that he has some rum in it. And fill a hot water bottle for him. I'm going back to sit with Magic. I'll take his milk and some water for another mash with me."

"He won't take it," said Uncle Arthur dully. He sat down on a kitchen chair. Grace re-lit the fire on top of the warm ashes.

"Sit by the fire," she instructed. "And stop worrying. He'll take a bit. He doesn't look that bad to me, and you said yourself he'd been nosing in his straw."

"You'll call me if he gets worse, won't you? said Uncle Arthur.

"I've promised I will," replied Grace. "Now drink that milk and go to bed. I'm going back to the pony."

She went out, taking the bucket of milk

and water and a saucepan of hot water with her.

"Is Magic a bit better?" asked Angela, as her Uncle drank his hot milk and rum.

"Possibly. Just a bit," replied Uncle Arthur. "Might not last, though. I hope Grace can manage. If he lies down, he won't be able to stand up again without help; leg's too swollen. Very good of her to try to help."

He went slowly up to bed at last, leaving the children to clear up as best they could. But they did feel slightly more cheerful as they went up to bed themselves.

Angela and Ian were woken the next morning by the sound of the back door closing very softly. Uncle Arthur was still asleep; they could hear him snoring slightly as they crept downstairs. Grace was in the kitchen, filling the kettle. She looked tired, but cheerful, and Ian said, "How's Magic?"

"Come and see," replied Grace. "Put your coats on. It's cold."

They followed her down the steps, feeling the frost rime cold and suddenly melting on the rail as they touched it. Moonshine was munching in his shelter, and Grace opened the shed door. An eager whinny greeted them, and Magic turned to face them, his head up and his ears pricked. His eyes were bright again, and his coat was no longer rough and staring. The only signs that he had been ill were some swelling still in his leg, and a hollow look about his neck just past the end of his rug. Clearly, his leg no longer hurt him, and his temperature had gone down.

"He's better," cried Angela.

"Yes," agreed Grace. "I don't think we shall need to worry about him much more."

Ian said nothing, but his face as he patted Magic was one broad grin. Then Magic raised his head sharply and gave a little whinny, and Ian and Angela turned round to see Uncle Arthur, wearing his dressing gown, standing in the doorway.

"My goodness, Grace, what did you do? Wave your magic wand?" exclaimed Uncle Arthur. "He looks terrific."

136

"I thought he seemed to be brighter than you thought last night," replied Grace. "He ate a bit of the mash I took him, and he lay down to sleep. I had to help him up a bit this morning, but after that he wanted hay and breakfast, and to be played with. I didn't have to do anything for him in the night. I even got some sleep."

"Well, that's marvellous. Marvellous," said Uncle Arthur. He rubbed Magic's ears, and patted him, until Moonshine called to remind them that he was being left out.

"He could come back in here now, couldn't he?" asked Grace, and Uncle Arthur agreed that he could.

Ian fetched him in, and Magic greeted his friend with a loud whinny.

"Well," said Grace. "I think we could all go in for breakfast now, don't you?"

Magic continued to get better steadily during the next few days, and by the middle of the next week he was able to go for his usual outings, although he was still a bit stiff. Jane and her brothers were as delighted as anyone to see him about again, and they and Angela and Ian accepted each other as friends in a way they had not done before the accident.

In spite of Magic's recovery, however, and the general cheerfulness, Ian and Angela grew quieter as the days passed. It could not possibly be long now before Aunt Mavis was ready to have them home. Already they had stayed longer than her last letter had suggested. Grace looked at them sometimes, and asked a few questions about life with their aunt.

Although they tried to be fair when they replied, they could not help showing that they were not looking forward to going back to Surbiton.

Since Magic's illness Grace was careful to come round every day. She obviously felt partly to blame for the state that they had got into when she did not know that there was anything wrong. Once or twice she and Uncle Arthur stopped talking rather quickly when Ian or Angela came into the room.

Ian hoped that it was not the accident that they were discussing. He still felt very guilty about that, although Magic was obviously going to be as sound and well as ever.

Then, at lunchtime on Saturday, when Grace was there as well, Uncle Arthur said that Aunt Mavis had written to him, and was coming home.

"She says she can have you back about the middle of the week," he told them. "She'll be home and have everything straight by then."

"Oh. I see." Ian looked down at his plate.

Angela said nothing. She knew that she would not be able to swallow any more dinner, and that if she said anything she would cry.

It was all over, the busy, exciting, sometimes hectic time at Uncle Arthur's. The feeling of really belonging somewhere, and with someone, was over, and Angela knew that she had never been happier anywhere.

"There is one possible alternative," said Grace. "One thing you could do instead."

She looked at Uncle Arthur, who cleared his throat and went rather red.

"Yes," he said. "Well. The thing is, Grace and I have decided to get married. I need

someone to keep me in order, and she says she doesn't mind trying. If you'd like it, she's willing to try to keep you two in order as well. And I'd certainly miss your help with Magic and Moonshine, not to mention

Angela's cooking. But of course, it's entirely up to you."

"We have mentioned the idea to your aunt," went on Grace. "Arthur suggested that there might be more scope for your energy here, as your aunt leads such a busy life, and has such a lovely home. What do you think? Would you like to live here properly?"

"Like it?" cried Angela. Her face was crimson, and her eyes shone. "Oh, Aunt Grace, we'd love it. Please. We really have been so happy here."

"Are you sure?" asked Ian, more quietly. "I mean, even after the accident?"

"Accidents can always happen," replied Uncle Arthur. "And I don't suppose you'd let that kind happen twice. Of course we're sure. It'd seem jolly quiet and dull here without you."

"Then we would like to stay. I can't think of anything we'd like better," said Ian joyfully.

For a few minutes there was chaos, while

Angela rushed round the table to hug both Uncle Arthur and Grace, and Ian leaped up to perform a war dance.

Partner shot up on top of the sideboard at all the noise, and Bluey began to screech in competition.

"Don't forget there'll be school now," warned Grace, but they were not at all dampened.

"I've got jobs lined up for you both already," said Uncle Arthur, when things had quietened down a little. "Grace and I will need a bridesmaid, and a footman to hold the ponies while we're in church."

"The ponies?" exclaimed Angela. "Will you take Magic and Moonshine to the wedding, then?"

"Of course," replied Uncle Arthur, looking shocked. "Couldn't leave them out. I know where I can get a beautiful little carriage for them, just the right size."

"Oh, Arthur," exclaimed Grace, laughing. "And Partner too, as coachman?"

"Why not?" asked Uncle Arthur. "Why

not? It's an idea, Grace. I might even try it."

And while everyone laughed Angela and Ian caught one another's eyes, and exchanged a private grin of complete satisfaction. Everything was all right now. They had found a real and permanent home at last.

Save the Ponies

Contents

1 · The letter

The sound of briskly trotting hooves in the quiet, drab London street made several people look round. Some children looked up from their game on the steps outside number ten, and two ladies with shopping baskets paused in their talk to stare. Someone glanced out of a lace-curtained ground floor window, and stayed there a moment, gazing out, and the milkman looked up from stacking crates on to his electric milk float.

The two tiny, cream-coloured ponies were in perfect step, their necks arched, their little ears pricked, and their creamy manes and tails floating. Against their pale coats the black, patent leather harness shone, and behind them the miniature landau carriage ran smoothly on its rubber-rimmed wheels.

On the driving seat sat a fair-haired girl of about eight. She held the reins lightly and carefully in her hands, and her face was intent. Her long hair, tied back with a blue ribbon, was blown by the breeze as they

149

moved along. Beside her sat a tall, thin, red-faced man with thin grey hair and thick bushy eyebrows. He, too, was intent on the ponies, and the way that the girl was driving.

Only the boy sitting in the lower, central part of the carriage behind them was less intent on the ponies. He was looking out instead at the passing terraces of rather sooty houses, the small shops, and the parked cars. To tell the truth, Ian was slightly bored. He was fond of Magic and Moonshine, the two little pantomime ponies who pulled Cinderella's coach on the stage each year, and who did their own routine of tricks as well, and usually he quite enjoyed going out with them in the carriage. Today, though, he felt slightly left out. He had felt like that quite a lot lately, now that Uncle Arthur was married to Grace, and she had taken the place of their mother, who had died with their father such a long time ago.

Until they had come to live with Uncle Arthur, Angela and Ian had moved about, living with different relatives, and it had been to Ian that Angela had turned for help or support. He had felt responsible for her, and the

150

two of them had needed one another. Now, Angela turned to Grace more than to Ian when she wanted help, and sometimes he felt rather on the outside of things. And it was Angela who had learned to drive the ponies most quickly, and who handled them the best.

"Steady now," Uncle Arthur was saying, as they approached the end of the street. "Back to a walk in good time, remember, and halt at the corner. Never let them go up to a corner fast, there might be something coming."

Angela tightened the reins, making sure to keep a steady, even pull on both reins, and the two tiny ponies bent their heads to their bits and slowed up. Uncle Arthur's hands were hovering over Angela's, just in case, but he did not have to touch them. Angela's hands, and her firm 'whoa' brought the whole outfit to a smooth halt in just the right place.

"Hop out, Ian, and make sure it's clear to cross," ordered Uncle Arthur, and Ian got out over the low door and went forward into the next quiet road to make sure that nothing was coming. With two ponies harnessed together extra time was needed to make a turn, and it was best to be quite sure that it was safe.

There was nothing coming. Ian signalled to Uncle Arthur, and he said, "Right. Remember now, Angie, don't let them come round too fast."

The ponies moved forward, at a walk now, Angela increased her feel on the 'off ', or right-hand rein, telling Magic, who was on the outside, to start turning. At the same time she kept a firm feel on the 'near' side, or left rein, preventing Moonshine from turning too fast and barging into his partner. The inside reins from both ponies' bits were fastened to those of their partners, and holding one pony back also helped to check the other.

As the little carriage with its miniature team came round Ian hopped back into his seat behind Angela and Uncle Arthur. He was trying not to remember the mess that he had once made of turning Magic and Moonshine. He had been in a hurry, hearing a car coming in the distance, and he had completely forgotten the need to steady Moonshine as well as pulling Magic's rein to bring him round. The ponies had started to turn much too sharply, scrambling round with the carriage skidding sideways behind them, and Uncle Arthur had had to take the reins from him quickly to prevent an accident.

"Everyone can make mistakes," Uncle Arthur had told him afterwards, but Ian had always felt humiliated by the incident.

The road into which they had turned led them through a square, past one of the overgrown, leafy gardens of which there were several in the district. As the ponies trotted past, the sound of their hooves echoing slightly from the tall, shabby houses, Ian

153

noticed that the leaves on the tall plane trees were just beginning to turn gold. The summer was almost over. School would be starting again soon, and for the ponies the busy season of stage shows and pantomimes would be beginning again. In two weeks Uncle Arthur was planning to take the ponies and their carriage to Horseman's Sunday, on Epsom Downs, when a special service was held for horses, and the day after that the autumn term began.

Ian knew that he was looking forward to school again, although he did get teased a bit about the ponies. That was different for Angela, too. The girls of her own age all envied and admired her for having an uncle who owned pantomime ponies, and she was popular because of them. That, too, had given her extra confidence to stand on her own feet more and need Ian's support less.

They were nearly home now. Ian jumped out again to conduct them across another road, and they were turning into their own street. This was a long street of terraced houses and a few small shops, with a public house at the end. Even in the bright summer sunlight it was rather dark, over-shadowed by

154

the tall office blocks behind it. Ian and Angela had thought at first that it was a dreary sort of street, but now it was home to them and they no longer noticed.

The ponies began to slow down as they approached the short row of shops where they lived. Uncle Arthur had the paper shop, and a board above the door read "A. Perry. Newsagent, Tobacconist, and Confectioner." It was the first shop in the row. Racks outside the door held copies of local and evening newspapers, and the windows were attractively arranged with displays of sweets and cigarettes, magazines, and plastic toys. Grace did the window displays now, sometimes with Angela to help her. They had taken the job over from Uncle Arthur, who had never enjoyed it much.

Outside the shop Angela brought the ponies to a halt, and Uncle Arthur stepped down from the seat and came round to the off side to take the reins from her. He was stepping back up when Grace opened the shop door. She was a nice-looking, dark-haired woman, quite a bit younger than Uncle Arthur.

"Hello," she said. "I'll put the kettle on,

and open up the gate for you."

"Thanks, Grace. We're coming right round," Uncle Arthur told her.

He drove the ponies on to the end of the shops, and the corner of the road where the pub stood. Round here, on the left, was the entrance to the cinder path which ran between the back yards of the two rows of houses, Uncle Arthur's row and the one behind.

It was a tight and ticklish job, turning the pair and their carriage into the narrow pathway, which was little more than the width of an ordinary car. Uncle Arthur, though, brought the ponies round with a practised touch on the reins, judging his distances exactly, and the ponies' hooves and the light wheels crunched on to the cinders. Magic snorted and the sound echoed back from the high fences and walls on either side. Grace had their own back gate open, and she went to the ponies' heads as they stopped outside. Uncle Arthur, Angela, and Ian got down, and Ian began to help Uncle Arthur to unhitch the ponies.

"Were they good?" asked Grace, rubbing Moonshine's nose as he breathed softly over her wrists. "How did your driving go, Angela?"

"They were very good," Angela told her. "And it was lovely. I hardly needed any help with them, did I, Uncle Arthur?"

"No, you did very well, very well indeed," replied Uncle Arthur.

"How about you, Ian?" asked Grace. "Enjoy the ride?"

"Oh, it was all right," muttered Ian, who was bending over one of Moonshine's traces. Grace looked at him hard, but he did not look round, and she said no more. Then he and Angela led the ponies through the gate into the little yard, and Uncle Arthur followed them pulling the light little carriage.

A long shed with a slanting roof was built against the wall at the path end of the yard, and this was where Magic and Moonshine lived. Inside it was divided into two by poles and wooden partitions, and a narrow gangway ran between the two halves, with hay stored at the far end of it. Grace had put feeds ready in both ponies' mangers, and after they had both had a drink they plunged their noses into the mixture of pony cubes, bran, and a scat-

157

tering of oats. They did not have too many oats, or they would have become fresh and naughty.

Uncle Arthur pushed the carriage into its place between the shed and the wall which divided the yard from that of their neighbour, and then he came in to make sure that all was well in the stable. He was followed in by Partner, the large ginger cat, who was a great friend of the ponies.

"Not sweating, are they?" asked Uncle Arthur, running a hand down Magic's shoulder. Although he never actually admitted it, Ian and Angela suspected that Magic was Uncle Arthur's favourite of the two ponies. He was the quickest and cleverest, and also the cheekiest of the pair.

"No, they dried off before we got home, and they haven't started again," replied Angela. "They feel quite dry now."

"Good," said Uncle Arthur. "That's the way. You know Grace, that carriage really was a good buy. It makes a fine advertisement for them. We might even get some bookings with it now that they've really settled to the job."

"And of course it did make a wonderful

wedding coach," added Grace, laughing, and Angela remembered coming home from Grace and Uncle Arthur's wedding. Uncle Arthur had been driving, with Grace inside the little carriage in her lovely dress, and herself and Ian perched on the step at the back. That was nearly six months ago now, before the ponies went away for their summer rest at grass, and before she and Ian had started to learn to drive. It seemed ages ago. Angela felt as though they had lived with Grace and Uncle Arthur always.

While they were talking and tidying up the stable Partner had paused for a moment in the doorway with one front paw raised and his whiskers pushed forward. Now he jumped up on to the partition on Magic's side of the stable. He stood there for a second, and then leaped lightly on to the pony's back. Magic glanced round at him, still chewing, with his ears pricked and bran dust clinging to his whiskers, and then he turned back to his feed. Partner turned round once and then lay down in the warm, broad hollow over the pony's loins and began to wash his face.

"Come on," said Grace. "Watching them

eat is making me hungry. Let's get our own tea."

The back door, at the top of a short flight of stone steps, took them into the kitchen, bright and shining since Grace had taken over. The children washed their hands at the spotless sink, sniffing the appetising smell of newly-baked cakes, and then went through to the living room, the only other downstairs room besides the shop.

Uncle Arthur's living-room was rather crowded. Chairs, tables, a shabby settee, a giant sideboard, an upright piano, and tall sets of crowded book shelves took up nearly all the space. The walls between the furniture were almost covered by Uncle Arthur's collection of old playbills, and his photographs of the stars of silent films. It was tidier than it had once been, however, for Grace saw to it that there was not too much clutter on the shelves and on top of the cupboard and the piano. The only things now on top of the piano were several framed photographs, one of Grace and Uncle Arthur after their wedding, one of the ponies on stage in a panto-mime, and one of Angela and Ian on a day out

160

by the sea. There was also a flourishing cactus garden in a green plastic trough. Over it all hung the cage where Bluey, the blue budgerigar, chattered to them, out of reach of tempting Partner into thoughts of catching him.

In the middle of the room the table was laid for tea, and the children's eyes went at once to the results of Grace's baking. There were scones and fairy cakes, a sponge cake with chocolate butter icing, and some sausage rolls. There was also a salad with hard-boiled eggs in it, plenty of bread and butter, a jar of Grace's home-made jam, and the cheese dish. Uncle Arthur rubbed his hands together in appreciation.

"My goodness, Grace, that looks good," he said. "You must have been working all afternoon."

"Not really." Grace put the tea-pot down on its mat, and sat down herself. "I made the pastry before June came for her piano lesson, and the scones are from yesterday, hotted up. I just had the sponges to make when June had gone. I had plenty of time, with its being early closing day, and I felt like doing some cooking."

"And we're all jolly glad you did." Uncle Arthur picked up the plate of bread and butter. "Now, who wants what?"

They had reached the cake stage when Grace suddenly said, "Oh, Arthur, there was a letter for you in the afternoon post. I'd forgotten all about it. It's behind the clock."

"Was there?" Uncle Arthur got up, his mouth still full of cake. "Better see what it is, I suppose."

He picked up the letter and came back to the table, passing his cup to Grace for more tea before he tore open the envelope. Angela went on asking Grace questions about making butter icing, and only Ian noticed that Uncle Arthur's face had gone pale, and that his cake was lying forgotten on his plate. The hand which was holding the letter began to shake slightly, and then Uncle Arthur said, "Oh, my goodness. Oh dear."

"What is it?" Grace looked up sharply. "Is something wrong, Arthur?"

"It's this letter. It's from George Manners, old Fred Manners' son." Uncle Arthur stared

162

at her down the table. "He's our landlord now, since old Fred died in July. He says the ponies have got to go. He says having them in the yard spoils the tone of the row and, as he's putting his property up for sale, he doesn't want the price kept down by the presence of backyard livestock."

"But can he do that?" asked Grace. "Didn't you have an agreement about them with Fred Manners?"

"Yes, I did. But only with old Fred. It was a gentleman's agreement really, nothing in writing." Uncle Arthur's eyes went back to the letter. "Oh dear, oh dear. And when we get a new landlord he isn't likely to want them back either. My goodness, what ever can we do?"

"I'm sure we'll think of something," said Grace encouragingly. "They aren't doing any harm out there. No-one round here objects to them, so surely we can persuade young Mr Manners to change his mind?"

"I doubt it, I really do." Uncle Arthur was staring down at the letter. "He's very much a business man, this George, quite different from his father. If he's decided that he'll get

a better price with them out of the way, then
he won't change."

"Has he given any date for having them
out?" asked Grace.

"Yes, yes, he has." Uncle Arthur looked
up. "He's given me three weeks to find them
a new stable."

"Well, that's quite a long time," Grace
pointed out. "We'll find somewhere before
then."

"I don't know." Uncle Arthur shook his
head. He had forgotten all about his tea.

"Most of the old stables round here are garages now."

"Oh Uncle Arthur, there must be somewhere," Angela's eyes were wide and anxious. "They're only little, they don't need much room."

"They need a proper stable, just the same." Uncle Arthur had handed the letter to Grace to read. "Oh dear, just when everything was going so well. I really don't know what to do."

The letter had spoiled the end of tea completely. No-one felt like eating any more cake or drinking more tea when soon Magic and Moonshine might be without a home. Grace stood up and began stacking plates together, and Uncle Arthur went out to the yard and the ponies. No-one followed him. Angela and Ian helped Grace to clear away, and then found tea-cloths to start drying up.

"What do you think Uncle Arthur will do?" Angela asked quietly, a few minutes later.

"Oh, he'll find somewhere, I'm sure," Grace told her cheerfully. "There's no need to worry."

"I thought the shop belonged to Uncle Arthur?" said Ian, drying a jug.

"No, he pays rent for it, but he has a long lease," explained Grace. "That's an agreement that he can stay here for a long time. But of course it doesn't apply to the ponies, only to people, although the old landlord didn't mind him keeping them here. He owned all this row from here to "The Red Lion" and the wine shop on the corner."

When Uncle Arthur came indoors again he was a little more cheerful. He said that he had thought of several places he could try for stabling, although it wouldn't be the same as having the ponies in the yard. But the atmosphere was happier by Angela and Ian's bedtime, and they even finished up the evening with a lively game of "Happy Families". Tomorrow, Uncle Arthur said, he would start asking round about new stabling.

2 · Horseman's Sunday

For the next two weeks Uncle Arthur searched the district steadily for new stabling for Magic and Moonshine. Gradually, as more and more people said that they could not help, his cheerfulness began to vanish again. All the possible places seemed to be already in use, for storage, or as garages, and although almost everyone said that they would like to be able to help, none of them actually could. By the weekend of Horseman's Sunday, just before Angela and Ian went back to school, even Grace's attempts to cheer him up were beginning to fail.

"I'm not sure that we ought to go," said Uncle Arthur, at breakfast time on Sunday. "There's a fellow I could see over at Balham, he used to keep a pony for his fruit barrow, but it's a long way out, and he's probably got a van in the stable now."

"I think we should go," said Grace. "After all, you might just as easily meet someone who can help us on the downs. And you said you'd

167

never missed a Horseman's Sunday since you got the ponies. It would be a shame to miss one now."

"All right." Uncle Arthur gave in, much to Angela's relief. In spite of the doubt about the ponies' future she had still been looking forward to Horseman's Sunday.

Having made the decision to go, Uncle Arthur cheered up once more.

"Come along then," he instructed the children. "It could be their last public appearance, but let's make it a good one. All hands to the grooming, now, while Grace gets on with packing the lunch."

The carriage, which was kept covered by a tarpaulin, had been washed down and polished the day before, for deep down Uncle Arthur had always intended to keep to the plan to go. It was only that at the last minute he had felt guilty about losing even a few hours of time that might have been spent stable-hunting. As well as helping to clean the carriage the children had helped to clean and polish the black, patent leather harness and to burnish the brasses which hung from it. They had worked on it in the kitchen, with

168

thick newspapers spread around to protect Grace's clean floor, and they were both proud of their share in achieving the shining result. He hadn't felt left out then, Ian realised, while they all worked on the same absorbing task. All that remained this morning was to get the ponies themselves ready.

Magic and Moonshine knew that today something special was happening. Uncle Arthur had been out early to feed them, and now they greeted him and the children with eager wuffling sounds as they entered the shed.

"We'll have them out in the yard for grooming," said Uncle Arthur. "It's a fine day, and we can see better outside."

Out in the yard Uncle Arthur started work on Magic, who was the smallest of the pair by two inches, but who sometimes needed a firm hand. He began by rubbing hard at the pony's cream coat with a soft body brush, scraping the grease and loose hairs out of it every now and then on the metal curry comb. Ian did the same with Moonshine, while Angela fetched a bucket half-filled with soapy water and started to scrub the ponies' small neat hooves.

169

At present they wore iron shoes, but later, when the pantomime season began, they would wear rubber shoes instead to prevent them from slipping on the wooden boards of the stage. Or they would if they were still here, Angela remembered unhappily, as she scrubbed Magic's feet with the small brush.

Uncle Arthur had washed both ponies' tails in soapy water the day before, and now he brushed the long hair out into soft, cream-coloured fans. Then he began to plait Magic's mane, weaving lengths of blue and red braid in with the hair as he worked. Angela had finished their hooves, and now she held Grace's small mending box for him, handing him needle and thread as he needed it to fasten each small neat plait.

When both ponies were groomed and plaited, and their manes and tails threaded with the coloured braid, Uncle Arthur went to fetch the van while Ian and Angela stuffed hay into two hay nets ready for the ponies to eat on the journey. Then Grace called them in to wash and put on tidy clothes, and by the time they were ready Uncle Arthur had loaded both ponies into the van.

170

Uncle Arthur's van was really rather spectacular. It was a tall, rather narrow-looking vehicle with a ramp at the back for the ponies to walk up. It was brightly painted, with red mudguards and wings, green bodywork, and yellow doors. Along both sides yellow letters were painted and read "Magic and Moonshine." Underneath, in smaller letters, was painted "Wonder ponies of stage and screen." Uncle Arthur thought that it was fair enough to say "screen" as well, because the ponies had once taken part in a television commercial, advertising shampoo.

Inside the van there was a padded partition, dividing the interior into two halves, one for each pony. They looked very comfortable and at home in there, as Uncle Arthur raised the ramp up into position behind them. The carriage had its own little trailer, which Uncle Arthur now hitched on behind.

It was rather a squash for them all in the cab, but they packed in somehow. Angela sat on Grace's knee, and there was just room for Ian between her and Uncle Arthur. The big basket of food had gone in the back, along with the hay nets, the harness, and the sack

171

containing the ponies' own lunches of pony cubes.

It was about an hour's drive to Epsom Downs. The van and trailer could only travel quite slowly, and Uncle Arthur always drove extra carefully when he had the ponies behind him.

When they got there the wide expanse of the downs was already crowded, with horses and ponies everywhere. Horse boxes, cattle trucks, and trailers mingled with hundreds of ordinary cars in the big chalky car parks and inside the oval made by the long sweep of the white-railed racecourse. Beyond the course the wide slope of short grass and scrubby bushes was black with horses and people. Away to their right, as Uncle Arthur parked the van, the children could see the great ugly bulk of the Grandstand, from which thousands of people each year watched the racehorses in the Derby and the Oaks flash past to the finish.

"They have the service over there, beyond this side of the racecourse," explained Uncle Arthur, pointing towards the massed crowd of horses gathering beyond the road which ran

172

alongside the racecourse straight. "See the loud-speakers in the middle of that clear space? Afterwards all the horses and riders and the vehicles parade round the road inside the course, and every horse and pony gets a rosette. It's quite a sight, there were nearly a thousand horses here last year."

"It's the biggest gathering of horses and ponies in the country, isn't it?" asked Grace.

"Yes. And they don't come to try to win prizes, or anything like that. They just come for the fun of it, and to have their horses blessed," replied Uncle Arthur.

"Is there really a service, like in Church?" asked Angela.

"Oh, yes. A short one, of course, or the horses would never stand quietly, but it is a real service," Uncle Arthur assured her. "There are prayers, and a reading from the Bible, a sermon, and a blessing for all the horses and ponies and the people with them."

The service was to start at twelve o'clock, and as it was now eleven-thirty they all got down from the cab, and Uncle Arthur un-hitched the trailer and lowered the van ramp to the sound of Magic's usual whinny.

Quite a lot of people gathered to watch as Ian and Uncle Arthur led the ponies out and started to harness them. Angela felt rather shy, but Magic and Moonshine, of course, were used to an audience. Magic began to "ask" by waving one front foot in the air.

"Can I give him a lump of sugar?" a little girl asked Uncle Arthur.

"Well, just one, then, before I put his bridle on," agreed Uncle Arthur.

Magic and Moonshine both received sugar lumps, and Uncle Arthur made them both go down on one knee to bow "Thank you." Then the bridles were put on, and the ponies were harnessed to the carriage. Uncle Arthur climbed on to the driving seat to take the reins, and Grace got in behind him. Ian and Angela perched on the step at the back, as they had done for the wedding. Then Uncle Arthur touched the ponies' backs lightly with the tip of the driving whip, and they were moving off, out of the car park and on to the road.

There was a policeman on duty at the crossing, where all the horses and ponies were converging to cross the road and the racecourse

174

beyond. Uncle Arthur brought both ponies to a halt to wait for him to hold up the traffic again.

"Oh Ian, look," gasped Angela, and Ian looked up the road towards a great oncoming rattle and clatter. A great, gleaming, dark-green dray drawn by four huge, magnificent black horses was coming towards them at a slow, jangling jog. Long "feathers" of black and white hair hung like silk from the horses' legs, and their long manes and tails were braided and plaited with coloured ribbons, far more intricately done than were Magic and Moonshine's. Gleaming brasses hung from their polished harness, and they arched their huge necks and chewed their shining bits, tossing white specks of foam on to the road. Their driver and the groom beside him wore dark-green uniforms, and there was the name of a big brewery painted along the sides of the dray in gold paint.

As they came closer the big horses made tiny Magic and Moonshine look like toys, but Magic arched his own neck harder, and whinnied a cheeky greeting.

"What are they?" Ian called to Uncle

Arthur, as the dray began to turn left across the road in front of them.

"Shire horses," Uncle Arthur called back. "Their ancestors were the horses that knights of old rode into battle. Those four probably weigh a ton each, and they can easily pull their own weight. I know that chap driving; I meet him around the shows sometimes when the lads are giving one of their displays."

The policeman was waving them on now, and the two tiny ponies crossed the road and went over the racecourse, crossing on to the inner road behind the towering dray.

The open, roped-off space from which the service would be conducted was by now surrounded by a mass of horses and people on foot. All the horse-drawn vehicles were on one side, and Magic and Moonshine were waved into position by a steward. They found themselves between the huge Shires with their dray and a coster-cart drawn by a fat skewbald coster pony whose driver wore the costume of a pearly king.

Once they had stopped Angela and Ian had time to gaze round at the massed ranks of horses and ponies. They were nearly all

176

very smart, their coats polished and their tack gleaming. The riders were neatly dressed, with well-brushed coats and shining boots or shoes, and many had a flower in their button-hole. Among them, looking just as smart and fit as the horses, were a number of donkeys, grey, chocolate brown, and skewbald, one or two with foals beside them. The driver of the big Shires beamed down at Magic and Moonshine, and Uncle Arthur raised his whip in greeting.

"Hello," called the Shires' driver. "Those shrimps of yours look well, Arthur."

"Bit small, beside yours," Uncle Arthur called back.

"Booked up for the season yet?" asked the driver.

"Not yet," replied Uncle Arthur. "Going to be a bit tricky this year, anyway. I'm losing my stabling."

"Got anywhere else?" asked the driver.

"Not yet. I've been trying, but without any luck," replied Uncle Arthur. "I've got another week to go, but I've looked just about everywhere."

"As bad as that?" asked the driver sym-

pathetically, and Uncle Arthur said that it
was. Then their attention was drawn back to
the present as a big black car slid slowly down
over the grass to stop at the edge of the open
space, and the Rector of a nearby village got
out and stepped forward to start the service.

The short service began with a welcome
from the Rector, and a prayer. Then a well-
known member of the British Horse Society
read the lesson from the Book of Job, the
verse about the war-horse, which made Ian

think of pictures he had seen of snorting Arabian chargers.

After the lesson the Rector talked for a few minutes about the trust that is given to all those who handle animals, and then he went on to lead the prayers. Among these was one for horses and ponies which Angela thought was beautiful, and determined to learn by heart from the service sheet which she and Ian were sharing. Then everyone joined together to say The Lord's Prayer, the words sounding firm but thin in the open air, and the service ended with a blessing.

During the service the circle of horses remained almost still, as though they sensed the solemnity of the occasion. A few ears and tails twitched, and one or two impatient forefeet pawed the ground, but Magic and Moonshine stood like statues, their ears pricked, and the breeze stirring the braid in their manes. Once a donkey brayed, and an aircraft droned overhead, but the quiet spell remained until after the blessing, when the mounted stewards moved forward to take up their positions to lead the procession over the downs.

The procession was led by the horse-drawn

vehicles, behind a steward, a girl riding a lovely grey horse. Magic and Moonshine were fourth in line, behind the coster pony. The Shires with their dray came after them, rumbling round the road until everyone reached the place where all the vehicles turned to commence the real procession. This would take them back past the place from which there would be a commentary given over more loud-speakers, then round the inside of the famous Derby turn at Tattenham Corner.

Coming down towards the commentator and the stewards who were handing out the rosettes, Ian and Angela could see the spectators packed solid in two deep rows on either side of the road. Magic and Moonshine pricked their ears and arched their necks, lifting their knees high like hackney ponies, and showing off as hard as they could. Uncle Arthur had a job to hold them in as the coster pony ahead pulled up for his driver to receive his rosette.

"And now we have Magic and Moonshine," said the lady commentator. "They are with us every year, and I always look forward to seeing them. Mr Perry has them in harness for the first time this year, and what a delightful turn-out it is; two cream Shetland ponies to a half-sized landau. I think I've only once seen a carriage like this before. Aren't they going well, and aren't they proud of themselves?"

Magic and Moonshine certainly were. They paused impatiently while Uncle Arthur received his blue rosette from a smiling steward, and then they were off at a brisk, gay trot, down the gently sloping road between the lines of people and past the clicking cameras and gasping children. Angela felt herself go scarlet under all the attention, but Ian was staring straight ahead, and it struck Angela that he seemed almost bored by it all.

At the end of the racecourse road, when Uncle Arthur slowed up the ponies and took them on to the grass, he and the ponies and carriage were immediately surrounded by people. They all wanted to pat Magic and Moonshine, and ask questions about them, and the ponies "asked" for sugar, and did some of their "yes" and "no" tricks as Uncle Arthur gave them the signals. The big Shires came crashing past a few feet away with their empty dray, and Uncle Arthur waved to his friend on the driving seat. Behind the last vehicle a seemingly endless stream of ridden horses began to come down the road, and after watching for a few minutes Uncle Arthur said that it was time they took the ponies back to the van and fed them.

They were unharnessing the ponies when the dray driver came over to speak to them. His four great horses were already loaded into the brewery horse box, and the dray had been run-up on to its trailer behind.

"About what you were saying, over losing your stabling," he said, as Uncle Arthur looked up from unfastening Magic's traces. "I might be able to help you. We're a team short in our stables at the moment, and we will be for another month or so at least. I reckon I might get you in there for a time. I'll have a word with the stable foreman if you like. We're not so far from your place."

"Would you really? That's awfully good of you." Uncle Arthur's face went even redder. "It really would be a load off my mind. It'd give me more time to find something permanent."

"I'll do that, then," promised the driver. "Be

a shame if you had to part with these two. Quite an eyeful, they are."

He rubbed Moonshine and Magic behind the ears, his hand big and firm and used to the great mass of the Shires, but both ponies pricked their ears and breathed at him in a friendly way. When he had gone Uncle Arthur turned to Grace and the children in great excitement.

"Well," he said. "Fancy that. I do hope he can get us in. Be a real relief, that, wouldn't it?"

"Won't they feel awfully small among all those huge horses?" asked Angela. Uncle Arthur laughed.

"Soon get used to it," he said. "It won't bother them, they're cheeky enough for anything. But my word, won't it be nice to get them fixed up, even if it is only temporary."

And as they collected their lunches and the ponies' feeds from the van, and led them away to find a quiet spot in the warm, pale golden September sunlight, they all, including Ian, hoped very hard that the driver of the dray really could provide Magic and Moonshine with a temporary home.

3·Among the giants

For the three days following Horseman's Sunday everyone at Uncle Arthur's lived in a state of great anxiety, waiting to hear some news from the brewery stable. School had started again, and each day Angela and Ian hurried home to see if there had been a message or a letter. Although Ian could not manage to feel quite so concerned about the ponies as Angela, he knew how much it would upset everyone else if they had to go. And really, when he honestly thought about it, he did not want them to go for good himself.

On Wednesday afternoon the shop was closed, and so Angela and Ian went in the back way, through the yard and past the stable. Magic whinnied to them as he heard their steps, but today they were in too much hurry to find out if there was any news, and they did not stop as they usually did. Uncle Arthur and Grace were both in the living-room, and with them was Uncle Arthur's friend from the brewery stables. All three of them looked

184

round and smiled at the children as they hurried in. Angela looked anxiously from face to face and knew at once that it was all right. Uncle Arthur's face was red and beaming, and Grace looked happy.

"Hello kids," said Uncle Arthur, rubbing his hands together. "Good news. There's room for us at the brewery stables; the lads can move in on Saturday."

"Oh good." Angela dropped her school satchel on the settee and went to hug her Uncle. "Oh, I am glad. So they won't have to go, not now, will they?"

"Well, not for two months, anyway," Uncle Arthur sounded a little less light-hearted. "But a lot can happen in two months."

"And it might be a bit more," put in his friend, who had in front of him a cup of tea and a plate with a slice of Grace's home-made fruit cake on it.

"Jolly good. I'm glad it's all right," said Ian, rather less whole-heartedly. Angela was standing close to Grace, and Grace had put an arm casually round her as she talked. Again, vaguely, Ian felt the odd one out. Of course, he was too old to want Grace to put her arm

185

round him, that was for girls, anyway, but Angela seemed so very much at home with Grace and Uncle Arthur. She seemed so much more able really to take part in their lives, with her complete enthusiasm for the ponies, and her interest in the domestic things that Grace did, like cooking, and the knitting that Grace had recently started to teach her. And she liked playing the piano. Grace had started to give them both lessons, but Ian had not been very keen, and he had given it up very quickly. And in spite of all these things that he did not really feel keen about he had nothing special of his own to take their place. Standing there, he felt distinctly left out.

Then Grace looked round and noticed him, and asked him if he would like some tea and cake. The way that she said it made it obvious that she considered him almost one of the adults, and as he went to fetch himself a cup Ian did feel slightly better.

Uncle Arthur's friend, whose name was Bill, went out to the yard with them before he left, and had a look at the ponies. He grinned at the sight of the stable and its miniature occupants, and said that it would certainly be a change for them at the brewery. Then he drove off in his clean and shiny Austin van, and Uncle Arthur turned to the children.

"Well, we'll have to get started," he said. "Must have all their stuff spotless by Saturday. They go in for a bit of spit and polish in those stables, you know. We don't want them thinking we can't do as well."

Uncle Arthur meant what he said. By Saturday he and the children had cleaned and polished every bit of leather, brass, and steel that the ponies possessed. The harness shone, the head collars and the little bridles were supple and gleaming, the lead reins that were used to take the ponies for walks in hand, and the long lunge reins on the end of which they were exercised were scrubbed and whitened. The carriage was washed and polished, and the feed and water buckets were scrubbed out. Grace made a few mild objections to the amount of time her sink spent filled with hot, soapy water while webbing reins and grooming brushes soaked, but she did not really mind. In fact, she did quite a bit of scrubbing and polishing herself.

Uncle Arthur did not forget the van in all

these preparations. He brought it up to the gate at the back of the yard, swept all the straw out of it, and hosed it down both inside and out, before leaving it with the ramp down to dry. Curious neighbours paused to comment, and nearly all of them were horrified to learn that the ponies had got to move.

"Why, they're no trouble, never have been," said one lady, who lived across the cinder path from Uncle Arthur's gate. "We hardly ever hear them, and we don't even smell them unless the weather's really hot and you've been clearing out that muck heap."

"Young fellow wants his head examined," remarked another neighbour. "Lowering the tone indeed. What about old Charlie Rogers and his rag-and-bone barrow? Leaves it parked right out in the path he does, too, smelly old thing that it is. What does that young chap think he's got to sell, Buckingham Palace?"

"Oh, he's out to get the best price he can, you can't blame him for that," said Uncle Arthur forgivingly. "It won't be so bad if I can get them fixed up somewhere near."

All the neighbouring children, too, were

sorry to see Magic and Moonshine moving out. Many of them had always come to visit the ponies frequently, bringing them gifts of titbits saved by their mothers for the purpose, and they would miss them very much.

"Perhaps they won't be far away for long," Uncle Arthur told them encouragingly, and Angela hoped that it was true, and he was not just saying it to cheer everyone up, including himself. But it was not a cheerful moment when the ponies were loaded, and Uncle Arthur raised the ramp behind them to drive them down the cinder path for the last time.

Angela and Ian went with Uncle Arthur and the ponies to their new stables, but Grace had to stay behind to look after the shop. It was about three miles from Uncle Arthur's shop to the brewery, and some of the roads were very busy. But the brewery itself was at the end of a quiet side street. From the front, as they drove towards it, it seemed to be enormous and rather forbidding, a high, blank looking, red brick building with the name of the brewers, "Champney's", in tall gold letters above a pair of high, wrought-iron

189

gates. These stood open this morning, and as Uncle Arthur slowed the van ready to turn in they all saw one of the delivery wagons coming out. It was different from the one they had seen at Horseman's Sunday, just a flat platform without sides, piled high with crates; the driver sat high above the horses on a small, fragile-looking seat with a tall hand-brake sticking up at his side. The horses were a pair of the magnificent black Shires, and they were moving at a slow jog trot, their great necks arched and the long white feathers on their legs flashing in the autumn sunlight.

At the sound of their hooves Magic whinnied, and peeping through the little window behind the driver's cab Angela could see him standing there in the dim interior. His tiny ears were very pricked, and his eyes shone. Angela knew that he was excited, and eager to know where they were going.

Through the gates the van was immediately stopped by the gatekeeper, who came out of a low brick building marked "Inquiries", and held up his hand like a policeman. Uncle Arthur explained who they were and where they were going, and the gatekeeper grinned.

"I thought you'd strayed from a circus," he said. "OK, carry straight on, and you'll find yourselves at the stables."

The main way through the brewery led past a maze of side turnings and blank-fronted buildings with big double doors and raised brick-built loading bays. Through some of the doors they saw pipes and cooling equipment, large vats, and a place for washing bottles.

Little metal tracks like miniature train tracks came out of other buildings, and down narrow side turnings, and they saw a man pushing a string of small metal barrels down one of these. Crates and barrels were stacked everywhere, and motor lorries were parked here and there at loading bays, waiting for their loads. There was also another wagon being loaded, the two black horses standing like statues, except for their nodding heads and ears as they chewed at their bits. Cats lurked among the crates and peered from doorways, and Uncle Arthur said that he betted there were plenty of mice about for them to catch. Over the whole place hung the smell of brewing, rich and sweet and full,

191

making the children feel hungry, and Uncle Arthur remark that he could do with a pint. And then they crossed another main roadway, and found themselves at the stables.

The stable building was in the shape of an E without the middle arm, and the centre part was in two storeys. In the yard were parked the spare wagons, and two drays with sides like the ones they had seen at Horseman's Sunday. A man was sweeping water down the yard towards a central drain, but as the van stopped he propped his broom against the wall and came to meet them.

"We've been expecting you," he said. "I'm Pat Massey, the stable foreman."

Mr Massey was big and rather fat, with grey-brown hair and a dusty-looking face, but his blue eyes were very bright. He was dressed in an ancient grey pullover on top of a faded blue shirt, and his old grey flannel trousers were held up by an enormous, shiny leather belt with big silver studs and a large gilt buckle.

"Bill's away at the show," he explained. "But you come with me and I'll show you where your two monsters are to go."

Uncle Arthur, Angela, and Ian followed Mr Massey across the cobbled yard to where a flight of steep, twisting stone stairs led upwards. Beside them was the entrance to a rather dark, cobbled ramp. They all clattered up the stairs, and at the top they found themselves at one end of the long upper stable. The top of the ramp came out close by.

"This is where we keep the show horses," explained Mr Massey over his shoulder. "The working horses are downstairs."

"Don't they all work, then?" asked Ian, surprised.

"No. They do a few years of travelling the shows, and then move on to the round," Mr Massey told him. "From May to October it's often practically empty up here. We travel them all over the country, showing in trade and heavy-harness classes, and in Shire breed classes. Then they give displays at agricultural shows, and at the "Horse of the Year Show" at Wembley. And they do their bit in processions, the Lord Mayor's Show is usually our last big engagement of the year."

"It doesn't sound so very much different to our game," said Uncle Arthur, and Mr Massey

193

said that he didn't suppose it was, except for the matter of size.

A wide gangway ran the length of the stable, with big stalls along either side of it. Light came in through high, clean windows on both sides, and the cobbled gangway was swept very clean. The stalls were deeply bedded down with a mixture of peat and wood shavings, and the green and white paintwork gleamed. There were enough stalls for twelve horses, six down either side, but only four were actually occupied. The great, dark hindquarters and thick, glossy black tails of these made Angela feel very small. Big, kind heads turned to look at them, and two of the horses greeted Mr Massey with a soft whicker.

"Midnight and Bomber," said Mr Massey. "They'll be due to retire from showing this autumn, they've done their bit of trailing round the country. You might not believe it, but it's a lot harder on them showing than doing the steady work on the round."

"Is it really?" asked Ian.

"Yes, too many changes, no regular routine," explained Mr Massey. "These other two down here are younger. Dandy's only a four year old, we're still breaking him in, and Clover's five. She's been with us a year now, haven't you, old girl?"

He went up to give the big horse a friendly slap on the neck, and Angela and Ian gazed almost in awe at the first Shire horse they had seen close to, from ground level.

"How big is she?" asked Ian.

"Seventeen hands three inches," replied Mr Massey. "She's not our biggest, not by quite a way. The record here at present is eighteen hands three, four inches bigger."

Clover looked quite big enough to Angela. Mr Massey was beckoning them into the stall beside her, but Angela hung back, although Ian went in quickly enough.

"It's all right, she won't hurt you. She's as gentle as a kitten," said Mr Massey, but Angela was not convinced. Ian, however, thought the big horse wonderful. This was a real horse, not a toy, like the ponies. Just standing there she radiated power, and when Ian put his hand on her shoulder, as high up as he could reach, he could feel the swell of huge muscles under the warm, silky hair.

Clover turned her head to look at him, and
Ian held his hand out to her. Big, warm lips
gently explored his hand, and a very long
tongue licked the salt taste off his palm. Her

196

head seemed half as long as Ian was tall, but her eyes were very kind, and he found that he was not at all afraid of her.

"She's lovely," he told Mr Massey. "Has she won many prizes?"

"Oh, she's been in a good many prize-winning teams," replied Mr Massey. He gave Clover a pat. "Well, we'd better get on. This isn't getting your animals settled, is it?"

He led the way out of the stall, and Angela looked admiringly at Ian.

"Weren't you scared of her?" she asked him, as they followed the two men on down the stable. "She's so big."

"She's gentle, though," said Ian. "But she's terrific, Angie. She feels strong, just standing there. She really is a horse."

Then they saw that Mr Massey had stopped at the two end stalls on the left. These had fresh but rather more shallow beds of peat and shavings down in them, and Mr Massey said, "Here you are. Will these be large enough, do you think?"

Uncle Arthur laughed. "One of them would almost do us," he said. "They'll think they've come to live in a palace."

197

"How will you shut them in?" asked Angela. "Or will they have to be tied up all the time, like the others?"

"Oh, they'll have to put up with being tied," replied Uncle Arthur. "They won't mind, they'll have long ropes and plenty of room. All right to bring them up now?" he asked Mr Massey.

"Yes, soon as you like," agreed Mr Massey.

Magic and Moonshine were delighted to be out of the van, and they gazed around them with great interest. Mr Massey grinned at the sight of them.

"Little all right, aren't they?" he said. "You'd better mind none of the big fellows eats them up for breakfast."

"Old Magic would give them indigestion if they tried," replied Uncle Arthur, laughing.

Angela had wondered if Magic and Moonshine would mind the ramp, but they did not seem in the least worried by it. Uncle Arthur went up first with Magic and Ian followed with Moonshine. Angela came behind carrying two hay nets, one slung over each shoulder.

The four big horses in the upstairs stalls

turned interested heads at the sound of Magic and Moonshine's little hooves clattering on the cobbles, and Clover whinnied. Magic whinnied back in his usual cheeky way, and Uncle Arthur said, "Now, now. You'd better mind what you say, my boy, until you've been here for a bit."

"Do you think they really say something, or are they just making a noise?" asked Angela, as they reached the ponies' stalls.

"Oh, they say something, I'm sure," replied Uncle Arthur. "That was probably 'Who on earth are you?' and I bet Magic answered 'Mind your own business'."

The two little ponies did look rather dwarfed by the big stalls with their high, solid partitions. They could not look over, and they had to stand facing the mangers, tethered by their head collar ropes. These were threaded through brass rings on the mangers and then through small blocks of wood known as "logs", which dangled on the rope, preventing it from being pulled through the ring, and also holding it straight, so that it could not tangle round the ponies' legs. All the Shires were tethered in this way, but it was not good enough for Magic. He objected strongly to not being able to see what was going on, and he began to paw the ground and jerk his head up and down, banging his log against the brass ring. Dandy began to move restlessly in sympathy, and the other three pricked their ears. Mr Massey appeared to ask what was going on.

"Cheeky little shrimp," he exclaimed, when Uncle Arthur explained. "So our stables don't suit him, eh?"

"He'll settle." Uncle Arthur did not want Magic to make a bad impression, but Mr Massey did not seem to be cross.

"Better let him have his way," he said. "There are some old bales out at the back. We'll sling a couple of those up for them, if you'll give me a hand."

"Bales" turned out to be heavy old doors, slung on their sides from two chains which fitted over the tops of the stall partition poles. Chains at the bottom also fitted to hooks in the floor, and Mr Massey and Uncle Arthur hung the bales low enough to prevent either pony trying to crawl under. With these in position across the open end of the stalls the ponies could be left loose, and Magic immediately hung out over his, eagerly gazing round his new home.

"We used to use those when we had a few lighter horses up here, vanners," explained Mr Massey. "The Shires are too big to leave loose in an ordinary single stall. They wouldn't be able to turn round safely, and they might get themselves cast."

"What's that?" asked Angela, forgetting to be shy in her interest.

"Cast? That's what it's called when a horse lies down or falls, and gets itself stuck, unable to get up again," explained Mr Massey. "A horse can't get up unless it's got room to get its legs in the right position. If it's too close to a wall or on a slope it may get 'cast'."

"Oh, I see." Angela imagined one of the big Shires unable to get up, and struggling. It was rather a frightening thought. Handling a frightened Shire horse would be a very different thing from dealing with Magic or Moonshine.

4 · Settling in

By now it was almost half past twelve. Down in the mews they could hear the clatter and rumble of the drays beginning to come in, for Saturday was a short day, and work stopped for the horses at one o'clock. None of the work horses came upstairs, but Ian and Angela went down with Uncle Arthur and Mr Massey to be shown the feed room, and to collect Magic and Moonshine's dinners, and found the yard full of them.

One pair was just being led into the stable by one of the stablemen and their driver, their harness still on them with the long traces neatly looped up. A second pair stood in the centre of the yard, still hitched to their empty dray. There was a light sheen of sweat on their necks and flanks, and one of them lowered his head to rub his big nose on his knee. Ian paused to watch the men unharness them, but Angela stayed beside Uncle Arthur, feeling safer well away from the big feet and great, silken-haired legs.

"Bit big for you, aren't they?" said Uncle Arthur, and Angela admitted that they were.

The way to the feed room led through the central stable, past a large double stall in which stood the biggest horse that Angela and Ian had ever seen. He was kept in just by a rope slung between him and the gangway.

"My goodness," exclaimed Uncle Arthur, stopping to marvel. "That arrangement wouldn't keep either of mine in for a moment."

"Do you think he bites?" asked Angela nervously, for the horse was leaning over his rope, and his huge head and neck extended the whole way across the gangway.

"Admiring Big Ben?" asked Mr Massey, catching up with them after pausing to speak to one of the men. "One of the biggest horses in England he is, eighteen hands three inches tall."

"So he's . . ." Ian did some rapid mental arithmetic. "He's six foot three inches tall."

"That's right," agreed Mr Massey. "At the point of his withers, that is. His neck's a lot higher, of course."

"And Magic's only thirty eight inches, or three foot two inches tall," said Uncle Arthur. "That's quite a difference."

Mr Massey laughed, and agreed that it was.

"And does that bit of string really keep him in?" asked Uncle Arthur, looking back at Big Ben's stall.

"His rope, you mean?" Mr Massey came past them and gave Ben a ringing, friendly slap on his enormous neck. "Oh yes, old Ben won't come out. He's quite happy in there, cadging tit-bits from everyone who goes past. He knows he'd lose his privileges if he started getting out."

"Does he bite?" asked Angela.

"Bite? Not Ben." Mr Massey let the horse lip his hand, and Ben's lips moved over his outstretched palm as gently as Magic's did. Angela, though, was not convinced. She felt as though the horse would only have to open his mouth to bite her head right off, but she followed Mr Massey and Uncle Arthur timidly past him, and through the door into the harness room beyond. Ian paused to pat Ben, thrilled by the immense size and power

204

of the magnificent animal, and Ben lipped his hands just as gently as he had Mr Massey's.

"This is the show horses' harness," Mr Massey was explaining, when Ian joined them. They were in a big room with a large stove against one wall, and pegs and racks holding harness all around them. Everything was polished to a brilliant shine, leather and brass glowed in the shadows, against the white-washed walls, and a glass case across the centre of the room protected several sets of especially beautiful harness. There were two big photographs on the walls, one of a team of six Shires in the show ring, pulling a dray, and one of a team pulling a coach in the Lord Mayor's Show. Several pegs were empty, and Mr Massey explained that they belonged to those horses who were away at the shows.

"We keep the working harness at the other end," he added. "There wouldn't be room for it all in here."

"There must be some work in keeping this lot clean!" exclaimed Uncle Arthur, and Mr Massey agreed that there was.

"Never finished here, that's us," he said.

"Start at six, finish at six, twelve hour day, and we still don't always get through without extra time."

But he sounded quite happy about it, and it was obvious that Mr Massey was content with his job.

The feed room was beyond the harness room, through another door, and was lined with big, galvanised bins. There were several sacks of carrots in one corner, and a pile of bundles of rich looking green-stuff, obviously freshly delivered. Uncle Arthur emptied the two sacks of fodder that he had brought into an empty bin, and then started to measure out Magic and Moonshine's midday feeds. Mr Massey grinned as he watched.

"That wouldn't go far with ours," he said. "One bite, that's about all."

"How much do they eat a day?" asked Ian.

"Oh, about ten bucketsful each," replied Mr Massey, and Ian thought for a moment that he was joking. Then he realised that the stable foreman was quite serious.

"Ten buckets?" exclaimed Uncle Arthur. "And how much hay?"

"We don't feed hay," explained Mr Massey.

"It makes a lot of extra work and litter, and doesn't give much return in nourishment that can't be given in short feed."

"But don't they get bored with no hay to chew at?" asked Ian, remembering the hours that Magic and Moonshine spent in contented munching.

"They get green meat at night," replied Mr Massey. "In season, that is. In winter they have mangels to chew. And we feed them as many carrots as they'll eat before they go out in the morning. Then it takes them quite a while to work through their four or five buckets of short feed each evening."

"I'll bet it does," exclaimed Uncle Arthur, while Angela tried to imagine Magic faced with five big buckets of food.

"When do they have the rest?" asked Ian.

"They have two in the morning, before work," replied Mr Massey. "A nosebag while they're out, then about three buckets when they come in and the rest in the evening. We feed a mixture of maize, bran, chaff, and oats. They don't go hungry, I can tell you."

Back upstairs with feeds for Magic and Moonshine they found that several of the drivers had gone up to look at the new arrivals. Magic and Moonshine were leaning over their bales, and Magic was showing off some of his tricks, asking with one front foot, offering to shake hands, and doing part of one of his dances. This was a sort of rumba, in which Magic swung his hindquarters from side to side and jiggled his hind legs, and it was raising quite a laugh from his audience.

"Quite a clown, isn't he?" said one of the men, as Magic stopped dancing to whinny to Uncle Arthur. "Can he do anything else?"

"Plenty." Uncle Arthur put down the buckets, and proceeded to put both ponies through more of their tricks. He made them both bow, and he talked to Moonshine until Magic pretended to be jealous, and leaned out to nudge him. Then he turned his back on Magic and the pony quietly took a handkerchief from his back pocket while Uncle Arthur pretended not to know what was going on. The men laughed, and patted the ponies, but it was clear that they did not take them seriously. They thought that Magic and Moonshine were just pets, like tiny dogs, and not capable of doing any real work. In fact, one of the drivers did say laughingly that Champney's was turning into a circus, with Magic and Moonshine in the stables. When they had gone, and the ponies were eating, Angela said, "They didn't think much of Magic and Moonshine, did they?" She was rather hurt. She was used to people admiring the ponies, not thinking them useless and rather funny, for she did not think that they were useless at all.

"Well, they are a bit small, aren't they?" said Ian, who rather shared the men's point of view. "After all, they aren't really working animals."

"They work jolly hard," exclaimed Angela, stung. "Look how much time they have to spend standing about in uncomfortable corners in theatres when the pantomimes are on, and look how they get driven about the country to appear at fêtes and shows in the summer. Even Mr Massey said shows were hard work. And they go beautifully in harness, they never try to be lazy."

"But it still isn't real work, not like pulling those drays, or ploughing a field," Ian pointed out. "What they do isn't really a job, it's not important."

"Of course it is. Look how many people have said how much they enjoy watching them," retorted Angela. "And Uncle Arthur's told us that Shetland ponies are very strong for their size, and up to a terrific lot of work. They pull all of us in the carriage, don't they?"

But Ian still thought that, compared to the Shires, Magic and Moonshine were like toys, and not really very much more use.

When they got home, rather late for lunch, Grace was very eager to hear how Magic and Moonshine liked their new home, and she was glad to be told that they seemed quite contented. Ian told her about the Shires, and all that Mr Massey had said about the way they were looked after, and he was surprised to find afterwards that he had talked almost all though the meal. But Grace did not seem to have been bored, she asked questions, and really listened to what he said, and she seemed to have enjoyed listening as much as he had enjoyed telling.

Of course, having the ponies three miles

away instead of in the backyard would mean a lot of extra work. Uncle Arthur would have to go over to the brewery stables early every morning to muck out and feed the ponies, and if he came home later in the morning he would have to return at lunch time to feed them, for he did not want to ask for any help from Mr Massey and his busy staff. Then he would have to go over again in the evening to feed them and settle them for the night. And there was still their exercising to be fitted in, either by driving them in the carriage, or lunging them somewhere as he often did on the recreation ground near the shop. It would mean that Grace must spend more time in the shop, and try to fit in the piano lessons she gave at times when she knew Uncle Arthur would be at home. In fact, it was not an ideal way to keep them, but for the time being they all knew that they would manage somehow.

The first complete day that the ponies spent at the brewery was a Sunday, a very quiet day for the Shires. They did not go out at all, and only Mr Massey and a few of the stable-men came in to do the essential feeding and mucking out. After seeing to the ponies in the morning Uncle Arthur, Ian, and Angela got home in time to go to church with Grace as they usually did. Then, while she finished cooking the dinner, they dashed over to give the ponies their feeds, and after they had been home for their own dinners Uncle Arthur, Grace, and Angela went back to take the ponies for a drive. Ian, however, did not go. He had arranged to play football with some school friends on the recreation ground, and although Angela missed him it was better than knowing that he was with them and feeling bored. Although why he should be bored with the ponies she did not know.

It was rather a grey sort of afternoon, with a slight mist about, and the streets were very quiet. Both Grace and Angela drove the ponies for a bit, and the eight little hooves tapped briskly along the empty Sunday streets and echoed sharply back from the tall, grey houses and the long, sooty terraces. In one overgrown square garden someone was burning leaves, and the sharp, tangy smell of the smoke drifted across their faces as the ponies trotted past. They all arrived back at the stables with glowing faces and tangled hair, and the sound of the ponies' hooves on the cobbles was greeted by a whinny from one of the resting Shires inside the stable.

As she helped Grace and her uncle to put the warm, prick-eared ponies away in their box-stalls and feed them Angela wondered how Ian could bear to miss such an afternoon. But when they got home Ian was just coming down the street, his football boots slung round his neck, and mud on his legs, shorts, and face, and he insisted that his afternoon had been just as good as theirs.

"Don't you like the ponies any more?" Angela asked him later, when they were alone in the sitting room for a few minutes.

"Oh, I like them," said Ian. "But I don't need to spend all my time with them, do I? The rest of you do that anyway."

"Well, why not? They're fun, and I like helping with them," Angela told him.

"So do I, in reason." Ian felt cross. He had enjoyed his game of football in a way, but he could not help feeling that once again he had been left out of the family. The fact that it had been his own choice did not help. "But

213

they're only like toys really, aren't they? It's all right for you, you're younger, and anyway, you're a girl."

"I don't . . ." began Angela, but then Grace came back into the room, and she stopped. Ian would only be cross if she let Grace hear them arguing about it, but she wished that she could understand why Ian seemed so touchy these days, and why he was no longer so keen on Magic and Moonshine.

On Monday morning the atmosphere at Champney's was very different. When Angela and Ian got there with Uncle Arthur, just before eight o'clock, after a very early breakfast, work was in full swing. Grace had not been very happy about them going to the stables before school, but they had both pleaded to go, and Uncle Arthur had promised to see that they had a good wash and got off to school in good time, and so she had given in.

Downstairs in the working horse section of the stables men were bustling in all directions, mucking out, carrying bags of shavings, or buckets of water, and starting to groom the big horses. Upstairs it was a little quieter, but

214

the six horses who had been away showing had returned the previous evening, and all the stalls were full. Magic was leaning out over his bale, watching the coming and going of the two men who were mucking out up there, and he greeted Uncle Arthur and the children with a shrill, greedy whinny.

"Yes, I know it's breakfast time," Uncle Arthur told him. "But mucking out first."

Ian helped him with this job while Angela began to brush Moonshine. Then, when the ponies had been fed and Uncle Arthur had started to groom Magic, he wandered away to watch the men working on the Shires. Now that really was grooming, he thought, watching one of the men at work on Bomber, a massive black horse with long white stockings on all four legs. The soft body brush skimmed across the shining black coat with a rhythmic, circular movement, the evenness of each stroke almost hiding the amount of weight that the man was putting into the job. At the end of each sweep of the brush the man scraped it across the metal teeth of the curry comb that he held in his other hand, and all the time he kept blowing a steady "sss" sound between

his teeth to keep the dust of his mouth. Then he turned to tap the grease out of the curry comb on to the floor and saw Ian watching.

"Bit different to grooming your pets, isn't it?" he asked.

"He's bigger," admitted Ian, who was not going to run Magic and Moonshine down to Champney's men whatever he might think himself. "But we groom ours just the same way. How big is he?"

"Seventeen two, this one," replied the man. "Not one of the biggest, of course, but he's a fair size to work on."

"I bet he's strong," said Ian, gazing admiringly at the big, shining horse.

"He is that," agreed the man. "He'd bowl one of your little ones over and not know he'd done it."

He turned back to his grooming, and Ian went on watching. When the man turned again to tap out his curry comb Ian said, "Could I have a go, do you think? At grooming him, I mean?"

"Not scared?" the man grinned at him. "He's got big feet, you know. You'd feel it if this one trod on your toe. And you'd need to put some weight behind the brush, no use tickling him."

"I'm not scared," Ian assured him. "I'd love to try."

"OK then." The man handed the brush and curry comb to Ian and leaned back against the partition by the horse's head to watch. Ian stepped in beside the big horse, very conscious suddenly of the great height and mass towering above him. Bomber turned his great, gentle head and Ian stroked his nose. Then he slipped his hand through the canvas loop on the back of the brush, flattening his

217

palm against the wooden back, and began to groom. Bomber stood quite still, and Ian concentrated on putting all his strength into each stroke of the brush. He was so occupied that he did not hear Uncle Arthur calling until the man said, "They're wanting you. Time for school, I should think."

"Are they?" Ian looked round, his face hot and crimson from the work. He tapped out the comb, finding quite a reasonable amount of grease in it, and the man looked quite impressed.

"Not bad," he said. "I didn't think you'd have an idea, but that wasn't bad at all. I can start the other side now."

He gave Ian a friendly smile, and Ian felt quite proud of himself as he went to join Uncle Arthur and Angela. He might have made mistakes sometimes with the ponies, but he couldn't be so hopeless after all.

Angela and Ian washed in the small wash room downstairs, and brushed the hay and shavings off each other as best they could. Uncle Arthur said when they rejoined him that they had better wear something old next time, and change when the ponies were done.

218

"Otherwise the whole of your school will smell of horses, and then I'll have your teacher after me," he said.

Most of the drays had gone out by the time Ian and Angela hurried out to catch the bus for school. Mr Massey had told them that the horses worked from eight thirty until three o'clock. In that time each dray did about three deliveries of beer to local public houses owned by Champney's.

"They'll be back before we get here after school," remarked Ian, as they dashed out of the gate.

5 · More like man's work

Angela and Ian went straight back to the stables after school. Angela was glad to find that Ian was as keen as she was to get back there. She had been afraid that he would want to do something else, and Uncle Arthur had said that she must not go alone, as she was not used to either the journey there or the big horses.

The drays were in now, as Ian had said they would be, standing idle in the yard, and the blacksmith was at work in the forge at the end of the left hand stable block. Uncle Arthur's blacksmith came round by van, and nailed "cold" factory made shoes on to the ponies' hooves in the more usual modern way. Uncle Arthur sometimes shook his head over their feet, and said that shoeing wasn't what it used to be when every blacksmith had made his shoes himself, but Angela and Ian had never seen this done. Now they paused, fascinated, to watch, for the brewery smith worked in this traditional way, heating the

metal in his coke fire and hammering it into
shape on the anvil. In the shadows of the
forge the fire glowed intensely red, and when
the smith placed the half-made shoe against
the hoof of one of the Shires to check the fit,
clouds of blue, acrid smoke blew out into the
yard from the singeing horn.

"Doesn't it hurt him?" wondered Angela, gazing at the calm horse.

"No. You know Uncle Arthur said that there's no feeling in the horny part of their feet," Ian reminded her.

When the shoe was shaped and fitted the smith plunged it into an iron tank of cold water with a tremendous sizzling noise, and then hung it with two others on the edge to cool while he started work on the fourth. He winked at the children over the fire as he pulled the handle to work the bellows, and they grinned back. Ian would have stayed to watch the shoes nailed on, but Angela pulled at his arm.

"Come on," she said. "We'd better find Uncle Arthur, and tell him we're here. He might want us for something."

Rather unwillingly, Ian let himself be led away, but when they got upstairs they found Magic bridled ready for exercise and Uncle Arthur bending over one of Moonshine's front feet.

"Only shod two weeks ago, and this shoe's loose already," he told the children. "That's cold shoeing for you."

222

"The blacksmith's down in the forge now," Ian told him. "He's making the shoes himself, like you told us some smiths did. Couldn't he do something about it?"

"Is he?" Uncle Arthur brightened up. "I'll go and have a word with him."

The blacksmith agreed quite readily to fix Moonshine's shoe, and Uncle Arthur told the children to take the pony to him while he gave Magic his run on the exercise ground behind the stables.

The big Shire was just coming out of the forge when the children and Moonshine got there, stamping out behind one of the stablemen on his ringing new shoes. The smith was sweeping up, and he grinned when he saw Moonshine.

"Cor, what a little 'un," he exclaimed. "He wants to be stood up on stilts for this job. Still, let's have a look at him."

Moonshine's hoof looked tiny in the smith's hard, smoke-stained hand, but he stood quite quietly while his shoe was nailed back on again.

"Rough old shoes, all the same, these factory ones," remarked the smith. "You tell your uncle I'll make a decent set each for this fellow and his mate before they go."

When Moonshine was finished the blacksmith showed them some of the shoes he had made ready for the big horses. There were hooks on the walls, with the names of the different Shires above them, and on some of these sets or odd new shoes hung ready. The smith took down one enormous shoe from Big Ben's peg, and handed it to Ian.

"Seven pounds, that weighs," he said, smiling at Ian's startled face. "Old Ben's a bit clumsy with his feet, and I shoe him extra thick. These'll last him seven or eight weeks."

"It's huge," exclaimed Angela. "Moonshine's foot would go right through the middle of it."

"Yes, there's quite a bit of iron in that shoe," agreed the smith, hanging it back on its hook. "Now, don't forget to tell your Uncle what I said about these little 'uns' next lot of shoes."

Uncle Arthur was out at the back with Magic, lungeing him in circles at the end of a long white webbing lunge rein. There was also a big Shire out there, Dandy, the

224

youngest of the show horses, being taught to walk quietly on a leading rein. It was Bill who was leading him, as he was not one of the delivery drivers, but worked mostly with the show horses. The children stopped with Moonshine on the edge of the big cinder-covered area to watch.

Out here, behind the stables, and cut off from the outside by a high brick wall, they might have been a hundred miles from London. Two tall elm trees in a corner shed drifts of golden leaves over the cinders, and the sun was bright and the light crystal clear. The air smelt of autumn leaves and damp ground, with the background richness of brewing, and a tang of horses. An old, heavy breaking cart for training the young horses stood in the centre of the cinder yard, its wood mellowed to a golden brown colour.

Magic circled Uncle Arthur at a brisk trot, his neck arched and his ears pricked, his coat a warm cream colour against the dark cinders. Beyond him the big Shire moved ponderously, but playfully, tossing his head, and every now and then waltzing heavily sideways until Bill steadied him with a quiet word and a touch

on the rein. Then Uncle Arthur called Magic
in and patted him, and came to take Moonshine.

"Can I put Magic away?" asked Angela,
and Uncle Arthur agreed that she could. Bill
was coming in as well now, with Dandy, and
Ian said, "Could I help you with him, do you
think?"

"Well, I don't know." Bill looked slightly
doubtful. "He's a bit touchy, and you're a bit
small to be around these big fellows, aren't
you?"

"I helped groom Bomber this morning,"
Ian told him.

"Did you now?" Bill smiled at him. "OK,
you come along with me. I daresay I can find
you a job."

In the end Ian spent the rest of the afternoon helping with the Shires. When Dandy
had been brushed over and settled Bill took
him down to the harness room, where two of
the stablemen were at work on the show
harness.

"Brought you a helper," Bill told them.
"He'd like to have a go at some full sized
harness for a change."

Ian felt a bit shy, but he did want to help. At first the men teased him about the difference between Magic and Moonshine's "fairy" harness, and their size, but soon they realised that he really did know something about cleaning harness, and did it quite well. Instead of teasing they began to offer advice, and to give him bits of their own sets of harness to clean, and Ian found that he had been accepted.

When the harness was done there were the late afternoon jobs around the stable to be attended to, and Ian helped to tidy up the stalls and check that all the automatic water bowls were filling properly. To start with the men kept an eye on him, not sure that he could move safely around the big horses, but Ian knew how to approach a horse. He knew that he must always speak to the horse before entering its stall, so that he did not startle it into kicking or shying, and that it was always safest to go round a horse under its head rather than round the tail. If he did have to go round behind a horse he remembered to keep close up to its back legs, with a hand on its tail, for a very close range kick was not dangerous, as there was no force in it. Also, keeping a hand on the horse told it where he was, and made it less inclined to move sud-denly backwards. He and Angela had both learned these things from being around Magic and Moonshine, and watching the way that Uncle Arthur handled them, and size made little difference when it came to things like that.

Angela and Uncle Arthur were ready to go before Ian had finished helping, and they had to go and find him.

"Hey, you're not taking our new stable boy away, are you?" asked Mr Massey, and Ian knew that he really had proved himself cap-able of being a help. As they drove home in the van he was feeling happier than he had for some time.

By the end of the first week it seemed to the children that the ponies had been at Champney's for ages. The journeys to the brewery from home and from school had already become familiar, and the routine of the big stable was becoming a part of their lives. Uncle Arthur still worried about finding new stabling for the ponies, but Ian, at least, was in no hurry for them to move. He found helping with the big horses the most absorbing, fascinating thing that he had ever done, and something that seemed to be entirely his own, for Angela was still very wary of them. Ian never grew tired of being close to their size and power, and he worked really hard to earn the approval of the men. For grooming, he often had to use the wooden steps which the men used for reaching the top of the biggest horses, like Big Ben, but he quickly became an expert at nipping on and off them, and none of the horses played up.

The only horse that Ian did not help with a lot was Dandy, but it was Dandy who seemed to have become Magic's special friend. The little pony always whinnied to the young Shire whenever Dandy went out or came in, and when Magic went out himself he would pause at Dandy's stall to whicker a greeting. Dandy always replied, turning his head as far as he could and pricking his ears at his small friend.

"Just so long as Dandy doesn't start trying Magic's tricks," said Bill, watching the two whinny to each other one day. "He's a bit big for shaking hands."

"Trust Magic to find a friend," said Uncle Arthur. "At home he's got Partner, now he's picked Dandy. Moonshine never makes friends like that."

At home, Partner was miserable without the ponies. He would wander into the empty shed, standing in the doorway and gazing round at the clean-swept boxes with a sorrowful expression on his face. Then he would turn away and go back into the house to curl up in a ball on a chair, or he would leap up on to the shed roof and sit there with his paws tucked under him, gazing out at the cinder path as though he was watching for Magic and Moonshine to come home.

Angela, too, hated seeing the empty shed, but to Ian life had become far more exciting and worthwhile now than it had been when Magic and Moonshine were in the yard.

"It must be jolly exciting, driving behind big horses," he said one day to Bill. "I always feel top heavy behind our two."

"It's a good feeling," agreed Bill. "Although I wouldn't really have called it exciting. Our teams are pretty sedate, no rodeo stuff from any of them. Even young Dandy will calm down when he gets in the breaking cart beside something sensible like old Ben."

"I'd love to go out on the round one day," said Ian longingly.

"There's no reason why you shouldn't," replied Bill. "One of the men would take you along on a Saturday morning, I expect. Of course, you'd have to ask your Uncle first."

Ian did ask, and Uncle Arthur agreed that he could go if one of the men would take him. Bill arranged for him to go with a driver called Frank, and Ian could hardly wait for next Saturday morning.

Angela was rather hurt by Ian's keenness on the big horses. Hurt on behalf of the ponies, that was. She felt that Ian was neglecting them, and when Ian had dashed off on Saturday morning to look for Frank she gave both ponies an apple to show that at least she had not abandoned them. Magic shook hands for his, and then kissed her for thank you, and Angela was quite unable to understand how Ian could prefer the big,

231

clumsy black horses to the charming little ponies.

"Why doesn't Ian like Magic and Moonshine any more?" she asked Uncle Arthur rather miserably.

"Oh, he does, he does really," Uncle Arthur assured her. "He just wants to have a go at something that looks more like man's work than these two. Might have felt the same myself once, before I stopped worrying so much about what other people think. Though I do think Ian's really keen on those big horses, handsome fellows, you know, can't help admiring them myself."

The Shires and their wagon were certainly a man's work. Just harnessing the two horses took all the height and strength of Frank and one of the stablemen, for one of the pair was Big Ben. His collar was an enormous thing, solidly-stuffed leather, with big brass guiding rings for the reins to run through, and big enough to slip over his big head and down his massive neck. His partner was Jasper, another big horse, although at eighteen hands he was three inches shorter than Ben.

"Do the same pairs always go out together?" Ian asked Frank, as he walked out beside him and Big Ben.

"Mostly," replied Frank. "It takes a bit of time to match a good pair for height and pulling ability. It's no use putting a lazy one with a willing one, or the willing one does all the pulling while the other hangs back with slack traces and shirks. But if you put two lazy ones together someone's got to do the work, so most often they both will."

"Are these two lazy?" Ian asked him.

"No, these are a good pair, good steady workers both of them," replied Frank.

Outside Ian was thrilled at being allowed to hold Jasper while Big Ben was "put too" or backed into his place on the right of the long wooden pole which divided the two horses. Frank linked up the traces to their rings and hooks, and then came back to take Jasper and back him into position on the other side of the pole. While Frank and the stable-man worked Ian looked more closely at the wagon. It was very solidly built, a flat timber platform on a heavy timber frame, and the wheels had big rubber tyres on them. Ian had noticed that one of the other wagons in the yard was of a different type. Instead of having a solid platform it had bars with spaces between, and its wheels had iron rims instead of rubber tyres. The wheels, too, were set at an odd angle, leaning slightly outwards from where the rims touched the ground.

"That one?" said Frank, when Ian asked him why these wagons were different. "That's one of the real old ones, one hundred and forty years old, that one is. We were using it up to this spring, but it finally had to be condemned. It's called a barrel dray, or an "old roller", we used to call them, for the noise those iron wheels made."

"Wasn't it much harder for the horses to pull, with iron tyres?" asked Ian.

"No, believe it or not those iron tyres ran easier, once they got it moving," replied Frank. "But rubber's better with a modern braking system."

"How old is this wagon?" asked Ian, as Frank gave Jasper a pat before mounting the high seat.

"Oh, about forty years," replied Frank. "They're mostly about that. It's not easy to get a decent wagon built these days, there aren't the wheel-wrights about to do the job now that all the young chaps can have it easier in a factory. They don't care about being craftsmen these days, all they want is quick, easy money. Now, you jump up on the back with Dave, and we'll get loaded up."

Dave was Frank's handler, who came along to help load and unload the crates, but who had nothing to do with the horses. He was a fair-haired, silent boy of about nineteen, dressed in jeans and a tough duffel jacket. He nodded at Ian as he scrambled up, but did not speak. Frank climbed up on to the high, single driving seat, released the tall hand brake, and clucked to the two horses. The wagon began to move smoothly down the cobbled yard. Ian saw Angela and Uncle Arthur waving to him from the stairs, and waved back. His own private adventure had begun.

6 · Horse power

It took quite a long time to load the wagon up with crates of beer, but at last it was fully laden, and once again Ian climbed on to the back with Dave. A small space had been left for them between the crates, and under him Ian felt the wagon start to move again. They clattered down the wide, cobbled way between the brewery buildings towards the main gates, and Ian saw the tall buildings and the stacked crates slide slowly past. Then they were out into the quiet road, heading for the busy main street.

At the turning the horses came to a halt, but only for a moment. Then, at a word from Frank, they moved forward again, turning into the stream of traffic. Remembering how close to Magic and Moonshine cars sometimes came Ian felt rather nervous. This road was much busier than the ones that Uncle Arthur usually took them out on. Dave, however, seemed quite unconcerned; he was chewing a piece of gum, and staring out at the passing

236

stream of cars, and soon Ian realised that there was no need to worry about the traffic. Cars and vans were eager to give them a wide berth, anxious not to risk their paint on any part of the heavy, slow-moving wagon, or to risk one of those huge hooves hitting any part of their vehicle.

Under Ian the wagon moved smoothly on its thick tyres, and in front, by peering round the crates, he could glimpse the big black hindquarters and the high carried tails of the two horses. Hooves and jangling brasses made music in the midst of the noisy roar of traffic, and people on the pavements looked round and most of them looked pleased to see the living horses in the middle of all the metal and machinery. Jasper and Big Ben went at a slow jog, keeping a steady course, except for pulling out now and then to pass a parked car or van. Each change of direction was carefully signalled first by Frank's long whip.

Their load was for "The King's Head", and almost before Ian had got properly used to the sensation of riding on the wagon Frank was bringing the horses to a halt outside. Dave stood up and hauled down the metal

trolly that was used to wheel in the crates,
and Frank secured the horse's reins round the
handbrake and dropped down to help.

"Shall I hold the horses?" asked Ian eagerly.

"Well, we usually have to trust them, but
it would make us safer if you were to stand
at their heads," agreed Frank.

And so Ian went to stand by Jasper and
Big Ben's heads while the wooden trap-door
in the pavement was opened, and the two men
began to wheel trolly loads of crates across to
it. The two big horses lowered their heads to
breathe at Ian, and most of the passers-by
paused to admire them. Ian felt very proud of

238

them. He had helped to groom them and worked on their harness, he had driven behind them, and now he was at their heads. He had a share in them. It was a good feeling, and he stood very happily, stroking the big, soft noses until Frank and Dave had finished and once again the wagon was empty.

Going back was, if anything, more fun, because there was nothing in the way now to stop Ian from seeing the horses. Jasper and Big Ben knew that they were going home now, and perhaps even that it was Saturday, and a short working day. They went at an eager jog, the fastest that they were allowed to go on the hard roads in case of damaging their legs, their necks very arched, and their ears pricked forward. In front of Ian the massive hindquarters rose and fell, and the traces lifted up and down above the horses' hocks to the rhythm of their jog. Above him Frank sat on the spidery driving seat as though it were a horse itself, his feet braced against the foot rest, and his shoulders squared as he held back his two tons of living engine power.

Watching him, Ian knew what he wanted to do himself when he grew up. It might be a

239

queer thing to want to do in these days, to drive a team of heavy horses, but for the moment it was what Ian wanted. Of course, he knew that he might change his mind, as he had about driving a fire engine or being a professional footballer, but for the time being Ian could think of nothing finer than sitting up on that slender metal seat and driving the two immense horses home to lunch. And whether or not he did become a driver, Ian knew for certain that a strong love of the great horses was settled deep inside him, and that it, at least, would never change.

"Well?" inquired Uncle Arthur later, when Ian had finished helping Frank and the stableman to unharness and rub down Jasper and Big Ben. "Did you enjoy yourself?"

"It was terrific," replied Ian. "And do you know, Frank says I can go out with them again next Saturday? Honestly Uncle, they're marvellous horses. They're such hard workers, and they're terrifically sensible. Do you know, the cars got out of our way this morning, instead of us having to get out of theirs? You can really respect horses like those."

He continued to chatter eagerly about

240

Jasper and Big Ben and his trip on the dray all the way home in the van, and all through lunch. Angela was inclined to be hurt because he so obviously thought them better than Magic and Moonshine, and even Uncle Arthur said, half jokingly, "Better keep quiet when you're with the lads, Ian, or they'll be jealous."

"No they won't," said Grace, as she got up to fetch the pudding. "They know there's room for both the workers and the entertainers, and for the very big and the very small. They're much too sensible to be jealous."

"Ian seems a lot happier these days," she remarked to Uncle Arthur, that evening, after Ian and Angela were in bed.

"Yes, he does, I thought that," agreed Uncle Arthur. "It's those big horses, he's really keen on them. It's surprised me, the way he's taken to handling them. I wouldn't have thought he had it in him."

"All Ian needed was a bit of confidence in himself as a person, apart from Angela and us," replied Grace. "Finding he can handle those horses, and getting interested in them, seems to have given it to him."

Time passed very quickly for them all during the next few weeks. Ian and Angela's time was completely full, with school, the brewery stables, and homework, and Uncle Arthur seemed to be constantly dashing between the brewery and the shop in his gaily painted van. Grace did a bit of everything, the housework and the cooking, minding the shop, giving piano lessons, and going along when she could to join the rest of her family at the stables. Sometimes Ian and Angela did the shopping on their way from the bus stop to the brewery, but very often that had to be Grace's job too.

Although Ian was quite happy with things as they were even he had to admit that it made life rather hectic, and Angela knew that Uncle Arthur was growing more worried about the future. A lot of the time that the ponies were to stay at Champney's had passed now, and he was still no nearer to finding a stable for them. And it was clear that they could not go on rushing about as they were for too long. It had been simple enough to fit the ponies into the daily routine when they were in the back yard, but the distance to Champney's did make it much harder. Already Grace had lost one piano pupil because she had not had the time to give the child the extra lessons that she wanted. Also, several times people had complained because they had been sent the wrong papers, after the rush in which Grace and Uncle Arthur had sorted them, and once or twice the shop had been closed when it should have been open. This meant that people coming to buy something found that they could not get it at Uncle Arthur's shop, and had to go somewhere else. All of this was very bad for business.

"We can't go on like this much longer," said Uncle Arthur one evening, after an especially frantic day. "I can't risk losing too many customers, and you don't want to lose any more pupils, Grace. We've got another three weeks or so at Champney's, this can't go on any longer than that, even if they offer to let us stay longer. We must find a handier solution somehow."

"If there is one," Grace pushed her long, slightly roughened fingers through her curly dark hair. "I honestly think we've tried everything, Arthur."

"The shop hasn't been sold yet, has it?"

asked Ian. "Mightn't the new landlord, when we get one, let Magic and Moonshine come back here?"

Uncle Arthur shook his head. "Goodness knows," he said. "Can't rely on it, not by a long chalk. There must be something else, we've just got to keep looking."

It was all rather depressing. Even Grace no longer seemed to be so optimistic.

"Surely Uncle Arthur will find somewhere, he couldn't ever sell them, could he?" Angela asked Ian, later that evening, when she and Ian were sitting on Ian's bed in the narrow room which was really half a room with a partition down the middle. On the other side of the partition Angela slept. They were both in their dressing-gowns, ready for bed, but Angela had felt too anxious to go straight to sleep.

"If he can't find anywhere, I don't see what else he can do," replied Ian.

"Would you mind if they did go, really?" Angela asked him.

Ian looked down at the floor. Would he mind? A few weeks ago he would probably have said "No", but now he was not so sure.

After all, Magic and Moonshine were the same creatures as his beloved Shires, even if they were in miniature. And if it hadn't been for them he would not have had the knowledge to be accepted as a helper by the stablemen. He owed them that, and also, he realised, he was and underneath always had been fond of them for themselves. It was just that he had been feeling lost and left out, and had blamed the ponies for it, when it was not really their fault at all.

"Yes," he said now. "Of course I'd mind. And think how Uncle Arthur would feel. He just wouldn't know what to do without them."

His answer made Angela feel quite a lot happier. At least Ian was on their side. She had hated it when she thought that he was not.

When Uncle Arthur and the children got home at tea time the next day Grace said that there was a message for Uncle Arthur from the theatrical agent who handled the bookings for the ponies. Uncle Arthur went to telephone him, and came back looking pleased.

"A job for the lads," he told his family. "Advertising a new film. We're to get ourselves up as a Victorian turn out, and plaster posters all over the carriage, then tour around hoping seeing us will make people want to see the film."

"When?" asked Angela eagerly.

"Next Thursday and Friday afternoons," replied Uncle Arthur. "And then we're to be outside the cinema when the première begins on Saturday evening."

"What, up in the West End?" exclaimed Grace.

"Yes, Leicester Square, no less," Uncle Arthur told them. "I'll take them up in the van, of course, too far to drive them at night anyway."

"Can we come?" asked Angela.

"You can come along in the van," replied Uncle Arthur. "No costumes for you to wear in the carriage, though, and any case we're to give the actress who plays the star part a ride up to the cinema entrance. But you can certainly come in the van."

"There was another thing, too," Uncle Arthur said, a few minutes later, when the chatter about the première had died down. "Quentin wanted to know about panto bookings. He said he'd had an inquiry about ponies for "Cinderella on Ice" at the Empire Pool, Wembley, and he wondered if mine would be available. It'd be a good booking, have to have them specially shod, of course, but I said I'd let him know. No use accepting bookings for the new year before we've found a place to keep them."

"But mightn't you lose it if you don't accept quickly?" asked Grace, who was handing round bread and butter. "Wembley would be the biggest panto booking they've had, wouldn't it? I should accept it, I think, you'll manage somehow."

"Maybe, maybe. I don't know. I'll give it until tomorrow, anyway," said Uncle Arthur. "Best not to rush into it at the moment."

In the end, rather doubtfully, Uncle Arthur did take Grace's advice, and accepted the pantomime booking. Angela felt that it was a good omen. Surely now he would have to keep the ponies somehow, for she knew that Uncle Arthur would hate to break an agreement.

Preparing Magic and Moonshine and their carriage for the film advertisement created a lot of amusement among the men at Champney's. The advertising agency who had booked them provided Uncle Arthur with two big plywood frames bearing posters for the film, and a Victorian coachman's outfit for himself. On the first afternoon he would drive down to the embankment, and along the side of the river to the Battersea Festival Gardens. On the second he would drive the ponies in the van across the river, and drive them around Chelsea and Kensington.

The plywood frames fitted into the body of the carriage, so that the posters stood up clear of the low sides. Both Ian and Angela helped to harness Magic and Moonshine, as they had also helped to groom them. Even to Ian the little ponies were, for the moment, more interesting than the Shires. Uncle Arthur left the children holding the ponies while he went away to change into his costume. When he came back they could hardly recognise him. He wore tight scarlet knee breeches and white leggings with black buckle shoes. His coat was dark grey, with long tails. On his head was a tall black hat with a white band round it, and a white cockade sticking up at the

248

side. He also wore a long, dark false moustache.

"You look lovely, Uncle Arthur," Angela told him.

"Do I, do I?" Uncle Arthur looked pleased. "Got to do the lads justice, you know."

With Uncle Arthur in position on the driving seat the effect was both dramatic and eye-catching. Most of the stablemen gathered to see them off, and a pair of Shires coming in late pulled aside to make way for the little ponies. There was a ragged cheer from the men as the turn-out started off, and more men came to the doors of the store rooms and malt houses to watch as the ponies went by.

"Makes quite a show, does your Uncle," said Mr Massey, as the little carriage went out of sight. "Not found a new stable yet, has he?"

"No, not yet," admitted Ian.

"Oh well, no hurry yet, so far as we're concerned," said the stable foreman. "We've had no news of the new pair coming, so he's got a while yet."

Uncle Arthur's drive round London went very well, he told them when he got back.

The ponies had behaved beautifully, and a lot of people had shown interest in them, as they could hardly help doing, thought Angela. Then, on Saturday evening, both ponies were loaded into the van, the carriage was run up on to the trailer, and they set out for the première in Leicester Square. Grace and the children went along as well, sitting up in the cab with Uncle Arthur as the van rumbled along the dark streets to the river, and drove on across the wide bridge, with the lights of London and the embankment coming up ahead of them, gleaming in the black water. Towards the West End the sky was a vivid pink as the clouds reflected the mass of lights, and they saw Big Ben's namesake lit up against the sky as Uncle Arthur drove along the embankment. Brightly lit trains crawled across Hungerford Bridge like yellow caterpillars, and as they turned away from the river towards the central theatre area of the West End the few people on the pavements became crowds.

Uncle Arthur parked the van in a quiet, dark street on the edge of Covent Garden market. When they got down from the cab the children could smell oranges and cabbage, and the thousand other mingling smells of the big vegetable and fruit market, closed and silent now for the night.

"Better get them harnessed," said Uncle Arthur. "We haven't got too much time."

Magic and Moonshine were excited by the strange place, and the nearby roar of traffic and the light at the end of the street. They snorted and tossed their heads, fidgeting so that Grace had to help hold them while Uncle Arthur and Ian got them harnessed. When Uncle Arthur, dressed in his coachman's outfit, stepped on to the seat they were immediately fretting to be off.

"All right?" asked Grace, still at their heads.

"Right," agreed Uncle Arthur, and Grace let go and stepped back as the two little ponies jumped forward. The carriage lamps were lit, gleaming golden on either side, and shining on the creamy tails and hindquarters of the ponies as they came past Ian and Angela, breaking into a trot towards Charing Cross Road.

"Come on," said Grace. "We'll have to be quick if we want to be there before them.

Arthur's only got to pick up Catherine Kerby, the actress, round the corner, and he'll be on his way to the cinema."

She took Angela's hand, and with Ian hurrying alongside they set off in the wake of the ponies.

7 · Not a joke any more

There was a big crowd in front of the cinema in which the première was being held. A red carpet ran down the cinema steps and across the pavement to where the cars pulled up with the various stars and guests inside, and flood-lights shone out across the street towards the green gardens in the centre of the square. Grace and the children edged their way forward until they had a good view of the steps and the street. They were just in time.

Faintly, they heard the sound of trotting hooves through the roar of traffic and people began to stand on tip-toe and peer to see what was coming. Then Magic and Moonshine came into sight round the corner of the square, and a loud murmur went up from the crowd. Both ponies were trotting briskly, ears pricked, and necks arched, with Uncle Arthur above them on the driving seat, splendid in his grey and red costume. In the carriage itself sat Catherine Kerby, the star of the film, dressed in a gorgeous white dress under a peacock blue cloak trimmed with white fur. Her blond hair was piled high on her head, and sparkled with shining jewels. Uncle Arthur brought the ponies round to the steps and they came to a flourishing halt right at the end of the red carpet.

"They look like fairy ponies," whispered Angela, and certainly Magic and Moonshine hardly looked real. They were cream and silver under the big flood-lights, champing their bits and tossing their heads while the doorman helped their passenger to alight. There was a round of applause from the crowd as she started up the steps, and she turned for a moment to wave. Then she had vanished into the brilliantly lit foyer of the cinema, and Uncle Arthur was driving Magic and Moonshine on out of the square, away into the traffic and the hurrying crowds back to the quiet street and the waiting van. Grace and the children edged their way out of the crowd and began to hurry after them.

Back at the van Uncle Arthur already had the ponies unhitched, and he was starting to remove Magic's harness while Moonshine stood tethered to the van.

"Good, weren't they?" he said. "Did they go down well, do you think?"

"They were wonderful," Angela told him. "They really looked lovely. Like fairy ponies."

And she put her arms round Magic and kissed him on the nose.

Just how well the ponies' appearance had gone down was shown the next morning. Almost all the papers had a photograph of them outside the cinema, and one of their neighbours was round early to tell them that the ponies had been on television, in a late report of the première. Then, on Tuesday, Uncle Arthur received a letter. He read it, and then handed it to Grace.

"What do you think of that?" he asked her.

Angela and Ian watched, their eggs and bacon forgotten, while Grace read. They both knew from Uncle Arthur's voice that it was something serious. Then Grace looked up.

"It's a good offer," she said. "But you needn't accept it, surely? Not yet."

"Well, not for a bit, perhaps," Uncle Arthur had taken the letter back and was gazing down at it. "But it'd be a good home for them. It's a big firm, they'd look after them well."

255

"Uncle Arthur, what is it?" asked Angela urgently.

Uncle Arthur did not answer, but Grace said, "It's from Swales and Lawrence, the department store people. They want a pair of ponies for advertising round London, like those grey horses that pull a carriage advertising Rothman's. They've made an offer for Magic and Moonshine. They saw the reports about them at the première, and they think they sound just what they've been looking for."

Angela and Ian did not know what to say. Suddenly, the ponies' going for good seemed terribly close. Angela looked down at her plate, and found that she did not want any more bacon and egg, and from the way that Uncle Arthur had begun to push his bacon about with a fork, neither did he. Grace looked round at them all, and decided that things needed cheering up.

"It hasn't come to accepting anything yet," she said briskly. "There's still plenty of time. Now, eat up your bacon, and does anyone want another cup of tea?"

But however much Grace might try to be cheerful Angela knew that she was not much

256

more optimistic than the rest of them about Magic and Moonshine's future.

In the end Uncle Arthur wrote back to Swales and Lawrence thanking them for their offer and saying that he would like to think it over. But there was a shadow over everything that they did, and even to Ian the brewery stables seemed suddenly less fun.

The next Saturday Angela and Ian stayed on at the stables alone to finish grooming the ponies while Uncle Arthur hurried back to look after the shop while Grace gave a piano lesson. They were hard at work, Angela on Moonshine and Ian on Magic, when they heard Bill take one of the Shires out. Magic turned round in his stall to whinny, and looking out Ian saw that it was Dandy who was being led towards the ramp and out for exercise on the cinder yard. The big Shire paused to turn his head and whinny back to his small friend, and then Bill led him forward again. The black horse looked very full of himself this morning, walking slightly sideways at Bill's side, and shaking his big head when Bill told him to "Steady".

"Easy now," Bill said to him, as they

reached the ramp, and Ian turned back to his grooming as they started down into the dimness.

Ian had only run the body brush once over Magic's quarters when there was a sudden uproar from the ramp, thumps and bangs, a shout from Bill, and a final, much heavier thud. Magic flung up his head to listen, and Ian dropped his brush.

"Whatever was that?" exclaimed Angela, from the next stall.

"I don't know. I'm going to find out." Ian was stepping over the bale.

"Wait for me." Angela's legs were not long enough for her to step over, but by getting right down on hands and knees she could crawl underneath. Moonshine gave her a friendly push as she wriggled under, and then she and Ian were hurrying down the stable towards the ramp.

There were voices coming from lower down now, out of sight round the bend of the ramp, and some heavy thumps.

"I'm going to look," said Ian, starting carefully down the rather slippery, worn cobbles. Rather nervously, Angela followed him.

On the bend Ian stopped short, and behind him Angela gasped. Dandy had slipped on the turn, and fallen, and now he was "cast", his head and back lower than his legs, which were pointing up the ramp. Bill was sitting on his head to prevent him from struggling, and Mr Massey and two of the stablemen were hurriedly spreading a bale of peat over the cobbles around him to make them less slippery.

"Have to turn him over," he said, straightening up. "He'll never make it in that position."

"There isn't room," objected Bill. "He'll get jammed on his back if we try to pull him over on this bend."

Mr Massey scratched his head, and Dandy made a heaving attempt to get his head free. Bill sat tight, soothing the horse with his hands and voice until Dandy lay still again.

"Fool horse," Mr Massey looked down at the big black shape. "What a place to start playing tricks."

"What about putting some ropes round him and pulling him down to the yard?" suggested one of the stablemen.

"There aren't enough of us," Mr Massey looked round. "Just three. We'll have to leave Bill at his head. We might move him, but it needs to be done slow and steady, and that means some behind to hold him back as well."

"There's us," said Ian, from the shadows behind Dandy. "We could help." Mr Massey looked up, startled.

"What are you kids doing there?" he demanded. "Don't come any closer, I don't want you getting hurt. This is no place for you, anyway."

"But we could help," insisted Ian. "We can both pull on a rope."

"You haven't the weight," objected Mr Massey. "No, we can't do it that way."

For a moment there was silence, while everyone gazed at Dandy and thought. Then, from up in the top stable, came a sudden, shrill whinny. Magic was curious, he knew that something had happened, and he sensed that it involved his friend, Dandy. Then he whinnied again, and suddenly Ian had an idea.

"The ponies!" he exclaimed. "Magic and Moonshine. Couldn't they help? They're pretty strong and sensible."

"Now that's an idea, Pat," said Bill. "There is a lot of strength in those little fellows."

"Have to get them down here first, though." Mr Massey looked doubtful. "I don't see how we'd do that, with the ramp blocked."

"They could get by," Ian was eager to prove that his idea could work. "They don't need much space, and they really are sensible."

Mr Massey made up his mind. "All right," he said. "Cut round by the steps and get their harness. We'll get some ropes round this fellow, and we'll see what they can do. There's no time to waste, certainly, a cast horse can panic at any moment, and if he really does that...." He shrugged, and the children knew that he meant Dandy could easily injure himself seriously if he was not rescued soon. They turned to hurry back up the ramp and down the stairs to the harness room for the ponies' harness.

Magic and Moonshine knew that something serious was happening. They stood quite still to have their harness on, without any of their usual playful sidling and nuzzling, and Magic stood with his ears pricked and head turned towards the ramp where he knew that Dandy had disappeared. When they were harnessed Ian took down both bales, and the ponies followed them quickly along the stable to the top of the ramp where Mr Massey was waiting for them.

"We've got some ropes round him," he said. "First awkward bit will be getting these two past him. Can you manage, or shall we take over?"

"I can manage," Ian told him. "What about you, Angie?"

"Yes, it's all right." Angela was a bit nervous but she was not going to hand Moonshine over to Mr Massey. If Ian could help then so could she. She took a firmer hold of Moonshine's rein and followed Ian as he led Magic on to the ramp.

There was a narrow space between Dandy's head and the wall, on the steepest angle of the ramp, where it turned. Usually they led the ponies down on the other side, where the slope took a wider, shallower turn. Magic pricked his ears and whickered when he saw Dandy's great, ungainly bulk spread across the ramp, with Bill sitting on his head.

Dandy's big nostrils fluttered, and he whickered back, a deep, anxious sound. Magic replied, almost soothingly, and Ian patted him.
Then, with Mr Massey anxiously watching,
he led Magic forward again. The little pony
picked his way neatly and carefully down the
extreme edge of the ramp, and it occurred to
Ian that for the first time the ponies were not
a joke to Mr Massey and the men. They were
being asked to do a difficult, responsible job,
one that none of the big horses could have
attempted in the confined space, and Ian
made up his mind that they were going to do
it well.

Magic was past Dandy by now, and glancing back Ian saw Angela leading Moonshine
down. Her hand was very tight on his rein,
and her voice as she encouraged him sounded
slightly shaky, but he knew that it was better
for he and Angela to handle the ponies
rather than the men, whom they did not know
as well. Then Moonshine was past Dandy as
well, and Mr Massey said, "Good. Well done.
Now, stop them just there, and we'll get them
hitched up."

There were ropes around the Shire's big

body now, and Mr Massey fastened one each to Magic and Moonshine's breast collars. Then he ran them round in front of the ponies' chests, and back to join the loop around Dandy. When he had finished both ponies were harnessed to the cast Shire, close together, but on separate ropes. Mr Massey checked the knots, made sure that there was plenty of peat spread on the lower part of the ramp and in the yard at the bottom, and rejoined the children.

"We're ready," he said. "Geoff, you and Steven get up behind him, and hold him back so he doesn't skid down too fast. Bill, keep by his head in case we have trouble. You've got the blind-fold tight, have you?"

Dandy now had a scarf tied firmly over his eyes to help prevent him from struggling when Bill got off his head.

"Yes, it's tight," Bill told Mr Massey.

Geoff and Steven had taken up their positions behind and above Dandy, the extra ropes that were fastened to him in their hands. Then Bill slowly stood up. Dandy gave one experimental heave, and then lay still.

"Right, now, start them pulling," ordered

264

Mr Massey. "Slow and steady, mind."

"Come on, Magic," said Ian.

For a moment Magic did not move. He turned his head to look back at Dandy, and he whickered again, long and deeply, so that his sides vibrated. It was as though he was telling the black horse that everything was all right. Then Ian urged him forward again, and Magic leaned forward smoothly into his collar. Beside him, Moonshine, encouraged by Angela, did the same, and behind them, slowly and gently, Dandy began to slide down the ramp.

"Keep it steady," said Mr Massey, who was hovering close by in case a stronger hand was needed for the ponies. But Magic and Moonshine might have been pulling cast horses down ramps all their lives. Smoothly and steadily they moved down the ramp, pulling easily in unison, their feet sure on the peat, their heads bent forward. Behind them Dandy slid slowly, back first, round the bend and on to the last, straight slope, with Geoff and Steven holding his weight back from too fast a slide and Bill staying close to his head.

"That's fine," said Mr Massey. "Just keep

them like that. We're almost there."

Ian's hands were damp by now, and sweat was running down his back as he concentrated on managing the pony. Beside him, Angela's face was pale, but she was keeping a firm, sensible feel on Moonshine's bit. They were nearly at the bottom now, the greyish daylight brightening around them. Ian had time to notice with part of his mind that there were several strangers out there, watching, and then Mr Massey's "Easy, now. Bring him down the last bit gently," brought his full attention back to what they were doing. Suddenly Magic and Moonshine were out in the yard, still pulling steadily, and behind them the big black bulk of Dandy was pulled slowly off the last slope of the ramp on to the flat, peat-strewn yard. The ponies' part of the rescue was over.

8 · The new landlord

When the ropes were finally off Dandy, and the blindfold removed, for a moment he did not move.

"Come on then, boy," Bill encouraged him. "You're all right now, you can get up."

Still Dandy did not try to pull his legs under him. Watching, the children wondered if he was hurt. Then Magic, who was watching as well, suddenly thrust his head forward and whinnied. Dandy raised his head, saw his friend watching him, and suddenly he drew his legs under him, stretched out his neck, and in one lunge he was on his feet. There was a subdued cheer from the men, and Bill began to pat Dandy, soothing the big horse. Sweat showed dark on the big body, and peat and shavings were stuck to his usually shining coat, and caught in his mane and tail. Magic was fidgeting to get closer, and Ian let him go across to nuzzle the big Shire. Dandy put his head down to the pony, and for a moment they stood quietly, nose to nose. Then Dandy took a deep, sighing breath, and Mr Massey said, "Better take him round to the back, Bill, and lead him round until he cools off. I'll get the vet up to have a look at him."

"That was a fine job your ponies did," said a voice beside Ian, as Dandy was led away. He looked round to see one of the strangers he had noticed in the yard smiling down at him.

"They were good," replied Ian. "I knew they'd be able to do it, although I don't think Mr Massey was quite so sure."

"Well, they certainly must have convinced him," said the man. "It looks to me as though they saved that horse from being seriously injured."

Then Mr Massey came back from seeing Dandy on to the cinder yard, and joined the children and the stranger.

"Good morning Mr Champney," he said. "You found us having a bit of difficulty, I'm afraid."

So this was Mr Champney, the owner of Champney's brewery, and of many of the public houses in the district. He was a big,

269

well-dressed man with grey hair and a pleasant smile.

"Morning Massey," he said now. "These two little fellows saved the day, by the look of things. I was just telling this young man that they did a fine job."

"They certainly did." Mr Massey felt in his pocket, and immediately Magic and Moonshine's ears shot forward, their noses went up, and they began to "ask" with their front feet. Mr Champney and his friends laughed, and came to pat the ponies while Mr Massey fed them on slices of carrot. Then Mr Champney asked how the ponies came to be at the brewery, and Mr Massey began to try to explain tactfully. There was no real reason why Mr Champney should object to the stable having an odd boarder now and then, but he felt that it should be carefully explained. But suddenly Angela interrupted. Before Mr Massey could say anything she had plunged into the full story of Uncle Arthur's new landlord, and the ponies having to be moved, and of their so far hopeless search for new, permanent stabling. Mr Champney listened in silence, his hands in the pockets of his elegant overcoat,

270

and Ian fiddled with Magic's mane and hoped that Angela was not going to make things worse by her story. But at the end Mr Champney merely nodded.

"Your Uncle's shop is near the "Red Lion", is it?" he asked. "Yes, I know the area. Well, your ponies are certainly very welcome to stay on here while Mr Massey has room. I wish I could say they could stay longer. I don't expect having them over here is really ideal for you, though, is it?"

"No, it's too far from the shop," Angela told him. "Grace has to look after it while Uncle Arthur comes over here, and then she can't give her piano lessons. And getting here in the morning makes sorting the papers a dreadful rush."

"So I can imagine," said Mr Champney. "Well, I'm certainly grateful to your ponies for what they did today, and as I say they can stay here as long as there's room."

He gave the ponies a final pat, and then Angela and Ian took them back to their stalls. On the way Ian said, "Whatever made you tell Mr Champney all that about them?"

"I don't know really," Angela was surprised

herself. "It just somehow seemed a good idea. Anyway, he did say that they can stay here as long as there's room, didn't he?"

"Yes. But it hasn't really got us much further," Ian pointed out.

Of course Uncle Arthur and Grace were very interested in the children's story of the morning's adventure.

"That'll show old Bill and the others that they aren't so useless after all," said Uncle Arthur jubilantly. "Good for you, Ian, for thinking of using them."

"Was Dandy all right?" asked Grace.

"Yes. But Mr Massey said he'd better not go back upstairs until the ramp's been resurfaced," replied Ian. "It is a bit worn and slippery. He's changed Dandy over with one of the working horses for now."

In spite of the praise which everyone showered on the ponies, and Mr Champney's assurance that they could stay as long as there was room, time really was getting short now. Uncle Arthur would have to decide soon about the offer from Swales and Lawrence, and only three days after Dandy's fall Mr Massey told Uncle Arthur that he had heard some news about the expected pair of new horses.

"They'll be arriving in about two weeks," he said. "We might still be able to find a corner for your two, but I'm afraid it wouldn't be so comfortable. We could convert a corner of the feed store for them, perhaps, or the forge."

But Uncle Arthur thought of the time he was spending away from the shop, and the fact that he had a family to support. And he thought of Grace's cancelled piano lessons and the late morning papers.

"No," he told Mr Massey. "I'll have them out by then. If nothing turns up closer to my place before that they'll have to go. Can't go on like this for too long, you know."

"I could feed them for you, if it'd help," offered Mr Massey, but Uncle Arthur shook his head.

"It's good of you," he said. "But if I can't manage to look after them myself they'd be better out of my hands altogether."

The next week was a miserable one for everyone at Uncle Arthur's. The thought of the ponies' being sold hung unhappily over them all, and even Grace could do little to cheer them up. The news spread to most of Uncle Arthur's customers, and they nearly all had something sympathetic to say when they came into the shop, but no-one could help. On Friday afternoon Angela and Ian went in through the back door while Uncle Arthur put the van away and found Grace in the living-room rather hastily taking off her coat and head-scarf.

"Mrs Randall's been minding the shop for me," she explained, as they looked at her in surprise. Mrs Randall had helped Uncle Arthur in the shop before he married Grace, but she was usually too busy these days with another part-time job. "I heard of somewhere that sounded possible for the ponies," Grace went on. "But it was hopeless. I didn't want Arthur to know, because I was afraid it might not be any good, and I didn't want to disappoint him again."

"You don't think he will find anywhere now, do you, Grace?" asked Ian soberly.

Grace looked at them sadly. "No," she said. "I'm afraid he won't. And I know that we shall miss the ponies, but Arthur will miss them much more."

"But he can't sell them," cried Angela. "He can't. Oh Grace, isn't there anything we can do?"

But it did not seem that there was. Sadly, the children took off their own coats and began to set the table for tea.

Besides the ponies' going, Ian had another thing to be sad about. Without Magic and Moonshine there he did not see how he could find a reason for going on visiting the brewery stables, and that would mean the end of his newly-found satisfaction in helping with the Shires. To Ian, that was almost, though not quite, as bad as Magic and Moonshine's being sold.

That weekend there was only another week to go, and Uncle Arthur began to talk about writing to Swales and Lawrence to accept their offer for the ponies. Several times he got as far as taking the note-paper out of its drawer, but each time he found an excuse to put it off.

On Sunday afternoon they all took Magic and Moonshine for a drive round the cool, grey November streets. It should have been the most exciting part of the year, with rehearsals for the pantomime starting soon, and Christmas coming, but of course it was not. Angela spent most of the drive trying not to think that it might be the last one they would ever have, and she knew that the others were feeling the same. Magic and Moonshine, however, were as gay as usual, trotting on together with a will, ears pricked, manes and tails flying, and little hooves sending echoes ringing between the tall, quiet houses.

Uncle Arthur drove them home more slowly, turning into the last street to the brewery at no more than a jog. No-one spoke until Ian and Angela were helping to unharness the ponies. Then Uncle Arthur said, "They'll have a good home, there's that. Light work, a groom to themselves, and six weeks at grass every summer. They'll be in clover."

"They will. A life of luxury," agreed Grace, as cheerfully as she could, and Angela hoped that she was not going to cry.

Breakfast on Monday was a silent affair. The children knew that while they were at school Uncle Arthur would write to Swales and Lawrence and the ponies would be sold. They were sitting down to scrambled eggs on toast when Uncle Arthur came in from the shop where he had been sorting the papers. He was carrying some letters that the postman had just left, and he dropped them on the table while Grace brought in the teapot.

"Anything interesting?" she asked, trying to sound as usual.

"The electricity bill," replied Uncle Arthur dismally. "And some sort of circular. I don't know what the other is, probably a letter from a cross customer."

"Hadn't you better open it?" asked Grace, as he picked up his knife and fork.

"I suppose so." Uncle Arthur was not very interested in his breakfast anyway. He picked up the envelope and tore it open, and for a moment no-one spoke. Then Grace said sharply, "Do you feel all right, Arthur?" and Ian and Angela looked up. Uncle Arthur certainly looked very peculiar. His face had gone white, and was now starting to go scarlet instead, and his hands were shaking so much that the sheet of notepaper he was holding rustled.

"Arthur," said Grace again, and this time Uncle Arthur looked up.

"Here," he said. "You read it. Tell me I'm not dreaming."

Grace took the letter from him, and as she read she too began to look excited.

"Oh, what is it? Please tell us." Angela could not bear it any longer.

"It's from Mr Champney, the owner of the brewery," replied Grace, in a tight, excited sort of voice. "He, or rather the brewery company, have bought all this property. They're going to develop "The Red Lion" and the old wine shop next door into one of their new pubs, with a grill-room for people to eat in. And . . . and he says that as far as he's concerned it will be quite all right for us to have the ponies in the yard again. He says he's glad to have the opportunity to thank them in some way for saving Dandy."

"You mean, it's all right?" Ian felt dazed. "They can come back?"

"Then they needn't be sold?" Angela felt her face going scarlet with excitement. "They really needn't?"

"No, they really needn't," Grace was looking across the table at Uncle Arthur. "You aren't dreaming Arthur."

"Hurrah," Ian was on his feet, his breakfast forgotten, and Angela was hugging first Grace and then Uncle Arthur. And Uncle Arthur's face was one enormous, beaming smile.

"Come on," he said, leaping to his feet. "Let's go and tell them. They know something's been up, they've probably been worrying themselves."

"Arthur, you haven't eaten your breakfast," protested Grace.

"The kids have. I can have something later." Uncle Arthur swung round the table, seized Grace, and gave her a smacking kiss. "See you later, love. Come on, you two, let's get down there."

Ian and Angela grabbed their coats and rushed after him, leaving Grace on the kitchen steps laughing and waving and shaking her head.

"I'll get the stable swept out if I have time," she called, and Uncle Arthur paused to wave and grin at her from the yard gate.

They brought Magic and Moonshine home that afternoon, after school. All the men at the brewery came out to wave them off, and Magic and Moonshine gave a last performance of their tricks for rewards of carrots and sugar from everyone.

"We shall miss them," said Mr Massey. "But I'm taking my wife and kids along to Wembley to see them in "Cinderella". Come round and see us some time, won't you? And if you want to go on giving us a hand with the big fellows, Ian, you'll be welcome any time."

"Thank you," said Ian, and beamed at Mr Massey with real gratitude. So he wouldn't lose his Shires after all. From inside the stable Dandy, hearing the disturbance outside, whinnied, and Magic whinnied back. Mr Massey smiled.

"There's another who'll miss them," he said. "But he'll be going in harness soon, and he'll find himself another pal then. But it's been a real experience for us all, knowing these two."

Most of Uncle Arthur's neighbours had come out to see Magic and Moonshine return home. Someone had even gone as far as to hang a strip of bunting across the end of the cinder path, and the ponies came down the

ramp to a royal welcome. All the local children had brought them "welcome home" gifts of food, and Magic and Moonshine nodded and bowed and kissed and shook hands until they were dizzy. Uncle Arthur was in the middle of it all, red-faced and beaming, and Partner watched from a grandstand seat on the wall.

But at last the ponies were through the gate and inside their own shed, and the neighbours had drifted away. Standing in deep, clean straw, with large feeds and crammed hay nets in front of them, the ponies seemed to look round and take deep, satisfied breaths. They had been happy enough at Champney's, but it was not their own place. This was, and

281

their contented expressions as they began to eat said that they were glad to be back.

"Here comes Partner," said Grace, and the big ginger cat stalked in through the door, paused, and then leaped lightly up on to the partition, and into his usual place on Magic's back.

"He's missed that," said Grace. "He's certainly glad to see them back."

"He isn't the only one," Uncle Arthur put his arm round her. "Do you know, I really thought I was going to have to sell them. My goodness, I'd have missed them."

"So would we all," replied Grace, hugging him. "Now, come on. Tea's waiting."

She led the way out into the yard, where Uncle Arthur closed the shed door on the contented munching. And as he followed the others across the yard Ian knew that the family was complete again, and that now, like the others, he really was a part of it.

Ponies in Harness

Contents

1 · Can they do it?

It had been a marvellous summer, perfect, blue, shimmering seaside weather, but here in London the air smelt stale and shut in. The few trees looked dry and dusty, and Angela Kendall, walking home with her brother Ian after their first day back at school for the autumn term, almost wished that it would rain. It was too hot for school and London, and she wished that they were all by the sea. All included herself and Ian, Uncle Arthur and Grace, with whom they lived, and Magic and Moonshine, Uncle Arthur's two clever little performing ponies.

'Uncle Arthur said he'd take Magic and Moonshine for a drive when we got in,' said Angela. 'They get so hot in the yard. He said we could go as well if we wanted.'

'Not me,' said Ian. 'I'm going to Champney's. You can go with Uncle Arthur.'

Ian spent a lot of his spare time at Champney's Brewery Stables, helping with the huge

287

Shire horses, and going out on the delivery drays. Angela, who was happier with Uncle Arthur's little ponies, missed having him there to share things with, but she was starting to get used to it. Ian and she always seemed to want to do things apart now, and it was no use worrying about it.

Uncle Arthur's shop was one of a short row, at the end of a street of small, terraced houses. The shop window was filled with boxes and jars of sweets, packets of cigarettes, plastic toys, magazines, and tins of tobacco. Ian pushed open the shop door, and Grace looked through the door from the room behind the shop to see if they were customers.

'It's all right, it's only us,' said Ian, ducking under the flap of the counter. 'Can we have some chocolate?'

'Yes, one bar each,' replied Grace. 'How was school?'

'All right. We've both gone up a class. I've got Mr Benbow now,' Ian took two chocolate bars from the shelf and gave one to Angela as she followed him through into the living-room. When they had first come to live with Uncle Arthur, Angela and Ian had been surprised by this room, with its crowded furniture, the books bursting out of the bookshelves, and the walls covered in Uncle Arthur's photographs of the stars of silent films, but now they were used to it. There were old posters for music halls and theatres between the photographs, and the only clear space was the top of the piano on which Grace used to give music lessons. There was only one photograph here, a big one of Grace and Uncle Arthur coming home from their wedding in the miniature landau pulled by Magic and Moonshine.

Bluey, the budgerigar, chattered in his cage which hung from the ceiling well out of reach of Partner, the big ginger cat, and the open window let in a gleam of afternoon sun, which lit up the gay new loose covers which Grace had made for the armchairs. All of this meant home to Angela and Ian, and they were very happy here.

'Arthur's outside, getting the ponies ready,' said Grace, who was ironing in the kitchen. The rooms behind the shop smelt of soap powder and the hot iron.

'Is it all right if I go to Champney's?' asked Ian, and Grace said that it was. Ian dashed off to change out of his school clothes, and Angela looked at Grace. She looked hot, her short, curly dark hair was untidy, and Angela felt that she ought to stay in and help with the ironing, but when she offered Grace shook her head.

'I've almost finished,' she said. 'There are only the sheets left, and I can do those tomorrow; they'll stay damp enough if I roll them up. You go out with Arthur, you need some fresh air after school.'

The back door was open, and Angela could see Uncle Arthur in the little yard, buckling on the last of Moonshine's harness. Both the little cream-coloured ponies were outside the shed that was their stable. Magic was already harnessed and was nibbling the rope which tied him to a ring in the yard wall. Uncle Arthur, a tall, rather thin man with thin grey hair, looked hot as well. His face was always rather red, but this afternoon it was glistening, and Angela knew that he had been working hard on the ponies' coats.

The shop bell rang, and Grace put down her iron and went to answer it. Angela put her satchel down on a chair and was about to go upstairs to put on her jeans when Grace came back through the shop door followed by a short, stocky man in a blue suit whom Angela recognized as Uncle Arthur's friend Bill, who worked with Champney's show horses.

'Angela, go and tell Arthur that Bill would like a word with him,' said Grace, and Bill smiled and said, 'Hello.'

'It's all right, I can go out to him,' he told Grace, but she was offering him a chair, and Angela ran out to tell Uncle Arthur, wondering what Bill could want.

Uncle Arthur said the same when Angela gave him the message.

'Old Bill?' he exclaimed. 'Wonder what he wants? Here, Angie, you stay and keep an eye on these rascals. Magic'll be up to mischief if he finds we're not going out straight away. I'll just nip in and have a word with Bill.'

He went off across the yard and Angela went to talk to Magic, who nuzzled her with his soft, creamy nose, his dark eyes gleaming under his silvery forelock. With their cream and silver colouring the ponies looked very pretty

when they and Uncle Arthur appeared on the
stage, and they were very clever too. They
could perform a great many tricks, and Angela
thought them the cleverest ponies in the
world.

Uncle Arthur was gone for about ten minutes,
and when he came out again he was smiling
and rubbing his hands together.

'Well,' he said. 'There's a turn-up for the
book. Bill wanted to know if the lads and I
would stand in for a friend of his in some
driving competitions. This friend and his
ponies were sponsored for the season by
Blakely Garages, but he's had an accident, a
crash in his car, and he can't finish the season
for them.'

'What's sponsored?' asked Angela, who could
not think what Uncle Arthur was talking
about.

'It means that someone pays you a fee, and
pays your entry money and expenses for shows,
on condition that you let them use you in their
advertisements,' explained Uncle Arthur. 'And
they add their company's name to your ponies'
names for the shows. The lads will have to be
"Blakely Magic and Moonshine" for a bit, but
they won't mind.'

'What sort of driving competitions?' asked
Angela. 'Sort of showing, like the carthorse

parade in Regent's Park?' They had all gone to that last year, riding behind Magic and Moonshine in their little carriage among the coster ponies and the Shires, the milk floats, and the private turn-outs.

'Oh no, not like that, not really,' Uncle Arthur was patting Magic, who was 'asking' for a titbit by waving one front foot in the air. 'There's quite a bit more to it than that, quite a bit. We'll need a different vehicle for a start. Bill says his friends' Shetlands go in a small four-wheeled dog cart. We'll be using that if we do it. Bill says the landau's two low and heavy.'

'Do you think we'll do it?' Angela thought it sounded exciting.

'I think we'll have a go.' Uncle Arthur's face was redder than ever, and Angela knew that he was quite excited himself. 'Why not? It could be fun. Go on, Angie, get your jeans on, and we'll take the lads for their drive.'

Angela ran back into the house impatient to find Ian, if he hadn't already gone, and see what he thought. Ian hadn't gone, but he was rather disappointing. He refused to get at all excited, saying that they'd all driven Magic and Moonshine before, in all sorts of places, and he didn't see why a show or two should be much different.

'Bill drives a team of six Shires in some shows,'

he told Angela. 'Now that is exciting. Six Shires – imagine the strength of them, all pulling together. I must go, Angie, Mr Massey's working one of the young horses about teatime, and I don't want to miss it.'

Feeling rather squashed Angela went into her own small room to change. It would be fun, she told herself, even if Ian didn't think so, but it would be nice if he'd get interested too.

Uncle Arthur was very busy for the next few days. He went to see Bill's friend, Robert Sheering, in hospital, and he went to see the Managing Director of Blakely Garages.

'They both suggested I should take over Mr Sheering's pair of ponies,' he told Angela, Ian, and Grace afterwards. 'But I said if I couldn't use my lads I'd rather not do it. Bob Sheering's place is down in Hampshire. I couldn't be chasing down there all the time and looking after Magic and Moonshine. They all saw that, and it's all right, they don't want to waste the entries for the last of the season's shows, and the chance of good publicity, so now Magic and Moonshine are officially the Blakely ponies, leased until the end of the year.'

'That isn't like them being sold to Blakely's, is it?' Angela asked, with a sudden horrible picture of Magic and Moonshine going away.

'No, no. Just an agreement that Blakely's

will pay all our expenses and give me a fee in return for calling the ponies theirs. The agreement says that the lads can't be used without me or my consent,' explained Uncle Arthur.

'What do they have to do in the shows?' asked Ian, who was sprawling on the floor doing a jigsaw.

'I must admit I don't really understand that yet,' said Grace. 'What sort of competitions are they, Arthur?'

Uncle Arthur felt in his pocket and brought out a sheet of paper.

'First,' he said. 'A week on Saturday, they're entered for the marathon and the obstacle driving in a harness show in Surrey. Then we go on to a combined driving event the next week, and finally they're entered for the Eldonian Double Harness events at The Horse of the Year Show at Wembley.'

'What is obstacle driving?' asked Ian. 'Does the driver have to get out and climb through tyres and things, like in our school obstacle race?'

'No, Bob says it's really a test of control at fast speeds,' replied Uncle Arthur. 'They put pairs of markers round the ring, a few centimetres wider apart than the wheels of the widest cart competing, and the competitors have to drive in and out of them as fast as they can without knocking any down. The fastest wins.'

'Can Magic and Moonshine do that?' asked Ian dubiously, and Angela opened her mouth indignantly. She was about to say that of course Magic and Moonshine could do it when Uncle Arthur said, 'We'll see, we'll soon see. I'm fetching Mr Sheering's cart tomorrow, then we'll take them down to the rec. and have a go.'

The new cart was there when Angela and Ian got home from school the next day. It was quite different from the low-slung landau, which had a high seat in front for the driver and lower seats inside for the passengers. The new dog cart had four wheels, two quite big ones at the back and two smaller ones in front, and there were two double seats, set well up above the ponies, with a dashboard in front against which the driver could brace his feet. It was painted dark green with yellow wheels, and the cushions on the seats were of fawn leather.

'Do you think Magic and Moonshine will like pulling it?' Angela asked Uncle Arthur.

'We'll soon find out,' replied Uncle Arthur. 'We were only waiting until you two came home to try it out. You run in and get changed and I'll harness them up.'

'I did tell Mr Massey . . .' began Ian, but Angela was pulling at his arm to hurry him inside, and he gave in. Even if he did say that he found the little ponies a bit of a bore these days Ian couldn't really resist seeing how they went in their new cart.

Magic and Moonshine went very well. The dog cart was much lighter than their own landau, and it ran so easily that they could

hardly feel it behind them. Uncle Arthur drove, with Angela sitting up beside him in the high seat, and Ian sat on the one behind. Angela could look down on the two little ponies as they trotted up the street, the harness moving with their jaunty steps, their sharp little ears pricked,

297

and their silvery manes streaming over their creamy necks. Eight hooves with iron shoes on made a lovely clatter, and people turned to stare and exclaim and smile.

'My word, this is fun,' exclaimed Uncle Arthur. 'The lads really like this. We'll take them back past the rec. and see what they can do.'

The recreation ground and playing fields were where Uncle Arthur usually took the ponies when they were led out for exercise. He had permission to lunge them there, that is, to give them a run round and round him on the end of a special long webbing rein, and there was plenty of space. Magic and Moonshine's ears pricked even more, and their heads went up high as they saw the grass in front of them. Uncle Arthur shortened up his reins a little, and clicked his tongue. The ponies started to canter, and Angela grabbed hold of the side of her seat as the cart rocked with their strides and the slight bumpiness of the ground. The wind whistled past her ears and caught at her long fair hair, and the ponies' hooves thudded.

'Go on, lads, stretch your legs,' Uncle Arthur encouraged the ponies, and Magic and Moonshine lengthened their strides and took the cart even faster. Halfway across the recreation ground Uncle Arthur brought them back to a slower canter.

'Now we'll try some turns,' he shouted, above the sound of the wind in their ears. 'Hang on, kids.'

He began to turn the cantering ponies to the left, driving with his hands well apart, and taking great care not to bring them round so sharply that the inner pony dragged the outer with him, which might have turned them over. Even so, the cart came round much more quickly than Angela had expected, and Uncle Arthur shouted, 'Lean over, lean into the turn.' Angela and Ian both leaned to the left, feeling the cart recover its balance, and then Uncle Arthur was pulling up, first to a trot, then to a walk.

'We'll certainly have to practise,' Uncle Arthur said when they were walking. 'And we've only got a week. Mustn't let Mr Sheering down by making a mess of things, goodness me no.'

'Are you going to try again now?' Ian asked, and Angela found herself rather hoping that he would say 'no'. She was not sure that she had liked the feeling of that precarious turn, with the cart tilting and skidding under her, but Uncle Arthur said, 'No time like the present,' and sent both ponies into a canter again.

Angela took a deep breath and a firm hold of the seat and hoped for the best.

'Turning right this time,' called Uncle Arthur. 'Lean to the right, remember. Come on lads, round you come.'

They were turning to Magic's side this time, and he came round quickly and neatly as Uncle Arthur pulled the rein, at the same time holding Moonshine back slightly so that he would not rush round and make them skid. This time it was much better, the cart came round smoothly, and they were scurrying across the field in another direction watched by an interested audience of two boys in football boots and an old man with a dog.

'That's it,' cried Uncle Arthur, as they straightened out. 'Much better. Come on, lads, let's try again. Left this time, kids.'

Again the turn was not quite so smooth, Moonshine was a bit inclined to plunge round, dragging Magic with him, but he always took a bit longer to learn anything new than his partner did, and Uncle Arthur looked pleased as he brought the ponies back to a walk again.

'Good lads,' he said. 'Soon get the idea, won't you? Next thing we must do is get some markers up, mark out a few gates, that's what Bob Sheering called the obstacles. We must take them for some longer drives, too, to get

300

them ready for the marathon. Then we'll have dressage to practise for the combined driving. Goodness, aren't we going to be busy?'

He sounded pleased, and Angela knew that Uncle Arthur liked the prospect of being busy when it was because of the ponies.

'Do you know,' said Ian later, when they were hanging up the harness for Uncle Arthur in the outhouse he used as a harness room, 'that was fun. I wouldn't mind coming again the next time he has a go at that.'

2 · Getting ready

The week before the first show was just about the busiest that Magic and Moonshine had ever spent. Uncle Arthur borrowed some plastic road-works bollards from a friend of his who worked for the council and he, Angela and Ian drove up to the recreation ground with them loaded into the dog cart. Angela held the ponies while Ian and Uncle Arthur measured distances with Grace's tape-measure, and then set out the bollards in pairs. Then Uncle Arthur climbed into the driver's seat and picked up the reins.

'Now to see what we can do,' he said. 'Oh, hang on a minute. Someone's got to be steward, and someone groom. Better toss for it, I think.'

The ponies stood with Angela still at their heads while Uncle Arthur fished a coin out of his pocket.

'Right,' he said. 'You call, Ian.'

'Heads,' said Ian, and Uncle Arthur tossed.

'Tails,' he said. 'All right, Angie, you ride as groom, I think that's the thing you'd pick, isn't it? This time Ian can put up the bollards, if we knock any.'

Feeling a bit guilty, Angela climbed into the back seat. If Uncle Arthur had left her to pick she'd probably have said 'Steward', because she knew that Ian would be keener if he had the ride, but it was true that she'd rather be in the cart.

'Ready?' said Uncle Arthur. 'Then off we go. Come on, lads.'

Magic and Moonshine started eagerly forward, and Angela stared at the bollards. There barely seemed room between them for two ponies and their cart. The first time Uncle Arthur drove carefully through at a walk and the wheels cleared the bollards by a few centimetres on either side.

'Now we'll go a bit faster,' he said, and the ponies broke into a trot. This time they went through clear as well, but then Uncle Arthur said, 'Now to try turning for them,' and the ponies started to canter. The first pair of bollards was on their left, and Uncle Arthur had to judge the right moment to turn if they were to pass through clear, for the courses at the shows would be full of twists and turns. Driving between them like this was a lot more difficult than it sounded. The first time Uncle Arthur

303

tried the cart swept straight across the bollards, sending them flying.

'That'd be five seconds to add to our time,' said Uncle Arthur, as he pulled up. 'We'll have to do better than that.'

Ian stood the bollards up again and Uncle Arthur took the ponies round for a second try. It was no more successful than the first, and Angela began to wonder if Uncle Arthur and the ponies were going to be able to manage it. Ian put the bollards up again, and Angela could tell from his face that he was wondering the same thing.

'Right,' said Uncle Arthur. 'Third time lucky, we hope.'

Magic and Moonshine were beginning to get excited. They liked galloping and they were enjoying the quick turns. This time they came up the recreation ground at a gallop, and to Angela, sitting in the back seat, it seemed as though they had gone past the bollards. Then, when she thought it was too late, Uncle Arthur turned. The ponies came round in their own length, with the cart swinging round behind them, and this time it was right. The cart swept through without touching the bollards as though it was the easiest thing in the world, and Uncle Arthur drew up triumphantly beyond them.

'Got it,' he shouted, as the ponies came back to a trot. 'That's how it's done. Almost past, wait until their hindquarters are level with the gate, then turn. It sounds unlikely, but that's it.'

He was right. From then on it didn't seem as though he and the ponies could go wrong. They cleared the bollards nine times out of ten, all round the course. Uncle Arthur was delighted, and even Ian was smiling and patting Magic and Moonshine. Angela jumped down to feed the ponies on slices of carrot, and Magic began to show off, shaking hands, nodding and shaking his head, nudging everyone in the back, and exploring their pockets with his nose.

'Home now,' said Uncle Arthur, after a few minutes. 'That's enough for today. We'll have a couple more practices before Saturday.'

Ian and Angela collected the bollards and the ponies headed for home. It was another hot day, but neither Magic nor Moonshine seemed to mind at all that their creamy coats were sticky with sweat and that there was lather under the straps of their harness.

'Do them good to sweat a bit,' said Uncle Arthur. 'They're fairly fit, but they could do with losing a bit of fat.'

They had several more practices before Saturday, and the ponies and Uncle Arthur certainly seemed to have got the knack of judging the obstacles. Ian continued to come up to the recreation ground with them. He even missed a few evenings at Champney's to help, much to Angela's delight. It was fun with Uncle Arthur, but it was even more fun with Ian there as well. Uncle Arthur seemed pleased too, and he even let Ian have a try at driving through some gates, though only at a trot. Ian managed quite well, only knocking two down, but when Angela tried she found that she was not strong enough to bring the ponies round quickly, although she could judge quite well when they should turn.

'You'll be fine when you've grown a bit,' Uncle Arthur told her. 'My word, Blakely's are doing well, three drivers for the price of one. I bet they never expected that.'

After school on both Thursday and Friday was taken up with getting everything ready for the show, although Uncle Arthur had done some of the jobs while Ian and Angela were at school. The dog cart had to be washed down and polished with soft cloths, and the wheels had to be greased. The van and trailer for the cart had to be hosed down, and all the harness had to be cleaned. Ian went to Champney's on Thursday, but he stayed at home to help on Friday, and Angela knew that he really was interested.

The harness took all of Friday evening. All the leather parts had to be washed and then rubbed with saddle soap, and the brass rings and fittings had to be polished. Then, when the saddle soap had sunk in, Uncle Arthur went over all the smooth outside surfaces of the black harness with shoe polish. Grace was teaching one of her piano pupils in the living-room while they worked in the kitchen and yard, and the sound of scales mingled with the clink and jingle of the harness and the sounds of brushing and polishing. Every now and then the shop bell rang, and whoever had the cleanest hands at that moment went to answer it.

It was well after closing time when everything was finished and ready for next day. The harness hung on the hooks that Uncle Arthur had fixed for it inside the van, and the dog cart was on its trailer. Magic's and Moonshine's tails had been washed, and they were eating extra large feeds. They both knew that something exciting was going to happen next day, and later that night Angela heard Magic stamping and walking round in his box and she knew that he was impatient for the morning.

When Angela and Ian woke on Saturday morning they knew almost at once that the weather was changing. The air felt heavier, and the sunlight through the windows looked less clear than it had for a long time.

'Do you think it's going to rain?' Angela asked Ian, as they met on their way downstairs.

'Hope not.' Ian jumped down the last few stairs in front of her. 'It would make a horrible mess of all our clean harness and everything after all that work.'

They helped Uncle Arthur to sweep out the stable and put down fresh straw, and they were all helping to groom the ponies when Grace called to tell them that breakfast was ready.

'Looks as if it might be stormy later,' said Uncle Arthur, as he scrubbed his hands in the sink. Grace was dishing up scrambled eggs, and she too looked out of the window.

'You'd better take your macs,' she said. 'And your boots. You know how quickly grass can get churned up if it rains hard.'

Grace was not coming with them today. Mrs Handry, their friendly neighbour who sometimes looked after the shop for them, was going to visit her mother in hospital, Grace had packed her usual picnic basket for them, however, and now, after another look at the sky, she added a flask of hot soup.

'If you do get wet, it'll help to keep you warm,' she said. 'I wish I was going to be there to keep an eye on you.'

'Don't worry, we'll be fine,' Uncle Arthur assured her. 'Won't we, kids? Come on, time we got the lads loaded. We mustn't be late.'

Soon they were all in, and Grace was waving from the gate.

'Goodbye,' she called. 'Good luck, and don't forget to put on those macs if it rains.'

'Goodbye,' they all shouted, and the ponies whinnied. A minute later they were round the corner and Grace was out of sight.

*

Their first show was being held just outside London, in Surrey, and so the trip in Uncle Arthur's gay, red, yellow and green van with the ponies inside and the cart on its trailer behind did not take too long.

People turned to stare at the van as Uncle Arthur drove it carefully through the bumpy gateway on to the show-ground, and Angela knew that they were reading the words that Uncle Arthur had painted on the sides. 'Magic and Moonshine, Wonder Ponies of Stage and Screen', they read, and several people smiled.

'It's like being with a circus,' Ian whispered in Angela's ear, too softly for Uncle Arthur to hear, and it was a bit. Not that it mattered, there were all sorts of horses and ponies and all kinds of different horse transport vehicles in the field. As Uncle Arthur parked beside a big cattle truck Angela saw a tiny black Shetland pulling a round-bodied trap, driven by a lady wearing a tartan cap and scarf. An elegant pair of tall grey horses went by pulling a carriage, and Ian pointed out a tall black Shire horse in a big-wheeled haywain.

There were skewbald coster ponies pulling flat, gaily painted London trollies, a grey horse with a milk-float, and a lovely, golden-coloured horse with a silver mane and tail pulling a pretty, light little trap with a lacey, open-work back which Uncle Arthur said was a stick-back gig. Some of the lorries had 'Cattle' written on them, others had the names of stud farms where horses and ponies were bred, there was a brewery horsebox from another brewery, not Champney's, and another box with the name and advertisement of a big London store painted on it.

'There's all sorts here, right enough,' said Uncle Arthur, as he switched off the engine. 'Lets get the lads out and let them have a look round.'

Magic and Moonshine were extremely interested in everything. Magic was sure that he was there to do his stage turn, and he started practising at once with his usual hand shaking, head tossing, and pocket picking. Moonshine was calmer – he never got as excited as Magic – but he was gazing round, and his dark eyes looked bigger and bulgier than usual. Quite a few people drifted up to watch, and Uncle Arthur let Magic demonstrate some of his tricks to settle him down.

'Will all competitors in the marathon please get put too and come into the ring?' said the loudspeaker, and Uncle Arthur patted Magic.

'That's all for now,' he told the little pony. 'Time for work.'

Ian helped Uncle Arthur unload the dog

cart from the trailer while Angela brushed out Magic and Moonshine's manes and tails. It was while they were doing this that Angela and Ian noticed the boy driving the grey pony. It was quite a big pony, and quite lively, with a very pretty head, and it was harnessed to a high, light cart with two big wheels. The boy was about Ian's age, elegantly dressed in a tweed hacking jacket and fawn slacks, and he was handling the lively pony with almost scornful ease. Uncle Arthur went to fetch the reins from inside the van, where they hung, and the boy, who had been eyeing Magic and Moonshine and Ian with interest, brought his grey pony alongside.

'Do you drive them?' he asked Ian, ignoring Angela, who was giving Magic's mane a final brush.

'Well, not usually. My uncle does that,' replied Ian.

'Won't he let you?' The boy sounded scornful.

'I do sometimes,' replied Ian, who was starting to go red.

'Only sometimes?' exclaimed the boy. 'Bad luck. Of course, Streamer here is mine. He's quite a goer, I can tell you. Shame those two aren't yours, we could have tried them out against mine in the exercise field. Two of that size should be about an even match for Streamer.'

'They might even beat him,' said Angela, who thought that the boy sounded as if he was showing off. The boy looked at her.

'This your sister?' he asked Ian. 'I've got a younger brother. Bit of a drag, aren't they? Well, see you later. Maybe we'll get a chance to try them out after lunch.'

'What a stupid boy,' said Angela crossly, as the grey pony bounded off with the high cart bouncing behind him. 'He was just showing off.'

'He wasn't so bad,' said Ian, as Uncle Arthur came back with the reins. 'And he's jolly lucky, having his own pony to drive.'

'Come on, come on,' Uncle Arthur was looking hot. 'Time we were ready, they're going into the ring for the marathon now.'

Moonshine was 'put too', or had his harness fastened to the cart first, then Magic was backed into place on his side of the pole. Uncle Arthur slipped the outside trace, or long leather strap, over its bolt on the front of the cart, and fastened the short inside strap, called a tug strap, to the front of the long wooden pole which went between the two ponies.

'Right,' he said. 'Up you get, Angie, and you Ian.'

Uncle Arthur stepped up on to the cart and gathered up the reins. Magic and Moonshine had been taught to stand until they were told to move off, but they were off with a bound as soon as Uncle Arthur clicked his tongue, and Angela saw the ring ahead, with horses and vehicles heading for it from every side.

3 · A stormy afternoon

In the marathon all the competitors had to go out on a drive, getting back to the show-ground within a set time, forty minutes today. When they came back they would be judged on the turn-out of the ponies and vehicle, and their condition after the drive. Everyone at the show seemed to have entered for it, and although the ring was quite big it was almost full. Magic and Moonshine trotted round with the rest, ears pricked and necks arched, until a steward gave the signal to follow on out of the ring to the road.

The drive was fun. Magic and Moonshine loved bowling down the road in the string of horses and vehicles, and they went with such a will that Uncle Arthur found it quite hard to keep them in their place behind a blue and white milk-float pulled by a grey horse with blue wool fastening the plaits in his white mane. It was certainly hot and hazy, and one or two of the horses began to flag. Magic and Moonshine were waved on to pass a very fat black and white pony pulling a round tub cart full of children, and they also passed a fat brown cob who seemed to have gone on strike, for he refused to do more than walk.

'Out of condition,' said Uncle Arthur, when Angela asked what was the matter with them. 'Can't expect a horse to trot five or six miles pulling a load unless he's pretty fit. You wait until we go to this combined driving event, you'll see some pretty fit horses there, I'll be bound.'

As the drive went on the vehicles became more strung out, and Uncle Arthur let several lengths stretch out between Magic and Moonshine and the milk float. The route was round quiet lanes, many shaded by trees, so that the sunlight flickered over the creamy backs of the ponies in bars and patches of light and shade. It was like being under water, thought Angela, as she watched the greeny-gold patches slide over the ponies' backs. They crossed a narrow bridge, where most of the vehicles slowed to a walk to avoid any danger of hitting the parapets, and began to circle back towards the show-ground. A few spectators had walked or driven out to watch the final mile, and Magic and Moonshine arched their necks and stretched out their toes, showing off to the onlookers.

'Rascals', said Uncle Arthur. 'Go on then, show what you can do.'

As they came back through the gate into the showground he let the little ponies stride out, and they swung back into the ring at their best, fast, high-stepping harness trot, manes and tails flying and harness fittings flashing in the sun. There was a round of applause from the spectators around the ring. Then Uncle Arthur brought the ponies back to a slower trot, and a few minutes later they were lining up for the final judging.

There could be no doubt about Magic and Moonshine's fitness and good condition, but the marathon was also judged on the whole turnout, and when the rosettes were handed out Magic and Moonshine were fourth out of the whole class. The winners were the pair of elegant greys in their carriage, with the lovely gold-coloured horse, which Uncle Arthur said was a palomino, second, and a smart black cob third.

The sky grew darker while they ate their lunch. It wasn't only haze now. Small, wispy black clouds were drifting fast under a grey sky, and the trees were beginning to stir in a gusty breeze. Uncle Arthur kept looking anxiously at the clouds, and the heaviness of the air made them all less hungry than usual for Grace's delicious picnic. Angela was also put off eating by feeling nervous about riding as groom in the next class. She and Ian had tossed for it, but she almost wished now that it was Ian who was going. It would be so awful if she did something wrong and spoiled their chances.

'Will all competitors for the obstacle driving please get put too and come to the collecting ring,' said the loudspeaker, and Uncle Arthur jumped to his feet.

'Here we go,' he said. 'We'll beat the storm yet.'

Magic and Moonshine were more excited now. They sensed that something exciting was going to happen, and they could feel the storm coming.

'Better give them a turn or two on the exercise field,' said Uncle Arthur. 'Come on, you two.'

Other people were practising in the open space at the end of the show-ground, some driving single horses or ponies, including Streamer and his boy driver, and two others with pairs, the elegant greys, now pulling a dog cart, and a pair of little Welsh mountain ponies not much bigger than Magic and Moonshine.

318

'They'll be quick. We'll have our work cut out to beat those two,' said Uncle Arthur when he saw them. The Welsh ponies were pulling a dog cart too, one a lot like Magic and Moonshine's, and their driver was a rather stocky lady dressed in a tweed jacket and skirt and a soft felt hat.

She gave them a friendly wave and drove over.

'I'm Mrs Patson,' she said. 'Haven't seen you at a show before. This your first one? Nice little ponies, prefer Welsh myself, though.'

Uncle Arthur introduced himself and he and Mrs Patson chatted for a few minutes before she drove off to give her ponies another turn round the field. Then Uncle Arthur said that he ought to take a look at the course.

'Here, Ian,' he said. 'Just keep them walking round. I won't be long.'

Ian climbed into the driver's place and took over the reins, and Uncle Arthur hurried off towards the ring.

'Uncle Arthur said to keep them walking,' Angela reminded Ian, as Magic and Moonshine bent their necks and pulled at the reins, and Ian said that he knew. There was a thud of hooves beside them and Streamer drew alongside the two little ponies. His neck was very arched, and his ears flickered quickly backwards and forwards, and Angela noticed that his neck was black with sweat and his eyes looked wild.

'Old Streamer always gets excited when there's a storm coming,' said the boy. 'Come on, let's have a trot, keeping up with us will make your two stretch their legs.'

'But we're only supposed to let them walk,' said Angela, wishing that Uncle Arthur would come back.

'Gosh, are you?' the boy sounded astonished and amused, and Angela saw Ian flush.

'A short trot won't hurt, Angie,' he said. 'It might settle them down.'

'But ...' began Angela, but Streamer was off, and Ian clicked his tongue and sent Magic and Moonshine after the grey pony. The little ponies were only too pleased to go, and they were beside the wheel of Streamer's cart as they went up the field. The boy looked round to grin at them, and then it happened. There was a sudden flash and a roll of thunder, and the grey pony shied violently, swinging right into the path of Magic and Moonshine.

Ian shouted, and tried to turn the ponies round, but the turn was too tight and sudden. Angela felt the cart skidding, and then tilting under her. She had a glimpse of Moonshine rearing as he tried to avoid the back of the other cart, and of Magic swinging hard round, and then the cart was turning over, rings and seat cushions were coming loose, she lost her grip on the side, and the hard ground came up to meet her with a thump that knocked most of her breath away.

The next few moments were complete confusion. Angela could hear people shouting, the thud of hooves, and the crack of splintering wood, and she heard Uncle Arthur's voice shouting, 'Steady, steady, whoa lads.' Angela scrambled shakily to her knees in time to see Magic and Moonshine brought to a stop by Uncle Arthur and another man, who had grabbed their heads. Their cart lay on its side behind them, and not far away she could see Streamer's cart, also over-turned, with one wheel off and the grey pony kicking and plunging furiously as several people worked to free him from the broken shafts.

'Angie,' said Ian's voice shakily beside her. 'Angie, are you all right?'

'I . . . I think so,' Angela got gingerly to her feet and bent down to pick up one of the seat cushions. Her legs felt most peculiar, as though something had happened to make her knees go loose, and breathing made her chest ache. Ian's face was white, with a long scratch down his cheek, and his shirt was torn.

'We'd better go and help Uncle Arthur, he

said unhappily. 'He's going to be furious.'

'Well, he ... he did say just walk,' Angela couldn't help saying.

They picked up the rest of the cushions, and the rug and whip, and started towards Uncle Arthur. The dog cart was upright again, and Uncle Arthur had left a man holding the ponies and was coming anxiously to meet them.

'Not hurt, are you?' he asked. 'Oh dear, oh dear, what a thing to happen.'

'My ... my legs feel funny and ... and my chest aches a bit,' Angela told him.

'I think she was winded,' added Ian.

'Better go and sit down for a bit. Wish Grace was here, oh dear,' Uncle Arthur's face was red and worried, and Ian said, 'I'm awfully sorry. I shouldn't have agreed to trot round with that boy.'

'Indeed you shouldn't,' Uncle Arthur

322

sounded stern. 'I thought I could trust you to be sensible, Ian. You might have killed your sister, not to mention Magic and Moonshine. That grey pony was half off its head with nerves before it thundered, I'd have thought you could have seen that, after all your experience at Champney's.'

Ian stared at the ground, and Angela said, 'Are the ponies all right?'

'Not hurt, just upset,' replied Uncle Arthur. 'I'll give you a lift up into the cart, and take you over to the van. You'd better sit quiet for a bit.'

'I . . . I can walk to the van,' Angela told him quickly, after a glance at the cart. Uncle Arthur looked at her.

'Now, what's all this?' he asked. 'Come on, up you get. I've got the lads now, remember?'

Before Angela could protest again Uncle Arthur had put the cushions back in the seats and lifted her in. Magic and Moonshine were sweating and jerking at their bits, and Uncle Arthur took the reins from the man holding them and got in beside her. Ian stepped quietly up into the back seat. A few yards away Streamer was being led towards the boxes, away from the wreck of his cart, and Angela was glad to see that he looked unhurt.

Magic and Moonshine jumped forward as

the man let their heads go, and Angela gasped and grabbed the side.

'Steady lads, steady now, settle down,' Uncle Arthur was talking in a calm, easy voice, and Magic and Moonshine turned back their ears to listen and started to go more steadily. It was starting to rain now, and the thunder rolled again, but the little ponies didn't mind thunder. With Uncle Arthur's hands on the reins, steadying them, and holding them back, they dropped their noses and took the dog cart back to the van at an easy jog.

'All right?' Uncle Arthur asked Angela, and she nodded, but riding in the cart no longer felt the same. She couldn't help remembering the horrible feeling of turning over, the tilt getting steeper and steeper, the confusion, and the thud as she hit the ground. At least she wouldn't have to go into the ring as groom now, though, for surely after that accident Uncle Arthur would withdraw and go home.

'Are . . . are we going home now?' she asked, as the ponies stopped by the van.

'Home? Can't go home yet,' Uncle Arthur looked at her. 'What about our class? We've got a job to do here, can't let people down. Chest all right now?'

Angela nodded, and Uncle Arthur patted her shoulder.

324

'Good,' he said. 'Get your mac on, and then hop back up. It'll be our turn in a moment.'

'C . . . couldn't Ian go with you?' Angela's heart thudded and she felt slightly sick at the idea of galloping round the ring in the cart, the sliding turns, and the speed.

'Now, Angie, you're not going to let me down, are you?' Uncle Arthur looked disappointed. 'Come on, I'm relying on you.'

Didn't he know how she felt? Angela supposed that he didn't. How could she explain? Then she knew that she wouldn't try. It was like going up the ropes in the gym, you felt horribly frightened before, but not trying felt even worse afterwards. If Uncle Arthur was going ahead and driving in the class she would have to go as well. Ian had fetched her mac for her, and was handing it up, and Uncle Arthur reached back and squeezed her hand as she started to put it on.

'Good girl,' he said. 'Come on then, lads, let's go.'

The ponies started forward, the thunder rolled again, and Angela realized that Uncle Arthur did know. He knew that she was scared, and he knew that not going with him would seem worse afterwards, and she suddenly wondered if he was a bit scared himself. It couldn't have been very nice for him to see his much-loved Magic and Moonshine in such trouble. As they drove towards the ring Angela knew that Uncle Arthur was a much tougher person than they had realized.

4 · Away for the weekend

Mrs Patson was the first person they met as they drove up to the ring to take their turn in the obstacle driving.

'Got them back on their legs all right, then?' she called, and Uncle Arthur called cheerfully back that they were fine. The steward was already calling their number, and Uncle Arthur shortened his reins.

'Ready?' he asked Angela, and she nodded. Then they were bowling into the ring, heading for the starting gate, and Uncle Arthur was leaning forward, his whip in one hand, a rein in each hand, and his feet braced apart against the dashboard. The starting bell rang, and the ponies' ears went forward and then turned back again as Uncle Arthur called to them.

'Go on, lads,' he shouted. 'Gee up, gee up, Magic, Moonshine.'

The little ponies jumped forward, and they were galloping as they went between the starting posts. The rain drove into Angela's face, making her half-close her eyes, and she clung to the side, her breath snatched away by the wet rush of air. Almost before she was ready Uncle Arthur shouted, 'Left,' and the ponies were turning, the cart coming fast round behind them. Angela hung over to the left, seeing the red and white bollard rush towards her, then they were through the first gate, and going at full speed towards the next. Magic and Moonshine's hooves thundered on the wet grass, and then they were turning right, quick and neat on their feet, with Angela hanging breathlessly over the right side of the cart. She had forgotten to be scared, forgotten everything except the thrill of the speed, and the wet wind lashing her face and pulling her hair, the creak of cart and harness, and the thud of hooves.

'Left,' shouted Uncle Arthur again, and almost at once, as they straightened out, 'Right.' Angela flung herself down the seat to balance the cart the other way, and saw the wheels spin past another bollard with only a fraction to spare.

'Now, go. Go on, lads.' Uncle Arthur was leaning right forward, urging the ponies on to their fastest, and they raced down the ring towards the last gate with the rain driving straight into their faces and mud and spray

328

flying from under their hooves and the spinning wheels. The last pair of bollards flashed past, and they were through the finish and Uncle Arthur was pulling up as thunder crashed across the sky again and the rain came down in a deluge.

It was impossible for the class to continue until the rain slackened a bit, and Uncle Arthur drove straight on to put the ponies into the van and start rubbing them down. Ian and Angela both helped, all of them crowded into the van together in the steamy warmth of the wet ponies, and while they were still working the loudspeakers announced that the class was over. Magic and Moonshine had won the pairs section with Mrs Patson's Welsh ponies second.

Uncle Arthur was delighted. Because of the rain the winners fetched their rosettes and prizes on foot, and Uncle Arthur fixed the big red ribbon to the windscreen below the one from the marathon.

'Make a real show, don't they?' he said happily. 'And now, home for tea. We're all ready for that, I'll be bound.'

'I am,' said Angela cheerfully. She had forgotten all about being scared, it had been fun after all, but Ian said nothing. Glancing at him, Angela knew that he still felt disgraced, and she had a sad feeling that he wouldn't be so keen on the shows again after today. It really was a shame that the accident had happened.

After the first show they all felt rather like sitting back and relaxing for a bit, but of course there wasn't time. They could have Sunday off, though, in spite of Uncle Arthur having to get up early to sort the Sunday papers for the boys to deliver. They all went to Church after a late breakfast, leaving the ponies with full

haynets to munch at, and after Grace's delicious Sunday lunch Uncle Arthur went outside to hose down the dog cart and to let Magic and Moonshine free to wander round the yard for a bit.

The weather was still hot, and soon Magic discovered the cool spray from the hose.

'Come and look,' called Uncle Arthur after a bit, and Angela, Grace, and Ian looked out of the door to see Magic standing with his nose stretched out into the cool spray where water was splashing off the cart. Uncle Arthur turned the hose so that the jet of water touched Magic's muzzle, and the pony snorted and then stuck his nose into the air, wrinkling his top lip back, before pushing his head into the spray again.

'Rascal,' said Uncle Arthur. 'That's enough, or you'll catch a chill. Go and beg for carrots with Moonshine.'

Moonshine had seen the rest of the family watching, and was 'asking' with one front foot. Angela fetched some carrots from the rack in the kitchen, and Magic soon left the water and came hurrying over to see what his friend was crunching.

After Sunday, however, the next week was as busy as the one before. The combined driving event was the next thing in front of them. On Monday the ponies were taken to the recreation

331

ground to practise for the dressage. Ian was not in the cart with Angela and Uncle Arthur, he had gone straight to Champney's after school, and Angela missed him.

'Poor Ian,' she said experimentally, as they drove towards the rec. 'He really was sorry about Saturday.'

Uncle Arthur looked serious. 'I expect he was,' he said. 'But he should never have let it happen. He really did let me down, Angie, he knows that, and Grace and I both feel that it's no use being too quick to forget all about it. I think knowing that I shan't trust him with the ponies again for a time is punishment enough, though I'm sorry about it. Ian could be quite a good driver if he didn't let himself get carried away, and learned to keep his head.'

Angela supposed that he was right, it had been silly of Ian, but she sighed as the little ponies swung along in front of her at their brisk 'working trot'. It was a shame that things had gone wrong.

This week the ponies' dressage and fitness were more important than their skill and speed in obstacle driving, for that would only be one part of the combined event. Uncle Arthur had marked out a part of the recreation ground, carefully measuring to make sure that it would be the same size as the one at the event, which was one hundred metres long by forty metres wide. There were letters at intervals along the sides and down the middle, and each different movement had to be started and finished at a certain letter. Uncle Arthur had written these on pieces of cardboard, which he now tied to short stakes round the arena.

'All ready,' he said to Angela, when this was done. 'Now let's see what we can do. You hold the test paper, and tell me if I forget anything.'

The dressage test had to be driven from memory, and Uncle Arthur had been learning it for a week now. There were all sorts of movements in it that the ponies had to do, three different sorts of trot, figures of eight, reining back, walking, and standing perfectly still. Uncle Arthur drove the ponies through it all once, only asking Angela twice what came next, and then he said that they would practise the different movements one by one, in a different order.

'If we keep doing the test all the time the lads'll learn it as well, and start rushing, and then we'll get bad marks,' he explained. 'Bob Sheering had a lot of advice about these tests, and that was part of it.'

So they went on to practise the movements in turn, starting with the three trots, the slow but eager 'collected' trot, when the ponies must go slowly but with great energy, the brisk, steady 'working' trot, and the fast 'extended' trot, when the ponies must take long strides and really stretch out over the ground.

'They look good to me,' said Angela, and Uncle Arthur said, 'Not bad, not bad at all. We'll soon get it taped.'

As well as dressage there was the long-distance, cross-country drive to practise for, and Uncle Arthur got permission to drive the ponies along some tracks and up and down hills in the grounds of a big hospital a few miles from home. Here also he practised timing their speed over different distances at different paces, for each part of the long-distance drive was timed, and penalty marks were given for being too quick, as well as too slow. Angela found it all fascinating, and she couldn't understand how Ian could resist coming as well, but he insisted that he would rather be at Champney's.

'Leave him,' said Grace, when Angela talked to her about Ian. 'He still feels ashamed about the accident, and he knows that only one of you can ride in the event as groom, and that after that Arthur will insist it's you.'

'But we could take turns,' said Angela, who would rather do that than have Ian miserable and out of it, but when she suggested to Ian that they should ask Uncle Arthur about this he said he'd rather not.

334

'He wouldn't want me,' he said. 'Anyway, I'm not that keen!'

And that was all he would say. Angela decided that Grace was right, she would have to wait until Ian felt less guilty before she could persuade him to join in again.

As the combined driving event was a two day show they would have to spend two nights away from home. The organizers were arranging places for the drivers, grooms, and teams to stay, and on Wednesday Uncle Arthur received a letter about this. He read it, and laughed as he handed it on to Grace.

'The lads'll enjoy that,' he said. 'Plenty of company.'

'Why? What is it, a riding school?' asked Angela eagerly. Ian said nothing.

'No, a stud farm, that's a place where ponies are bred,' replied Uncle Arthur. 'And it belongs to someone we know, Mrs Patson. She says she'll be happy to put us all up, not just me and the lads, jolly kind of her.'

'What about the shop?' asked Grace. 'Mrs Handry said the other day she'd be free if we wanted her.' replied Uncle Arthur. 'We'll have to get off early on Friday, so that we have time to look at the cross-country course. I say, you two have the afternoon off this Friday, don't you? Staff meeting, or something, wasn't it?

That's a bit of luck, we can get off about one.'

'We'd better have everything packed and loaded in the morning,' said Grace. 'So if Mrs Handry can come in for the day it would help. I think I'd better set up house in that van.'

Uncle Arthur looked up from Mrs Patson's letter slightly anxiously.

'Sure you don't mind?' he asked her. 'Lot of rushing about, I'm afraid, but it won't be for much longer now.'

'No, of course I don't mind,' Grace assured him, giving him a pat on the shoulder as she got up. 'It'll be fun.'

Uncle Arthur looked relieved. 'Good,' he said. 'Here, come along you two, it's gone half-past eight, you'll be late for school.'

'Do you think Grace does get a bit tired of the ponies?' asked Angela, as she and Ian walked down the road a few minutes later.

'Oh, a bit I think,' replied Ian. 'So do I, come to that. You and Uncle Arthur are really gone on them, aren't you?'

'So were you, once,' said Angela, rather crossly. Ian was a bit much sometimes. 'And you'd got quite keen again, until . . .' she stopped.

'Until last Saturday,' Ian sounded sulky. 'Everyone keeps digging that up, as if I'd meant it to happen or something. I suppose

336

these driving events are all right, but I'd still rather have real horses, like Champney's Jasper and Big Ben.'

'We don't keep digging . . .' began Angela, but their bus was at the stop, and Ian jumped on to the platform ahead of her. Best not to say any more, decided Angela, as she followed him inside.

Mrs Patson's pony stud had once been a farm, but now all the fields were surrounded by neat wooden rails instead of wire, and the buildings round the yard were all stables or barns for storing fodder or vehicles. Several pretty pony heads appeared over loose box doors when Uncle Arthur's van stopped, and Mrs Patson came out of a door to meet them.

'Hello,' she called. 'All in one piece again after last Saturday?'

'Yes, we're ready and rarin' to go,' replied Uncle Arthur, as he unhitched the trailer with the dog cart and lowered the ramp of the van.

Magic and Moonshine thought Mrs Patson's yard a very exciting place. They stared round with very high heads and pricked ears, and exchanged whinnies with several of the watching ponies. Mrs Patson patted them.

'Pretty little fellows,' she said. 'Not as broad as some Shelties I've known. That's the trouble

337

with Shelties, wide as they're tall, some of them are. Come along now, let them have a look at their boxes.'

Magic and Moonshine's boxes were big and roomy, and well bedded down with thick wood shavings. They looked fine, until Uncle Arthur came out and closed the doors, and then it was obvious that there was going to be trouble. The doors were Welsh pony height, just a bit too high for Magic and Moonshine to see out, and Magic objected at once. Several heavy thuds shook the door as he banged it with his front feet, and then his head appeared as he rose up on his hind legs to see over.

'Hey, behave yourselves now,' commanded Uncle Arthur, but Magic wanted to see out. There were several more hefty thumps, and now Moonshine started banging and whinnying as well. The Welsh ponies were getting excited, one young one was dashing round inside its box, and a beautiful dark grey one with a very arched neck and flowing mane was rearing and screaming in a high-pitched way that Angela and Ian had never heard before.

'I say, listen to Southwind,' exclaimed Mrs Patson. 'He's my best stallion. I can't have him making that racket, he'll be breaking out before I know where I am. Shall we shut the top doors on those little fellows?'

338

'Don't think that'd work, just make Magic and Moonshine angry,' replied Uncle Arthur. 'Would you have a couple of wooden boxes about anywhere, good strong ones?'

'Yes, I think I can lay my hands on some,' Mrs Patson turned away. 'Mandy,' she shouted. 'Get me two of those empty apple boxes, will you?'

Mandy, a tall girl in jeans with fair hair, nodded and hurried into one of the barns, to come out carrying two solid-looking wooden

boxes. Uncle Arthur thanked her, and opened Magic's door.

'What's Uncle Arthur going to do?' Angela asked, but Grace and Ian shook their heads. Mrs Patson was smiling. 'Think I get the idea,' she said. 'You chaps watch a minute.'

Magic backed up at a word from Uncle

Arthur, and he set the box on the ground just inside the door. Then he came out and closed the door behind him. A moment later Magic's head appeared over the door, ears pricked, gazing eagerly round the yard. Angela stared at him. What had Uncle Arthur done? Then she realized.

'He's standing on the box,' she exclaimed. 'He's got his front feet up on it.'

'Thought that was it.' Mrs Patson laughed. 'Your uncle certainly knows his ponies.'

Uncle Arthur put the second box in Moonshine's stable, and now both little ponies could see out. The yard was suddenly peaceful.

'That's settled them,' said Mrs Patson cheerfully. 'Now, come and see where you're to sleep, and then we'll all pile into the land rover and take a look at tomorrow's course.'

Mrs Patson's house was an old Sussex farmhouse, built mostly of flints, with low ceilings and oak beams inside. Uncle Arthur and Grace had a tiny room to themselves, but Angela was sharing with Mandy, the girl groom, and two others.

'I'm afraid it'll be a bit of a squash,' said Mrs Patson. 'But they're nice girls, grooms to the other two teams I'm putting up. I've set your bed up at the end of the passage, Ian; hope you can manage.'

There was a screen across the end of the long upstairs passage and behind it was a camp-bed. It would be like camping, thought Angela, and she rather envied him. Sleeping with Mandy and two other almost grown-up girls rather frightened her; strangers were bad enough in the day, but sharing a room with them would be an ordeal.

'You'll be all right,' whispered Grace, as they followed Mrs Patson downstairs again. 'If you're really worried, I could ask her if you can come in our room.'

'No, don't do that,' Angela did not want Mrs Patson and Mandy to think her babyish. She was there as Uncle Arthur's groom, and she was going to show that she could behave like one, and do the job as well as the older girls.

Outside again they began to pile into the land rover – Dan Halliday, driver of one of the other teams, Uncle Arthur and Mrs Patson in front, and Angela, Mandy and a girl called Sarah, who was Mr Halliday's groom, in the back. Ian stayed back with Grace, but Mrs Patson called, 'Aren't you coming then? Plenty of room.'

'You go,' Grace told Ian. 'I'll stay here and sort out our things.'

Ian still hesitated, and Angela knew that he was thinking that he'd be the odd one out, the

341

only one not going on the drive tomorrow, but Mrs Patson was revving the engine, and Grace gave him a gentle push.

'All in, then?' asked Mrs Patson, as Ian made up his mind and got on board, and the land rover jerked forward.

The driving event was being held in the parkland surrounding a stately home a few miles from Mrs Patson's farm, and to Angela it all seemed very confusing. The cross-country course was marked with red and white discs, nailed to trees and posts and gates, and there were five separate sections, each to be done at a different speed. There were tarmac roads, grassy tracks, some tracks through forestry land, between tall, dark pine trees, and one short stretch of quite busy road. There were narrow bridges and gateways, a place where the course zig-zagged between trees, steep hills up and down, and a water splash. This was one of the places where Mrs Patson stopped the land rover and they all climbed out to look.

'It's got a gravel bottom,' said Mrs Patson, as they walked down the slope from the road bridge to the ford through which the vehicles would drive. 'Quite safe, I think.'

Uncle Arthur and Dan Halliday did not take her word for it. They were both wearing boots and they waded into the water, testing the bottom with their feet, and exploring on both sides to make sure there were no holes or rocks under the water to catch a wheel or their ponies' hooves.

'Seems all right,' said Uncle Arthur at last, and Dan Halliday agreed. They both made notes on the maps of the course that they had been given, and started back to the waiting land rover. Following them up the hill with Ian beside her Angela found herself yawning. It seemed to be years since they had set off to school that morning. She couldn't imagine how Uncle Arthur was going to remember all about the course, but she was too tired to worry. Even sleeping with the older girls no longer seemed so bad, it would be nice just to be in bed.

Back at the house Angela woke up enough to help Uncle Arthur feed and settle Magic and Moonshine, and to eat cold ham and salad and apple pie for supper herself. Then she started yawning again, and Grace quietly said, 'Bed now, or you'll be too tired to make Arthur a good groom tomorrow.'

'I think I'll go as well,' said Ian, and Grace looked at him in surprise. Ian looked away, and again Angela knew that he was feeling out of it. If he stayed up, it would be to watch and listen to everyone planning their drive, and he and Grace would be the odd ones out.

'I've got a book,' he told Grace. 'Can I read for a bit in bed?'

'If it's light enough up there,' agreed Grace, and so Ian and Angela went up together.

'I wish you could come as well tomorrow,' Angela told him, but Ian shrugged.

'Oh, I'd as soon watch,' he said casually. 'That way, I'll see the big horses as well as the shrimps.'

He went off along the passage to his screened camp-bed, and Angela turned into Mandy's room. By the time the other girls came to bed themselves she was fast asleep, to dream of driving round the course beside Uncle Arthur with Ian running behind.

5 · The longest drive

It was already morning when Angela woke up. Sarah, Mandy and the third girl, June, were getting dressed, and outside a thick mist was pressing against the windows.

'It should be fine when this lifts,' said Mandy, peering out. 'I say, Angela, your uncle's up early, I just saw him go out.'

'Did he?' Angela scrambled out of bed and began to pull on her clothes. If Uncle Arthur was up it was time that she was out helping him.

Ian's screen was still closed across the end of the passage. When Angela put her head round it she could just see his hair over the top of the blankets.

'Ian, it's morning,' she told him. 'Are you getting up?'

Ian groaned and mumbled, 'It's too early. Go away.'

Angela hesitated. She suspected that Ian

345

wasn't really as sleepy as he looked; he couldn't be, in a strange bed, with all the noises of people getting up around him.

'Uncle Arthur's gone out,' she said, but Ian just twitched the blanket higher over his head.

'Good for him,' he muttered. 'You won't need me, then. Surely two of you can get Magic and Moonshine clean?'

Sighing, Angela knew that he wouldn't come. It would have been fun if they could both have gone out together, with everything so strange and exciting, but she'd have to enjoy it alone. It seemed as if Ian wanted to show that he really didn't care about the ponies, and so wasn't bothered by being the one not to take part in the event.

Outside, the mist was thick and damp. Drops clung to Angela's hair and to her eyelashes, and there were rows of silver drops on all the twigs and fences and on the spiders' webs in the grass.

Uncle Arthur was mucking out the boxes while the ponies ate their feeds, and Angela helped to sweep the floors and put down fresh straw. Then Uncle Arthur fetched the brushes, and they started grooming. It was important for the ponies to look their best, as they were judged on how they looked, before they did their dressage test.

While Angela brushed Moonshine, getting all the straw and stable stains off his creamy coat, she could hear Uncle Arthur talking to Magic

in the box next door. The other little pony was excited, and as usual he was showing it by playing all kinds of tricks on his master. Angela heard Uncle Arthur tell him to put down a brush, and to pick up his feet, and she heard him say a firm 'No', when Magic tried to pick his pocket. Moonshine never got so excited, and he went on eating hay while Angela tidied him up. Uncle Arthur would come in when he had finished Magic to give him a final polish.

With the ponies groomed, they went into the house for breakfast, and to get ready themselves. Angela and Uncle Arthur had to look their best as well as the ponies, cart, and harness, and everything has to look right, and go with the look of the whole turn-out. Uncle Arthur was wearing a dark grey suit and a bowler hat, and he had a dark red carnation in his buttonhole. He was also wearing gloves.

'Don't you think Uncle Arthur looks smart?' Angela asked Ian, who had only come down in time for breakfast.

'I suppose he does,' Ian refused to be impressed. 'You should see Bill when he's driving the Shires in a show.'

Again Angela sighed. It would be so much more fun if Ian would be enthusiastic too. 'Come on, Angie,' urged Grace. 'Time you were dressed as well', and Angela followed Grace up to her bedroom, where her own clothes were waiting.

Deciding what Angela was to wear to look like a suitable groom had been harder. In the end Grace had bought her a pair of brown cord trousers, which she needed anyway with winter coming, and she wore her school shirt with one of Ian's ties and an outgrown sports jacket of Ian's that fitted her quite well.

'Should have a hat,' said Mrs Patson, seeing her in the yard while Uncle Arthur was loading the ponies into the van for the short journey to the event. 'Think I can find the right thing. Mandy, get that small hat out of the tack room cupboard, will you?'

Mandy brought out a small black riding cap and put it on Angela's head. It was just a bit too big, but Grace padded the lining with newspaper, at Mrs Patson's suggestion, and when she put it back on Angela knew that at least it wouldn't fall off in front of the judges.

'That's very good of you,' said Uncle Arthur. 'You should be out to sabotage us, not help us. After all, we're rivals.'

Mrs Patson laughed. 'It isn't that cut-throat, not yet,' she said. 'New sport like this combined driving has everyone mucking in and helping each other. That's how it should be. I'll be sorry when it gets too big for that, like show jumping has, all big money and everyone out to win.'

'She's nice, isn't she?' said Angela to Ian, as they drove out of the gate a few minutes later, and this time Ian agreed with her quite cheerfully.

After leaving Mrs Patson's everything seemed

to Angela, who was starting to feel nervous, to happen much too quickly. All at once, it seemed, they were in the big field where the horse boxes were unloading. Magic and Moonshine were harnessed and impatiently pawing the ground, and she and Uncle Arthur were sitting in the cart with Grace and Ian wishing them good luck in the presentation and dressage.

'We'll be up there watching,' called Grace, as Ian let the ponies move off for a drive round to warm them up and settle them down.

The dressage arena was marked out smartly with white boards, very different to the big stones and pieces of cardboard that Uncle Arthur had used on the recreation ground. When their number was called Magic and Moonshine went into the arena at a jog, and halted for the judges to examine the turn-out and condition of them and their cart. Feeling the judges' eyes on her Angela sat up very stiff and straight on the back seat and hoped that they wouldn't notice that her hat was too big. It was important that the ponies stood still. Angela knew that Magic was longing to be off, but Uncle Arthur had trained both his ponies to stand when they were told for their stage act, and except for shaking his head and making a sly face at Moonshine Magic did stand.

'Right, thank you,' said the steward, when the judges had finished, and Uncle Arthur drove out of the arena again to circle and come back in to do his test.

Angela thought that Magic and Moonshine went very well. They walked without jogging when the test asked them to, they trotted slowly, with great energy, when they were supposed to be collected, went on smoothly at the faster working trot, and stretched their legs and strode out when Uncle Arthur asked them to extend. They did their figure of eight round the arena neatly, and their backing was straight. Quite a lot of people clapped as Uncle Arthur drove them out after their final halt, and both ponies arched their necks and pricked their ears, pleased to have people clapping them.

'Well, what did that look like? Not bad, eh?' Uncle Arthur asked Grace and Ian, who came to meet them. He was out of the cart now, patting the ponies and giving them slices of carrot as a reward.

'They looked lovely,' said Grace, and Ian said, 'They went better than the ones we watched before you. They kept cantering!'

'When do you know your marks?' Grace asked, and Uncle Arthur said that he didn't know.

'It'll take a bit of time for the judges to add

them all up,' he said. 'Then they've got to get them up on the board. We'll have a look in about half an hour.'

When Angela and Ian went to look at the scoreboard a bit later, while Uncle Arthur was busy with the ponies, they found Mrs Patson there, looking at her own team's marks. She turned to beam at Angela and Ian.

'Your uncle's done well,' she said. 'Six marks better than my two, in fact. He's standing fourth at the moment, Lewis Stanton's Hafflingers are at the top.'

'Fourth!' Angela was delighted, but as they started back to the ponies Ian said, 'There's lots to come, remember, the marathon, and the obstacle driving tomorrow. I shouldn't think being fourth halfway through the dressage tests means much.'

'It isn't bad, all the same,' retorted Angela, and Ian shrugged. Angela didn't know whether to feel cross with him or sympathetic. It was horrible to feel left out, she knew, but he was being a bit sulky about it.

All the competitors could get food at the refreshment tent at special prices, and they had a lunch of cheese salad, bread rolls, and slices of fruit cake. Then it was time to get Magic and Moonshine ready for the longest and hardest part of the event, the cross-country marathon drive.

'We'll walk out to the water splash to watch,' said Grace. 'That should be one of the high spots, shouldn't it, Ian?'

'I suppose so,' agreed Ian, and Grace looked at him, but he was looking at the ground and she did not say anything.

'Well, time we were on our way,' said Uncle Arthur, and he and Angela got into the cart.

'Good luck,' said Grace, and Ian echoed her. Then the ponies were moving off, and Angela waved. She couldn't help feeling a bit unhappy about Ian, and Uncle Arthur guessed, because he said, 'Ian's turn will come another day, Angie, don't worry. It's quite fair for you to be riding today, after what happened, and Ian knows it really.'

Then they were at the start of the cross-country course, and there was no time to worry about anything else for a bit.

For this part of the competition all competitors had to have a referee riding in the cart with them, to make sure that the team went at the right pace in each section, that no one but the driver handled the reins, and that they obeyed the rules. The referees also timed each section on a stopwatch. Uncle Arthur's referee was a cheerful young man wearing a sheepskin jacket and a soft hat with a little feather in the band. He carried his scorecard clipped to a board, and he held a stopwatch. He smiled at Angela, and then got into the seat next to Uncle Arthur, from where he would have a good view of the ponies and be able to see what they were doing.

'My name's David,' he said. 'You've got three minutes before you go. All competitors are sent off at ten-minute intervals, and the team in front of you has been gone seven minutes.'

Magic and Moonshine moved up to take their places at the start, which was on one of the made-up roads through the estate.

'All right, Angie?' asked Uncle Arthur, and Angela said that she was. The starter was

354

looking at his watch, and as they reached the last minute before their start he began to count backwards, 'Sixty, fifty-nine, fifty-eight,' down to 'Three, two, one, off.' Uncle Arthur released the brake and clicked his tongue, the referee pressed down the button of his stopwatch, and they were off on section A of the marathon.

At first it seemed easy. Magic and Moonshine were bowling gaily along at their steady working trot, the cart riding lightly behind them on the smooth tarmac. As Mandy had forecast the early mist had quite cleared by now, and it was a lovely, bright autumn day. The leaves on the trees were turning from green to brown and gold, and the air on Angela's face smelt of damp earth and trees with a faint tang of woodsmoke. She could smell the warm horse smell of the ponies, and the leather of their harness and the fresh paint on the cart, the wheels hummed on the road, and the ponies' feet tapped out a sharp rhythm. Then, ahead, Angela saw the red and white markers on either side of a gateway into a grass field track, and she knew that the easy part of the course was almost over.

The gate was easily wide enough for Magic and Moonshine, and beyond it the track curved across a field. Uncle Arthur kept the ponies going at their steady trot, but the cart no longer ran so smoothly. There were bumps and ruts in the track, and for a bit it tilted the cart the wrong way, tipping slightly to the right while the way curved to the left, and making Angela feel very unsafe. A herd of bullocks gazed at them over a fence, and as they approached the next gate, which would be the end of section A, a rabbit shot across the track and vanished into a bush.

'Five miles done,' said Uncle Arthur, as he slowed the ponies to a walk in the non-scoring area between sections A and B. Their referee was writing on his scorecard, and now he said, 'Half a minute early, I'm afraid. Three penalty marks. They're fine little fellows, though.'

'Oh dear, have to do better than that, won't we?' said Uncle Arthur, and Angela asked why being half a minute early mattered.

'You get one penalty mark for each ten seconds early at the end of a section, and two for each ten seconds late,' explained David. 'Don't worry, everyone collects a few.'

Section B was to be done at a walk, and was a good bit shorter, only half a mile. The track led through a forestry plantation of pine trees, deep and cool and sweet-smelling. There were pine needles on the sandy track, and Magic and Moonshine's hooves and the cartwheels made hardly any noise on them. It was very peaceful,

356

but Angela knew that Uncle Arthur had not relaxed. He was driving all the time, keeping Magic and Moonshine walking out well, and guiding them round any rough or too-soft-looking parts of the track which would make their work harder, and tire them more quickly. Then, ahead, Angela saw the end of the section and the first compulsory halt, where quite a few people and land rovers were gathered in a sort of lay-by beside the track.

Here everyone had to stop for ten minutes, to allow their teams to rest and have a short drink, and to give the drivers a chance to check their ponies' legs for injuries and their feet for loose shoes or stones. There was a vet and a black-smith with a portable forge for anyone who needed them, and there were buckets for water.

Everyone got out of the cart, and Angela held the ponies while Uncle Arthur looked them over. Then Magic and Moonshine were offered a small drink, not too much, as a big drink would make it harder for them to work, and very soon the ten minutes were up, and it was time to set off again on section C, which included the water splash.

Section C was to be driven at a faster trot, and soon they left the soft forestry track and Magic and Moonshine's hooves and their little iron shoes struck sparks from the stretch of made-up road which they had come to. This part of the course was uphill, and it was followed by a shallower downhill slope which led at the bottom to the water splash. Angela could see it ahead of them as they came over the crest of the hill, the stream winding through the fields, the road bridge, and the track at the side of it dipping through the ford. There were a lot of people there, and rows of cars and land rovers parked on the road, and something was going on in the water. There were horses there, and a vehicle, and men wading about.

'Someone's tipped over,' said David. 'Keep going, be ready to pull up when I give you the word. I'll stop your time until the way's clear.'

'I hope no one was hurt,' Angela stared down at the scene below. Two of the horses were being led out of the water while the other two were still plunging about, with men at their heads and others undoing their harness.

'Got two out, anyway,' said Uncle Arthur. 'Ah, there go the second pair now.'

The back pair of the team of four, the 'wheelers', were being led after the pair of 'leaders', while other men hauled the vehicle back on to its wheels. As Magic and Moonshine trotted on down the hill towards the water splash Angela could see the water pouring out of the tipped vehicle, and then she saw Grace and Ian watching from the bridge.

'Pull in now,' said David, and Magic and Moonshine came to a rather impatient halt at the side of the road. They had been enjoying swinging along fast on the easy slope, and they were not pleased at having to stop.

'All right, lads, stand. You're getting a free breather,' Uncle Arthur told them, and David and Angela laughed. Below them the big four-wheeled cart was being pulled up the slope out of the water, and a minute or so later the steward down there signalled that the way was clear.

'Off you go then,' said their referee, and the ponies started forward.

'Our turn for a shower bath,' said Uncle Arthur. 'Gee, lads, keep going.'

Magic and Moonshine turned down the slope to the ford still at quite a fast trot. Unlce Arthur was steadying them slightly, but they were keen to get through. They arched their necks and tucked in their noses and took the water splash with a will. Spray burst from under their hooves and from the wheels in a great cloud, Angela was blinded, her face and clothes spattered with drops, her breath snatched away by the sudden cold splashes. The ponies went through like a train, the cart

359

rocking, and their wake sending waves leaping
up the banks. In the front seat Uncle Arthur
and David had their heads tucked in, and
David was hanging on to the seat. Then they
were through, going up the slope on the other
side still at a spanking trot, with sparkling
drops flying from the wheels and the spectators
on the bridge laughing and clapping.

'Good lads,' said Uncle Arthur, as they

swung back on to the road. 'That's the way,' and David laughed.

'I began to think I was in a submarine,' he said. 'These little chaps of your certainly do go.'

With the water splash behind them the rest of section C seemed quite simple. They had been a little bit slow, four penalty marks went down on David's card, but Uncle Arthur still looked pleased.

'Now for the really tricky bits, though,' he said, as the ponies walked, stretching their necks and swishing their tails, through the non-scoring area between sections C and D, and Angela remembered the narrow bridge and the zig-zags round the trees. They were still far from finished, she realized, even if they had passed the water splash.

6 · One wheel off the wagon

Section D was another walking one, but it contained some of the tricky obstacles, as Angela had remembered. The narrow bridge came first. It was a little hump-backed one, with the stone parapets narrowing towards one another in the centre. Uncle Arthur aimed right at the middle of it, and the ponies took the cart over easily, without touching at all. Angela took a deep breath of relief, and then the red and white markers appeared ahead on another gateway and once again they left the road for a forestry track, and the tree zig-zags were in front of them.

'Steady now, lads,' said Uncle Arthur, and the little ponies approached the first pair of trees at a steady walk, with their ears pricking as they sensed that here was something more difficult.

Very carefully, Uncle Arthur turned them between the first pair of trees, the cart bumping as it went over some half-buried roots, and Angela caught hold of the side. There was quite a sharp turn to go between the second pair, and the ground was sloping slightly sideways, pulling the cart that way. Angela kept hold of the side and watched the next tree go past very close to her. There was a slight bump, and Uncle Arthur said, 'Touched that one. Round you come, lads.'

Two more pairs of trees went safely past, and they came to the last pair, up on the steepest part of the slope, their red and white markers looking vivid against the dark pine trunks and the thicker trees beyond.

'Now lads, very steady, this looks nasty,' said Uncle Arthur.

Magic and Moonshine steadied, their hooves rustling in the pine needles. Angela could feel the cart slipping sideways very slightly, the ponies were between the trees, and there was a slight grate as the hub of a back wheel touched. Then they were through and Uncle Arthur was straightening the ponies out for the rest of section D.

With section D over only the last section was left. First there was another ten-minute halt, and while she was helping Uncle Arthur with the ponies Angela saw Grace and Ian get out of a land rover.

364

'Hello,' she called, and Grace waved. 'Enjoying yourself?' she asked Angela, and Angela agreed that she was.

'One of Mrs Patson's friends gave us a lift here,' said Ian. 'I say, you weren't bad at the water splash. Some of the teams have been terribly careful there, and wasted ages, but Magic and Moonshine seemed to be going at top speed. We couldn't see you for spray.'

'They were good,' agreed Angela, pleased that Ian seemed quite enthusiastic again. Then Uncle Arthur was warning her that it was time to get back in the cart, and two minutes later they were off on section E, with the ponies swinging along at a working trot, and Grace and Ian waving them away.

Section E started along a sandy track, and at the end of it was a gateway with quite a sharp turn out on to one of the tarmac-covered estate roads. Uncle Arthur steadied the ponies, making them shorten their strides a little and pay attention, and the steward on duty at the gate waved them through. Afterwards no one could say whether Uncle Arthur misjudged the turn, or whether Moonshine, on the side to which they were turning, was a bit too eager to get home, and turned short. Uncle Arthur always said that it was his fault, but whatever the reason Angela suddenly realized that they were too close to the gatepost, and next minute there was a bump, the ponies checked sharply, then the cart bounced forward with a nasty cracking noise, and suddenly they were sagging to the left, and Angela was scrambling along her seat to the right in an attempt to stay on board.

'The wheel's gone, hang on.' Uncle Arthur was bringing the ponies round on to the road, steadying them, and they were all instinctively leaning over to the right, David as well. The steward was hurrying towards them, but Uncle Arthur had not stopped the ponies.

'We're balancing, we're still up,' he said. 'Keep going, lads, easy now. Everyone hang to the right.'

'Are you stopping?' shouted the steward, but Uncle Arthur called back, 'Only a mile and a bit to go, we'll try it. Come on, boys, keep trotting.'

There were no more obstacles, only ordinary bends in the road. Could they really still finish the course, wondered Angela.

Magic and Moonshine knew that something was wrong, their ears were turning backwards and forwards, and Magic was tossing his head, but Uncle Arthur kept talking to them, and they settled down. They were getting tired now, but they sensed that they were almost home, and in spite of the broken wheel they were determined to finish with a flourish. Soon Angela was starting to ache with the effort of keeping still, and keeping her weight to the right. In front of her David was leaning over as far as he could beside Uncle Arthur, and Uncle Arthur was driving very, very carefully, looking out for every bump or slope in the road that could spoil their balance.

There were quite a few spectators lining the route now to watch the competitors come home, and the broken cart raised exclamations and applause. Almost at the finish Grace and Ian were waiting, and Angela saw their startled expressions when they noticed the cart. Then the Finish sign went past them, and David pressed down the button on his stopwatch, without changing his leaning-over position. People were rushing forward to hold the cart steady as Uncle Arthur pulled up, and suddenly it was all over, Angela found herself standing on the road, while the ponies were led out of their places and the broken cart was pulled to one side.

Of course, Grace and Ian wanted to know what had happened, and there were plenty of people to ask questions and praise them for finishing, and for a few minutes Angela thought that it was all rather exciting. It was only when Ian said, 'So that's that, then. We'll be out of it now, with no cart. I suppose we shall go home,' that she realized what the broken wheel meant. However clever Uncle Arthur had been to finish he could not drive a three-wheeled cart round the obstacle course. Suddenly it was all an awful anti-climax.

Now that they were out of it there seemed no point in waiting to see their marks. Better to get Magic and Moonshine home to their well-earned feeds and rest. Angela realized that she was sore and stiff, and as soon as the ponies were settled in their boxes at Mrs Patson's

Grace sent her upstairs to have a bath. When she came down again twenty minutes later the others were in the big farm kitchen, and Angela knew at once that something good had happened. Uncle Arthur was beaming, and Grace had a smile on her face. Even Ian looked pleased. Mrs Patson was perched on the kitchen table, eating a biscuit, and she waved a hand towards the tin.

'Help yourself,' she told Angela. 'There'll be proper food in an hour or so, when they're all back. You were standing sixth, by the way, when I left. Good challenging position for tomorrow.'

'But . . .' began Angela, but Uncle Arthur said, 'Yes Angie, Mrs Patson's rescued us. She's very kindly lending us a cart. So we're not out of it after all.'

Suddenly everything was different. The evening sun seemed brighter on the plants in the window, and Angela realized how hungry she was.

'Couldn't have you dropping out now, not after your great show today,' said Mrs Patson. 'Oh well, I must get back to work.'

She jumped off the table and strode out of the kitchen, and Angela turned to Uncle Arthur.

'So we're still in,' she said. 'Oh, I am glad.

It would have been awful just to go home.'

And from his face she knew that even Ian agreed with her.

They tried Mrs Patson's spare cart next morning, in the flat field behind the stables. It was a bit larger than their own, but Magic and Moonshine handled it well, and soon Uncle Arthur was steering them between pairs of bollards as fast as ever.

Some of Mrs Patson's staff and visitors leaned on the gate to watch, and Mrs Patson said to Ian, 'Your uncle's got a good eye for distance. That cart must be a couple of centimetres wider than his own, but he's got it measured. Well done,' she called, as Uncle Arthur drove back to the gate, with Angela sitting in the cart behind him. 'You'll be beating us yet.'

While Uncle Arthur was unharnessing the ponies Mandy brought out a pair of Mrs Patson's ponies, different ones from those she had in the competition, and began to harness them to a flat exercise cart. Ian went to watch, and soon Angela noticed that he was helping Mandy. When Mrs Patson went over she spoke to Ian, who looked pleased.

'Is it all right if I go for a drive with Mrs Patson?' he asked. 'She says we won't be long, she's just taking these two down the road. They're young ones she's schooling.'

'Yes, go ahead,' said Uncle Arthur, and Angela was pleased to see that Ian looked far happier as he got into the cart beside Mrs Patson.

The two young ponies set off with a bound, one breaking straight into a canter, and as she watched them bounce down the drive with Mrs Patson holding them back as lightly and tactfully as she could, Angela knew that she would have felt rather scared. Ian, however, looked quite happy, and Grace said, 'I'm glad Ian's cheering up. He was a bit fed up yesterday, I'm afraid, although he didn't say much. I know he deserved to be in disgrace for a time, but enough's enough.'

It was half an hour before Ian got back. The ponies were going much more calmly now, and Ian was beaming. He jumped down as they stopped, and went to the ponies' heads in an experienced way, and when the ponies were unharnessed and stabled he came over to Moonshine's box, where Uncle Arthur and Angela were washing the cream pony's tail.

'Enjoy yourself?' asked Uncle Arthur, rinsing soapsuds off in a bucket of warm water.

'Mrs Patson let me drive for a bit,' replied Ian. 'It was fabulous. They're a super pair of ponies. She's hoping to drive them in competitions next year.'

371

He was much more cheerful for the rest of the morning, and when they set off for the show-ground after lunch he was as excited and eager as anyone. Angela was very relieved. It was horrible when she knew that Ian was not enjoying himself.

The course for the obstacle driving looked much the same as other obstacle courses. Looking at the list of placings after the first day they found that Magic and Moonshine had finally finished seventh, with Dan Halliday fourth, and Mrs Patson third. The team of black Austrian Hafflinger ponies was still in the lead. There were twelve teams of ponies altogether, being judged as a separate class from the horses, and so they were just over halfway down the list.

'Not bad, after the accident,' said Uncle Arthur. 'And we could still pull up a place or two if we're lucky.'

'We can't win, can we?' asked Angela, and Uncle Arthur said that he didn't think so.

'The first four teams are well ahead,' he said. 'Still, it's not bad for our first try, not bad at all.'

Magic and Moonshine had seen the bollards, and they knew what was coming.

'Want to be off, don't you, lads?' said Uncle Arthur. 'Won't be long.'

Magic and Moonshine would be going

seventh, in order of placing. Mrs Patson's ponies did a good round to keep their third place, but Dan Halliday's pair got excited, and dropped down to fifth after hitting three gates. Then it was Uncle Arthur's turn.

Magic and Moonshine seemed to know that they had a chance to pull up a place. They went at top speed, swinging round the turns, thundering down the straights, and weaving from side to side down the mid-ring serpentine so fast that Angela almost got left behind in her attempts to swing her weight over in time In spite of the bigger cart they came up to the last gate with all the bollards still standing, and as the cart swept through Angela knew that they might have passed the team in front of them.

'Smashing,' cried Ian, coming to meet them. 'Gosh, didn't they go? I'm sure you've done it.'

'Good lads, good lads.' Uncle Arthur was out of the cart, patting the ponies and feeding them on scraps of carrot.

'And that round moves Blakely Magic and Moonshine up into sixth place,' said the loud-speaker.

So that was the result. Magic and Moonshine were sixth, exactly halfway down the field, and everyone was pleased.

'Good chaps, well done,' said Mrs Patson. 'I've always gone for Welsh myself, but these fellows almost make me change my mind. They're real little characters.'

The event was almost over. The prizes and rosettes were presented, and they said Goodbye and Thank you to Mrs Patson and Mandy. They were to drop the cart and its broken wheel at a carriage makers that Mrs Patson knew on the way home, and the firm had promised to have the cart ready by Wednesday.

'Just give us time to get back in practice for Wembley,' said Uncle Arthur.

'Well kids, enjoyed yourselves?' he asked, as they drove out of Mrs Patson's gate with the trailer rattling behind and Magic whinnying because he knew they were on their way home.

'Oh yes,' said Angela, and Ian nodded. 'Mrs Patson's terrific,' he said. 'I wouldn't mind helping in a place like hers. It's almost as good as Champney's.'

Magic and Moonshine were glad to be home, and Partner was delighted to see them. He rubbed himself all round Uncle Arthur's ankles, then round everyone else, and then went to twine himself round Magic and Moonshine's feet before jumping up on to Magic's back and settling down to sleep.

'It's fun going away, but I like coming home as well,' said Angela, as they sat down to supper in the crowded living room, with Bluey chattering in his cage above them and the crisp autumn dusk filling the yard outside.

'Even when it's school tomorrow?' Grace teased her gently, and Angela laughed. She didn't mind school, and it was still good to be back.

7 · Uncle Arthur out of action

As the carriage menders had promised, the cart
was ready by Wednesday, and when Angela
and Ian got home from school it was in its
usual place beside the stable, with its tarpaulin
cover strapped over it to protect it from the
weather.

'Are they always that quick with repairs?'
asked Ian, and Uncle Arthur said that they
weren't.

'It was a special rush job, because of Wembley,' he explained. 'Blakely Garages paid for
it, of course. Couldn't have afforded it otherwise. This driving can be an expensive business.'

They took the mended cart for a drive next
day, and it seemed as good as new. The
repaired wheel was glossy and smooth, and its
pneumatic tyre, a rubber one with air inside
like a motor tyre, was firm and tight. Older
carts had traditional wheels with rubber tyres
clamped to them with wire, or fitted into a

clench in the wheel, but not many people were left who could repair and fit these old wheels, and so the modern sort which had to be pumped up were often used instead.

On the way home from their drive Uncle Arthur said, 'We'll have a practice tomorrow, probably our last one. The rec. gets too crowded at weekends for us to charge about on it, and the show's on next week. Our first round is on Tuesday.'

There were two classes for pairs at Wembley, the Eldonian Double Harness Stakes, and the Scurry. Both were run in heats, and the winners stayed on for the finals of each class, one on Tuesday and one on Thursday evenings. The best from both classes, both horse and pony sections, could compete in the Eldonian Double Harness Championship on Friday evening, but it was expecting a lot to hope to qualify for that on their first try, thought Angela.

'Are you coming to the rec. tomorrow?' Angela asked Ian while they helped Grace to set the table for tea.

'No, Champney's have got a late delivery and Frank said I could go out on it,' replied Ian. 'He sometimes lets me drive part of the way home if the roads are quiet. You can put out the bollards for Uncle Arthur, can't you?'

'Of course,' replied Angela. 'But, well, it's more fun when you do come.'

'I don't see why.' Ian looked down at the knives and forks he was putting round. 'Uncle Arthur would rather just have you along, he doesn't trust me much with the ponies now.'

'He does. He's said we can take turns to ride as groom at Wembley,' Angela reminded him, but Ian said he'd told Frank he'd be there, and they'd be expecting him. So it was just Angela who went down to the recreation ground next day, riding in the back of the cart with the bollards under her feet.

Magic and Moonshine knew where they were going, and they went on to the grass with a jump and a whisk of their tails.

'Steady, steady,' said Uncle Arthur. 'You'll have your run in a minute. Hop out, Angie, and set up the gates. You can see the marks where they've been. We'll have the serpentine in the course today.'

There were dabs of white on the ground in the places that Uncle Arthur had the gates, to save measuring every time, although the course could be made different by not always using all the marks. Angela soon had the plastic bollards in place, and she got back into the cart for the first run.

378

The ponies went well, and Angela found herself thoroughly enjoying it. All too soon, it seemed, Uncle Arthur said, 'Just one more run, then we'll call it a day. They're so good they'll be getting stale if we go on too long.'

He brought the ponies round for the final run. Angela gripped the sides, and they were away, racing up the field, Magic's ears pricked, and Moonshine's flicking back as they came to the first gate. Round a sharp turn, up the winding serpentine, left, right, and left again, and the final two gates were coming up.

'Left,' called Uncle Arthur, and the ponies turned, the cart beginning to skid round behind them, and it was then that it happened. There was a sudden *pop*, the cart lurched, tilted sharply sideways, and then dropped back on to all four wheels, and suddenly Uncle Arthur wasn't there any more, Angela was alone in the back seat, the reins dragging, and Magic and Moonshine were galloping faster and faster down the recreation ground, with the cart bumping and lurching after them.

For a moment Angela just sat there, clinging to the side, too scared and startled to move. Magic and Moonshine were running away, scared by the suddenly loose reins, and missing Uncle Arthur's feel on their mouths and his voice talking to them. She had got to do something, Angela realized, she'd got to stop the ponies before they overturned the cart, or headed for the roads and home.

Taking a deep breath, she let go of the side of the cart, grasped the back of the driving seat, and scrambled over into Uncle Arthur's place. The cart lurched as she dropped into the seat, and for a horrible moment she thought they were going over. Then they were back on four wheels again, and she was leaning precariously down, reaching for the reins that trailed over Magic's hindquarters, and dragged just within reach at the side of the cart.

'Whoa, steady, steady, Magic, Moonshine,' her voice sounded shrill and shaky, but the ponies heard her, and Angela managed to sit up, holding the reins, and to take a pull at the ponies' mouths. For a moment nothing happened, and she thought they weren't going to stop, then Magic lowered his head and began to slow up, and Moonshine did the same. Angela went on talking to them, giving and taking on the reins as Uncle Arthur had taught her, until their gallop slowed to a canter, then to a trot, and she could pull up and turn them and drive slowly back, her hands shaky on the reins, to find out what had happened to Uncle Arthur.

He was coming slowly to meet her down the length of the recreation ground, and from the

way he was walking Angela knew that something was wrong. He looked hunched up, and he was holding his right arm with his left hand, and as he came closer Angela saw that his face looked very white.

'Angie, my goodness, are . . . are you all right?' he asked her, and Angela said shakily that she was.

'Wh . . . what happened?' she asked him, and Uncle Arthur said, 'Think the tyre . . . burst. Jerk . . . tipped me out.'

Then he climbed awkwardly into the seat beside her, and leaned back, closing his eyes.

'Hurt my . . . arm,' he said. 'You'll have to . . . drive them home, Angie.'

It wasn't really very far from the recreation ground to home, but it seemed too far that day. Angela didn't dare to let Magic and Moonshine go faster than a walk, as she could feel the flat tyre bumping along, and with Uncle Arthur just sitting there, not advising her or anything, she found crossing the roads and steering through what traffic there was very frightening. She was very glad when, about halfway home, Uncle Arthur seemed to feel better. He opened his eyes, and began to give her rather shaky-sounding directions, Magic and Moonshine were glad to hear his voice again, too. They had been crawling uncertainly along, but now they perked up and began to look about them and toss their heads and tails in more their usual style.

They didn't pass many people on the way home, but those they did pass turned to stare at the cart with its bumpy wheel, at Angela driving with a red face and an anxious expression, and at Uncle Arthur sitting limp and white beside her, still holding his arm.

Angela was very glad when at last they turned into their own street. The ponies tried to jog, and she pulled them back, turning them slowly and carefully into the cinder-strewn passageway between the back yards. Magic and Moonshine stopped outside their own gate with almost visible relief, and Magic gave a shrill whinny.

'Grace,' shouted Angela, who didn't trust the ponies to stand if she went in, and wasn't sure if Uncle Arthur could hold them. 'Grace.'

Hearing her shout Magic whinnied again, and Angela heard Grace's footsteps crossing the yard behind the wall. Then the gate opened and a very surprised Grace was standing there.

'Whatever's the matter?' she asked. 'What have you ... Arthur! What's happened, Angela?'

She went round the cart to help Uncle Arthur down, and both Angela and Uncle Arthur began to explain.

'We'd better go down to the hospital,' said Grace. 'Can you manage the ponies, Angela?'

'I ... I think so.' Angela had often helped Uncle Arthur to unharness and stable the ponies, but she had never done it alone.

'It's all right, Grace, there's no rush. It's only my wrist,' said Uncle Arthur. 'Made me feel a bit queer, but it's not so bad now.'

And to Angela's relief he stayed until she and Grace had got the ponies out of their harness and into the stable. Then Grace insisted that Uncle Arthur went indoors and sat down while she telephoned for a taxi to take them to the casualty department at the hospital. She came out to the stable again wearing her coat.

'Will you be all right on your own for a bit?' she asked Angela. 'I've asked Mrs Handry to come in. She'll be round to see to the shop in about ten minutes. Arthur says you can feed the ponies, you know what they have, but remember to water them first.'

'I know,' Angela assured her. 'And I'll be all right. What do you think's the matter with Uncle Arthur?'

'I think he must have broken that wrist,' replied Grace. 'Look, if we seem to be stuck at the hospital for hours I'll ring up, and if you need me I'll leave Arthur down there and come back.'

She hurried away, and Angela went back to the ponies. They were both sweating after their fright, and the galloping, and she rubbed their damp coats dry with handfuls of clean straw before giving each of them a bucket of fresh water. The shop bell rang while she was doing this, and she went in to serve a small boy with bubble gum and a lady with matches and a magazine. She was just giving the lady her change when Mrs Handry hurried in, her hair in curlers under a headscarf.

'Hello Angie, all right, love?' Mrs Handry

ducked under the counter flap to join her. 'Sorry to be such a time, I was just washing my hair when your auntie called. Dear, dear, what a nasty thing to happen, and just before that big show. Put an end to that now, I suppose.'

For the first time since Uncle Arthur had fallen out of the cart Angela remembered Wembley. Mrs Handry was right, of course. Uncle Arthur couldn't drive in competitions if his wrist was really broken.

Angela was rather sadly stuffing hay into the ponies' nets while they ate their feeds of pony nuts, bran, and carrots when Ian came dashing down the yard.

'Angie, what's happened? Mrs Handry said Uncle Arthur got hurt driving. How?' He stopped breathlessly beside Angela, and she began to explain.

'But what about Wembley?' exclaimed Ian. 'It's only four days until our first heat?'

'I . . . I suppose we shan't be able to go.' Angela felt her lips trembling and turned back to the hay nets. 'I don't see how we can.'

'What foul luck.' Ian looked almost as disappointed as Angela felt. They finished filling the nets in silence, and hung them from their rings in the ponies' boxes. Magic and Moonshine's coats were almost dry by now, and they started contentedly to eat hay.

'They're all right, anyway,' said Ian, as they shut the stable door and went drearily indoors to start getting the tea.

It was after closing time when a taxi stopped at the door, and Grace and Uncle Arthur got out. Uncle Arthur had his wrist in plaster and held in a sling, and he looked as dreary as Angela and Ian felt.

'Well, looks as if that's that,' he said, dropping dejectedly into one of the armchairs. 'Won't be able to handle the lads in the ring for a couple of weeks or more. Looks as if I've let Blakely's down good and proper, not to mention Bob Sheering.'

'It wasn't your fault, Arthur,' said Grace

reasonably, as she put the teapot on the table. 'They'll understand.'

'Not the point,' said Uncle Arthur gloomily. 'Oh well, no help for it, I suppose.'

'Couldn't someone else drive them?' suggested Grace. 'There must be someone. Why not ring Mrs Patson? She might have some ideas?'

'Wouldn't trust the lads to just anyone,' said Uncle Arthur. 'Still, won't hurt to ask, I suppose.'

He began to get up but Grace said, 'Have your tea first. Half an hour won't make any difference.'

They had tea, with Grace trying to cheer everyone up without much success, and then Uncle Arthur went into the little passageway at the side of the shop, and picked up the telephone.

'Well, could she help?' asked Grace, ten minutes later, when he came back into the room.

'Sort of,' Uncle Arthur was looking thoughtful. 'She did suggest someone.'

'Who?' asked Angela eagerly. 'Do tell us, Uncle Arthur.'

'She suggested Ian driving,' replied Uncle Arthur, unexpectedly. 'She said she thought he drove very well with her that day. Well, Ian, what do you think? Like to have a go?'

387

'Me, drive them at Wembley?' Ian looked astonished. 'But would you let me?'

'We can see how you shape, anyway,' replied Uncle Arthur. 'Have to get that tyre mended, of course. Bill would very likely help me with that. Only a puncture, so long as driving on it didn't tear it up too much.'

'Bill from Champney's, do you mean?' asked Ian, and Uncle Arthur nodded. Suddenly everyone was looking more cheerful. Grace was humming as she washed up, and Ian looked happier than he had done for ages.

'I must make a go of it,' he said to Angela later. 'I didn't think Uncle Arthur would ever trust me like this, and I'd love to drive in a show. Not just any show, either. Wembley must be terrific.'

Angela thought that if it was her she'd be too scared to find it terrific, but she was glad that Ian was going to try. It was lovely to know that he was really happy again.

8 : Wembley

Bill and Uncle Arthur mended the tyre on
Saturday morning, and on Saturday evening,
latish so that the recreation ground was quiet,
Ian had his first practice. He didn't drive as fast
as Uncle Arthur, but after the first couple of
tries he didn't hit any bollards either, and
Uncle Arthur said that he would do.

'You mean I can do it?' asked Ian. 'I can
really drive them at Wembley?' Uncle Arthur
said that he could.

'Mind you, it'll be a lot of work for you and
Angie,' he said. 'You'll have to do most of the
cleaning, with me one-handed. Sure you don't
mind?'

'We'll manage,' Ian assured him. 'It'll be
fun, won't it, Angie?'

'Yes.' Angela wasn't quite so confident, but
she wasn't going to say so. Wembley would be
Ian's big moment, and she wasn't going to risk
spoiling it for either of them.

389

Since Magic and Moonshine lived in London they did not qualify for stabling at Wembley arena, but would have to travel to and fro in their own van each time they competed.

'Can you drive with that wrist?' Grace asked doubtfully, but Uncle Arthur said that it was good enough for driving the van, though not pulling excited ponies.

'What about school?' asked Angela. 'It'll mean us having two afternoons off, won't it?'

'Don't worry,' said Grace. 'Your headmistress is very nice. I think she'll let you go. Tuesday is mostly P.E. and art, isn't it, and you both have games on Thursday. You won't be missing anything terribly vital.'

Grace was right. Mrs Merle, their headmistress, was very understanding, and said that it would be all right for them to miss the two afternoons. They would have dinner at school as usual, and Grace would meet them outside afterwards and take them by tube to Wembley. Uncle Arthur would take the ponies over in the van earlier.

Ian had a second practice on the recreation ground on Sunday evening, and on Monday, after school, they all took part in an enormous session of harness- and cart-cleaning, and pony-washing, and polishing. When they left

390

for school on Tuesday morning everything except the ponies was already inside the van, and the cart was up on its trailer.

'See you later,' said Uncle Arthur. 'Don't get your sums wrong thinking about driving, mind.'

'We'll try not to,' promised Ian, but Angela didn't think that she'd be able to get a single thing right. Now that the show was so near she was almost wishing, as usual, that it wasn't going to happen at all.

Dinner at school that day was stew and treacle pudding. Angela could hardly swallow, although she could see Ian at the next table eating away as though it was an ordinary day. All their school friends were very envious about Wembley, and even Ian's friends had stopped their usual habit of pretending to find the ponies funny. What with trying to eat her dinner and answer all the questions Angela was glad to get outside and find Grace waiting for them. At least now she could stop trying to act as if everything was ordinary.

Angela and Ian had been to Wembley before, to see an ice pantomime, but it looked very different today. The big cinder-covered car parks were being used as exercise rings by the competitors, and at the back of the huge Empire Pool building were the stables, rows and rows of temporary loose boxes, made of wood and canvas, and the horse box park. Caravans for the competitors who were living at the show for the week were parked beyond the stables.

Uncle Arthur's van was easy to spot, and Angela and Ian were at work almost straight away, giving the ponies a good brush over, and then helping Uncle Arthur to harness them. It was hard to concentrate on their work, with so many other horses and ponies, and such a lot of coming and going, around them, but Uncle Arthur kept them at it until Magic and Moonshine's coats were shining and their silvery manes and tails were clouds of clean, soft hair.

'Get yourselves ready now,' said Uncle Arthur, when the ponies were ready to be put into the cart, and Angela and Ian went into the van to change. Angela was wearing the clothes she had worn in the combined driving event and Ian wore slacks, sports coat, and a bowler hat borrowed, like Angela's hat, from Mrs Patson.

'You look fine,' Grace assured them when they were ready. 'Come on now, Arthur wants to get down to the collecting ring.'

The collecting ring was a peat-covered square surrounded by large, shady trees. Some

big horses that Uncle Arthur said were show jumpers were exercising there, and Ian recognized one of them as a famous horse they had seen jumping on television. Angela could hardly take her eyes away from a beautiful grey with a lovely, airy canter, ridden by a pretty girl with fair hair and a union jack on her saddle cloth.

'The saddle cloth shows that she's ridden for England in the British team,' explained Uncle Arthur.

There were some other pairs of harness ponies in the collecting ring, and Ian drove

Magic and Moonshine on to the peat to join them. Uncle Arthur told him to drive round a bit to get the ponies used to the different surface, and certainly there was more drag on the wheels from the peat. They didn't go quite so fast as usual, but the ponies seemed quite happy.

'And they're used to being indoors, in theatres and places,' said Ian. 'So they won't mind that.'

There was a click and a crackle and the loudspeaker burst into life.

'Will all competitors in the second heat in the Eldonian Double Harness Stakes please go to the indoor collecting ring,' it said.

'That's us,' said Ian, and Angela felt hollow inside as he turned the ponies to go out of the collecting ring.

The indoor collecting ring was a peat-covered circle under the stepped seats, with a tunnel leading from it into the big arena. The two ponies in front of Magic and Moonshine stopped and spooked at the big double doors that led into it, and a steward came forward to lead them in, but Magic and Moonshine went in without hesitating.

There were five teams in their heat, and Magic and Moonshine would go second. The first two pairs would go on to compete in the final that evening. 'And let's hope we're one of them,' said Ian to Angela as the first team, the nervous ponies, went into the arena.

'Don't go too fast this time,' Uncle Arthur told Ian, as they waited for their turn with Magic pawing the ground, and Moonshine listening with pricked ears to the echoing sounds of the indoor arena. 'This event isn't on time, remember, not unless two pairs have the same number of faults. Go a bit steady, let all of you get used to it.'

There was a groan from the crowd and the click of plastic hitting wood as the team in the arena sent a bollard flying, and a minute later they came dashing out, sweating and excited, with their driver tugging at the reins.

'Sixteen penalties,' said the loudspeaker, as Uncle Arthur said, 'Good luck,' and Magic and Moonshine started towards the tunnel.

To Angela the first glimpse of Wembley arena was frightening. The big oval of dark peat was brilliantly lit, and surrounded by the steep, dark tiers of seats. The crowd was small as this was only Tuesday afternoon, and the competitions were only just getting going, and the seats were scattered with the flashes of coloured clothes and the white blobs of faces. There were lights in the box where the band sat, and flowers were banked in the corners.

Only the bollards looked familiar, red and orange plastic against the dark ground, with the white start and finish posts close together near the entrance.

'Number one three six, Blakely Magic and Blakely Moonshine, driven by Ian Kendall,' said the loudspeaker. 'Ian is the youngest driver in this competition.'

The spectators clapped, and the bell rang. Magic and Moonshine were already cantering, and they swung back across the arena to go between the starting posts.

'Hang on, Angie, we're off,' said Ian, and they were through the first gate and swinging down the arena to go through the next.

'Left,' called Ian, as they came through this, and Angela leaned over, feeling the cart turn, and seeing the next bollard go past. Next came a row of gates, all slightly out of line with each other, down the middle of the arena, and for these Ian slowed right down, although Magic was fretting to go faster. Angela knew that they weren't quite right just before they hit the last pair, but the groan from the spectators startled her. As Ian turned the ponies for the next gate she knew that they were with them, willing the ponies to be clear.

As Magic and Moonshine's speed increased for the last dash between the final bollards the crowd began to murmur, and there was a crack of pleased applause as they galloped through and on to stop the clock. Magic and Moonshine liked being shouted for as well, and they left the arena at a brisk trot, ears pricked, and heads high, and the loudspeaker said, 'Well done. That was only four penalty marks for Magic and Moonshine.'

'Jolly good, jolly good,' said Uncle Arthur, meeting them with his face red and shiny from excitement and Grace smiling beside him. 'Well done, lads, and Ian. Never know, you might get into the final.'

'They liked us,' Angela was climbing down to give the ponies their carrots. 'The audience, I mean. They wanted us to do well.'

It was an anxious wait while the rest of the afternoon's competitors drove, but at last it was over, and the loudspeaker was announcing the finalists.

'We're through,' cried Ian, hearing their number. 'Hurrah.'

'Good, good ponies.' Angela hugged them, and Grace opened a packet of polo mints and gave the ponies one each as a treat.

'Fine, fine.' Uncle Arthur was scarlet. 'Come on, let's take them back to the van and give them a drink and some hay. They'll need to be at their best tonight.'

The arena seemed very different that evening, in the dark. It felt strange to drive down from the stable area, through the dark car parks and the dimly lighted paths, to the doors into the indoor collecting ring, and Angela was glad that Uncle Arthur rode down in the cart with them to give Ian directions.

Once inside the arena they could tell at once that the audience was bigger this evening. A jumping class was just finishing in the ring, and the gasps and groans and the applause were louder. Two tractors with trailers waited by the tunnel to drive in to move the jumps as soon as the class ended, and the other three teams in the Eldonian Stakes final were also in the small collecting ring. To Angela and Ian's delight one pair of ponies was Mrs Patson's.

'Jolly good,' she called, when she saw them. 'I knew you had it in you, Ian.'

Ian grinned and thanked her, as the last of the show jumpers came out, its rider ducking on to its neck under the low tunnel, and the tractors roared in to clear the ring.

The course for the final wasn't quite the same, the gates were placed a bit more awkwardly, and Mrs Patson's team, the first to go, came out with four faults. Magic and Moonshine went next and, although Ian and the ponies did their best, and the audience shouted for them, two bollards went flying, and they came out with eight faults.

'Never mind,' said Uncle Arthur, as Ian started to apologize. 'I'd probably have done worse myself, and you're still in with a chance. This team's knocked two flying already.'

That team's final score was twelve, and the last pair went in.

'One gone,' said Uncle Arthur, as the crowd groaned. Then, seconds later, they groaned again, and Angela said, 'That's another knock.'

'Two gone, the same as you,' said Uncle Arthur, as the team came dashing out, and the loudspeaker announced 'Eight penalties.'

'Now what?' asked Ian.

'Ssh,' Uncle Arthur was listening to the loudspeaker.

'As Blakely Magic and Moonshine are also on eight penalties, time will decide their placings,' the announcer was saying. 'And so, by one and a half seconds, Magic and Moonshine take second place.'

Everyone started thumping Ian on the back, the spectators cheered, and Mrs Patson beamed at them.

'Go on, get your rosette,' said Grace, and Ian and Angela climbed back into the cart to follow Mrs Patson back into the arena to collect their rosette and the prize of thirty pounds.

'That's given you a good start towards the championship,' said Mrs Patson, later. 'The three teams with the most points in each height class, ponies and horses, go in for it. You've collected six points tonight.'

'Wouldn't it be terrific if we did qualify?' exclaimed Ian, and Angela knew that from then on he was determined that they should.

Wednesday seemed a bit flat, suspended between the two days that they had to be at Wembley. They watched part of the show on television at tea-time, and in an interval in the jumping the compere said, 'And now we'd like to show you some of the highlights from the rest of this great show. First, a couple of delightful little characters who are competing in the Eldonian Harness classes, Blakely Magic and Blakely Moonshine and their very young driver and his groom, Ian and Angela Kendall.'

And there they were, racing round the arena, Magic and Moonshine their familiar selves, and those two children in the cart who must be Angela and Ian. It was like a dream, thought Angela; did they really look like that? She could hardly recognize herself. Then the bit of film ended, and Ian was thumping her.

'That was us,' he cried. 'How fantastic. Do we really look like that?'

'You're famous,' said Uncle Arthur, laughing.

400

'You and the lads. If that isn't publicity enough for Blakely's it should be. Keep up the good work, Ian, you'll be the stars of the show.'

The second Eldonian class was the Scurry, and for this Ian knew that they must go faster. Magic and Moonshine were only too pleased, and they thrilled the Thursday afternoon audience by scurrying round at top speed, sending the peat flying, and also sending one bollard flying with it. But it was good enough to get them into the final, and that evening they came third, with Mrs Patson second and a stranger first.

'Have we qualified for tomorrow?' Ian wanted to know, but no one was sure. There was an agonizing wait while the judges added up, but at last the announcement was made. Magic and Moonshine, along with Mrs Patson's pair and the stranger's Exmoors, would go through to compete in Friday evening's championship against the three top teams of bigger horses who had been competing in the classes for their height.

Neither Angela nor Ian slept much that night. They felt strung up, caught high in the fast, exciting life of the show, and on Friday it was school that hardly seemed real. Most of their friends had seen Magic and Moonshine on television, and Angela and Ian found themselves the centre of attention. Ian thoroughly enjoyed it, but Angela was too shy, and she was glad when school ended, and they could go home. There was no need to miss any school today, as the championship was in the evening, and they could all travel to Wembley together in the van.

Friday and Saturday nights were the high-spots of the show, with all tickets sold out months before, and people willing to pay twice the price of the ticket to get a seat. The arena buzzed with life and tension, the air was smoky and it prickled their skin like static electricity. Angela felt weak and sick with nerves. Magic and Moonshine's heads were high, and every hair on their creamy bodies seemed to prickle with excitement.

'Relax,' said Uncle Arthur, who didn't look at all relaxed himself. 'You've as much chance as the others. Steady lads, settle down.' He patted the ponies, but it was impossible to really damp down the tension, and Magic began to paw the ground, digging a hole in the peat floor of the collecting ring, staring excitedly at the other two pony teams and the three teams of bigger, powerful horses.

'It's starting,' gasped Angela, as the steward called the first team, the Exmoors, into the

402

ring, and Grace said, 'Take a deep breath, and don't worry.'

Inside the arena the bell rang, and the championship had begun.

The Exmoors didn't do very well. It must have been luck that got them through to win the night before, thought Angela, hearing groan after groan from the crowd. With all the penalty seconds for knocks to add to their time it was a very slow one, and their driver looked very disappointed as they came out. Two teams of horses went next, but did even worse, and their drivers expressions were very disappointed as they drove out.

And now it was Magic and Moonshine's turn. They burst out of the tunnel into the arena with necks arched and noses in, and Angela hanging on to the side. To her surprise applause burst over them straight away from the crammed seats, and there was even a blast blown on a hunting horn to welcome them. Magic and Moonshine loved it. They were the favourites, and they were out to show what they could do.

Afterwards Angela could only remember it as a thrilling muddle of the brown peat whirling past, the swing and sway of the cart, and the lights hot and bright above them. The ponies' feet were almost soundless on the soft surface,

and the plastic bollards wheeled by as Ian
turned and twisted the cart between them.
Left, right, right, left, and a long run down
the centre.

Surely they must hit one soon, thought
Angela, as the last gates came towards them,

and the crowd began to shout. Magic and
Moonshine pricked their ears and galloped,
and the shouting became a solid roar. 'Come
on, come on, Magic, Moonshine,' and the
ponies responded. Faster and faster they went,
silver manes and tails flying, the cart leaping
after them, both Angela and Ian leaning forward. Then the last gate flashed past them, and
they were between the white finishing posts and
pulling up under the roar of the crowd. They
were clear, but what was their time? Was it

enough, or would Mrs Patson or the last pair of horses catch them?

The applause was still roaring round the arena as the ponies went out, and Mrs Patson, smiling and flourishing her whip, drove in. Then Uncle Arthur, scarlet-faced, was at the ponies' heads, and they were all listening intently to the sounds from the arena as Mrs Patson drove.

'She's clear so far,' said Uncle Arthur, but then there was a break in the sound from the crowd, a groan and a shout, and suddenly Mrs Patson's team was coming out.

'Four penalty seconds to add,' said the loudspeaker, and Angela gasped and grabbed Ian's arm. The last team, high stepping half-bred hackneys, were entering the arena. They looked unbeatable, but incredibly the click of flying bollards showed that they had faulted. Again, four to add.

Was it enough? Then the loudspeaker was saying, 'And so the result of the Eldonian Double Harness Championship is, first, Blakely Magic and Blakely Moonshine . . .' and the crowd was going wild. Cheers, stamps, and the hunting horn shook the stands, and Angela, Ian, Grace, and Uncle Arthur were hugging the excited and surprised ponies and being slapped on the back by everyone in sight.

'Mr Perry, would you come over here a moment, please, and Ian and Angela.' It was the television compere, leading them over to a camera in the corner of the collecting ring. 'Just a few questions. Stand here, please.' Then they were in front of the camera, with Uncle Arthur explaining about his wrist, and Angela and Ian being asked their ages, and Magic and Moonshine being hurried over by Grace to join in. Magic nudged Uncle Arthur in the back, and Uncle Arthur looked round in supposed surprise.

'Well, what's this?' he asked. 'Want to be on television too?'

Both ponies nodded, and the compere laughed and held out the microphone to the ponies. At a signal from Uncle Arthur Magic whinnied, and amid laughter and congratulations the interview was over. It was time to go back into the arena to meet the applause and drive round in a lap of honour with the huge Wembley rosettes on the ponies' bridles and the spotlights following them round the darkened arena. And then they were back in the collecting ring and the next class, one for show horses, was streaming into the tunnel.

'Now we can go home,' said Uncle Arthur, but Mrs Patson, who had laughed finally came third, after the hackneys, 'Not yet,' she said. 'At least, you'll have to come back tomorrow night. You'll be wanted for the cavalcade. Aren't you glad you took my advice about young Ian here?'

'I am, very glad,' agreed Uncle Arthur. 'He's done a tremendous job, couldn't have done better myself.'

Ian beamed, and Angela knew that everything was right again. She and Ian were as close as they'd ever been, and the show wasn't over yet. There was still the Horse of the Year Show cavalcade to look forward to, with Magic and Moonshine taking their places among the winners and the horse personalities of the year, and after that, who could tell? Life was certainly never dull with Magic and Moonshine about.